SHELTER
FROM THE
Storm

SHELTER FROM THE Storm

Volume Four of the Jayson Wolfe Story

A Novel

Anita Stansfield

Covenant Communications, Inc.

Published by Covenant Communications, Inc.
American Fork, Utah

Printed in Canada
First Printing: May 2009

16 15 14 13 12 11 10 09   10 9 8 7 6 5 4 3 2 1

ISBN 10: 1-59811-835-8
ISBN 13: 978-1-59811-835-3

Acknowledgments

Through the writing and publication of this story, I have been greatly blessed with the love, support, and help of many wonderful people. It only seems right that I take a moment and express that appreciation.

To Kathy, Managing Editor Supreme, who takes such good care of me in so many matters, and has facilitated miracles in the extreme rush of this particular volume. To Shauna, who edits my work with such grace and graciousness. You are both truly great women, and great friends, and you do the editing world proud. And of course, everyone else at Covenant: thanks for all the hard work on my behalf.

I have been blessed with many wonderful friends who have believed in this project and who always believe in me. Thanks for holding me together. You know who you are.

And to my family, for your patience, support, and understanding through all the loud music, obsessions, eccentricities, intense weeks of being consumed by the story, and all the other side effects of the roller-coaster ride. Thanks for hanging on with me through the ups and downs.

To my readers, for loving Jayson almost as much as I do, and for letting me know that what I'm doing is worth it.

Last, but never least, to my Heavenly Father, who gave me the ability to hear the stories and music in my head, and for blessing me with the means to share that vision with others.

CHAPTER 1

Highland, Utah

On a hot August day, Jayson Wolfe got into his SUV and turned the key in the ignition. The radio volume had been left on loud, as it usually was when he'd been driving alone. He liked it loud. But he was a little taken aback to hear his own voice crooning familiar lyrics through the stereo speakers. It happened now and then, and usually he changed the station. But today he listened to the tender words he'd written for Elizabeth. He'd given her the song as a wedding gift, and then it had become the title track of his solo CD. The fame felt like a faraway dream. The love he shared with Elizabeth that was clearly expressed in the song was one of two great constants in his life. The other was the religion he'd embraced that had changed his life irrevocably. And today, it all felt neatly summed up in the lyrics he was hearing on the radio.

"I'm a man who believes in miracles, and lady you're the one . . . who turned around and took my hand and said, 'We've paid the price. The fiddler's tired, the band's expired, but we still have time to dance.' I'm a man who knows beyond a doubt that God smiles on fools like me. I'm a man who got a second chance."

When the song ended, Jayson chuckled to hear the DJ state the title of the song, then he heard his own name attached to the words "destined to become a classic." Is that what he'd become? A potential classic? It hadn't been so long since his work had been high on the music charts and rocking the world. Not *so* long. But long enough to make it feel like a dream.

Jayson turned off the radio before another song began. His mind preferred silence at the moment. The lyrics he'd written and carefully composed into music now played comfortably in his mind where they had first germinated. And he smiled. He *was* a man who'd gotten a second chance. A whole slew of them, actually. Life hadn't worked out exactly how he'd planned, and the road had been hard, but the results were better than he'd ever dreamed possible. Not only was he blessed; he was happy. His high-school sweetheart, the love of his life, was now his wife and eternal companion. It had taken time for them to come together, and therefore they were a blended family. But her children and his daughter were all mutually loved and cared for as much as the children that he and Elizabeth had brought into this world together. Their days were typically filled with chaos and a string of minor challenges, as any family's life would be. But they were happy, and he was grateful. After years of such unfathomable *un*happiness, loneliness, and confusion, the life he lived now was not something he took for granted.

Jayson's cell phone rang, startling him. A quick glance at the little screen showed it was his daughter's cell phone. Macy was happily married to a fine young man who treated her like a queen in spite of her troubled past, which she'd left behind to embrace the gospel and commit herself to a better life. Macy and Aaron were currently living with Aaron's family while they waited for an apartment to become available. But they lived nearby, and they were all able to spend time together regularly. Another blessing worth counting.

"Hey, baby," he answered, entirely unprepared to hear her frantic voice reply, "Dad?"

"What is it?" he demanded. "What's wrong?"

"I'm at the hospital," she said, and his stomach tightened. "I think I'm losing the baby. Aaron's on his way, but . . ." Her tears made her words barely discernible. "I need you too, Dad. Can you come? Can you—"

"I'm on my way," he said firmly and made a U-turn. "Don't you worry, baby. Everything will be all right. I'm only five minutes away."

He hung up and dialed the house, where Elizabeth's father Will, and Will's wife, Marilyn, were watching the children. He explained the situation, and Will assured him that they could stay as long as they needed to. Jayson was grateful to have them living close and actively involved in their lives. Will had been like a father to him since his youth; being married to Will's daughter just made the whole package all the better.

Jayson arrived at the hospital in record time, even without breaking any speed limits. He was taken immediately to the private area in the ER where Macy was being monitored. She started to cry when she saw him, and he eased onto the edge of the bed, wrapping her in his arms. After she'd cried for a few minutes, he wiped her tears and asked, "Are you in much pain?"

"It's better since they gave me something, but . . . they say it's inevitable. I *am* going to lose it." She got teary again. "It just doesn't seem fair." Once again she pressed her face to his shoulder and cried.

"No, it's not fair, baby," he said and just held her, feeling teary himself. How could he not think of his years without Macy? She'd run away from home in her youth and he'd had no contact with her for years. She'd returned pregnant and scared. Through the process of bringing that child into the world and putting it into an adoptive family, Macy had changed her life and her heart. She had eagerly embraced the gospel and was now happily married to a good man. But she'd had trouble getting pregnant, and now the baby wasn't going to make it. Jayson almost felt angry at the sick irony of such a situation. He could never say that giving up that baby was as hard on him as it was on Macy, but it had still been hard. He'd shed many tears over seeing his grandchild go into someone else's life. They had all known it was right, but right and easy were rarely synonymous. He'd longed for Macy to have another child, certain it would fill a hole in all of their lives. Surely it would happen with time, but right now that hope felt vague and obscure. And he knew that such words would likely sound trite to Macy at such a moment. Right now she just needed to grieve this loss and have time to get beyond it. The best thing he could do was to love her and let her cry.

Even when she seemed all cried out, she continued to cling to him in silence until Aaron arrived. Jayson hovered in the room while Aaron tearfully took Macy in his arms. The grief they shared was as evident as the depth of their love for each other. Jayson kissed Macy and hugged his son-in-law tightly.

"Thanks for being here," Aaron said, wiping at his eyes.

Jayson just nodded and said, "You hang in there, kid."

It was appropriate for Jayson to leave his daughter in the care of her husband, but there were moments when he found that difficult. He told them both he'd be in the waiting room if they needed him. Aaron promised to keep him posted. Jayson rushed through the waiting room and outside where he could be alone enough to vent his own tears. He'd inherited a high water table from his mother and was prone to crying easily. He always had been. The grief he felt now spilled down his face, but he fought to quickly get it out of his system before he tried Elizabeth's cell phone. Just as Macy needed Aaron, he certainly needed his wife. She'd gone to the temple with a couple of friends, and he knew her cell phone would have been left in the car. But he left her a message, saying simply, "Don't freak out or anything, but Macy is losing the baby. We're at the hospital. If you get this message before you leave the temple, have them drop you off here. I need you. I'm in the ER waiting room."

He hung up and called the house to make certain all was well. Will answered the phone and assured him they were fine. Will asked about Macy, and Jayson started to cry again. But he'd been crying to Will for more years than he could count. He often wondered what he would have ever done without this man in his life, and this was one of those moments. Jayson had first met Will Greer when his newly acquired friend Derek had taken Jayson home with him during their high school days. Jayson had been a part of the family ever since. He had been around when Will's wife had left him and the family had struggled to cope with the divorce. Jayson had been an expert on that, since his own parents had been divorced, an event necessitated by his father's alcoholism and violence. Jayson's mother and Will had become close over time, and for a while they all wondered if the two of them might get married. But it hadn't worked out, and Leslie had passed away years ago. Will was now married to Marilyn, a wonderful woman who had helped make Will's life complete. The active involvement of Will and Marilyn in their lives was one of Jayson's many blessings, and he was keenly aware of that blessing now when he needed a fatherly shoulder to cry on even more than he needed a babysitter.

Jayson went back inside and sat there for more than an hour before Elizabeth came through the door, rescuing him from feeling completely alone in a room full of people. He rose, and she wrapped her arms around him. He touched her curly blonde hair and kissed her brow, grateful to have her in his life, and to know that she was, and always had been, more of a mother to Macy than her own had ever been—at least once she'd gotten out of diapers.

"Is she all right?" Elizabeth asked.

"I haven't heard anything since I called you," he said. "Aaron is with her."

They sat next to each other and held hands while Jayson told her everything he knew. Then they sat in silence until Aaron's mother arrived, having gotten the news while she'd been at work. They updated her on all they knew, then the three of them sat together in silence. Layla had raised Aaron and his younger brothers and sisters mostly on her own. Aaron was the oldest of seven children. His parents were divorced. He never heard from his father, who had run off with a younger woman, and Layla worked hard to support and care for her family. She was a good woman, and Jayson and

Elizabeth both liked and respected her a great deal. They had all been mutually thrilled with the prospect of having a grandchild, and now they were grieving its loss together.

Aaron finally came out to talk to them, crying a little as he told them that it was over and everything was fine, but Macy was pretty upset. He sat down with them and talked for a few minutes, and his grief and concern were readily evident. While Elizabeth and Layla went to sit with Macy, Jayson took his son-in-law to the hospital snack bar and bought him a sandwich, insisting that he needed to eat something.

"Talk to me," Jayson said. "I'm the only dad you've got."

"And boy am I grateful I've got you," Aaron said.

"We have that in common, you know . . . growing up without a dad."

"Yeah," Aaron said. "I guess that's one of many reasons you understand me."

"You okay?"

"No, I'm not okay," Aaron said with a cracked voice. "I think I'm in . . . shock. I never expected something like this to happen."

"I know *exactly* how you feel," Jayson said. "But we're family. We're going to get through this together."

Aaron nodded and they talked through their feelings and concerns while Aaron ate, admitting he was more hungry than he'd thought. Jayson was grateful that his daughter had found such a fine young man. In his own life, he'd witnessed more bad marriages than good ones, and he was glad to see that his daughter had a good one. He told Aaron so as they were walking back to see Macy. When they arrived, the two mothers left the room. Jayson sat and talked with his daughter for a few minutes, and they cried together a little. He tried to give her some hope, but he knew it was just going to take time for all of them. Then once again he left her in Aaron's care, hugging them both before he reminded them to call if they needed anything at all. The hospital was going to keep her overnight, and Jayson had to leave with Elizabeth and get home to see how the other children were doing.

Of course, Will and Marilyn had everything under control. They were both on the living room floor playing with the little ones and having a marvelous time. The two children that Jayson and Elizabeth shared biologically were busy playing with a variety of toys and making a delightful mess. Derek, named after Elizabeth's brother and Jayson's best friend who had been killed in high school, was going on two and a half and into everything unless he was being watched every minute. Thankfully his grandparents were very good at that. Harmony had turned one last month and was just learning how to get some speed into her recently acquired skill of walking. The two of them kept Jayson and Elizabeth both very busy, but it was a joyful kind of busy. And being with them now helped ease their mutual grief.

Jayson and Elizabeth sat on the floor with the rest of them and gave a report to Will and Marilyn that the babies were oblivious to. They talked for a while about the physical impact on Macy, and the emotional effect it would have on her and everyone who loved her. The conversation was becoming hopelessly repetitive when Addie came into the room.

"You're home," she said with a concerned face as Elizabeth guided the child to her lap. "Is Macy okay?"

Elizabeth explained the situation in simple terms, and Addie started to cry. She was a sensitive child and close to Macy. Their age difference and the fact that they shared no blood relationship in no way detracted from the bond they had formed as sisters since their parents had married. Addie would soon be starting third grade, and she was tall for her age. She looked very much like her mother, with curly blonde hair that hung down her back. Addie was instinctively maternal to everyone around her, no matter their age. Her gift in that regard was a huge blessing in the way she helped look after Derek and Harmony, and it compensated a great deal for the way she had to be nagged to do her chores, and for the fact that she hated keeping her room clean. Now, her concern for Macy was readily evident as she clung to Elizabeth and cried.

The situation had barely been explained to Addie when Trevin came in from his usual Wednesday Young Men meeting. Trevin and Addie were both from Elizabeth's first marriage, and they shared the same tall, lean frame and blonde curly hair—although Trevin's was cut too short for the curl to be evident. He would soon be a sophomore in high school, approaching his sixteenth birthday—and he had sprouted up to Jayson's height in the past year. He was a good kid with a strong spirit, and they never had to worry about him getting into trouble. If anything, Trevin was quick to remind other members of the family to keep up with scripture study and prayer. Elizabeth's son Bradley who had been older than Trevin had been killed in the same drowning accident that had taken Elizabeth's husband, Robert, from her. The event had been traumatic and life-altering. But years had passed, and the family they had become was strong and eternal—a fact that was made evident when Trevin too showed emotion and concern for Macy. With everyone there, the family knelt together to say the usual evening family prayer, but there were extra blessings requested on behalf of Macy and Aaron and everyone else who felt sorrow over this loss.

After Will and Marilyn had gone home, Jayson and Elizabeth worked together to help Addie with her homework and get the little ones to bed. After kneeling by the side of their bed together to pray, they crawled between the sheets and held hands as they typically did. After several minutes of silence, Elizabeth said, "You're having a hard time with this."

"And you're not?" he asked.

"Yes, of course, but . . . you're having a harder time than you're letting on."

"And how do you know that, Lady?" he asked, mildly facetious. She'd always been able to read him.

Elizabeth eased her head to his shoulder. "I've known you most of my life, Jayson Wolfe. You can't hide anything from me."

"That's true," he said, pressing a kiss into her hair. "But that works both ways, you know . . . Mrs. Wolfe."

"How wonderful."

"Indeed," he said and sighed loudly. "Yes, I'm having a hard time with this. I was really looking forward to that baby coming. I think a baby will help heal a great deal . . . for all of us, but especially for Macy."

"I'm sure you're right . . . but it will happen. It just won't happen as soon as we'd hoped." She leaned up to kiss Jayson. "Everything will be all right."

"I'm sure it will," he said. "Somehow it always is." He kissed her again. "But it's been easier to believe that since you finally agreed to be my wife."

"I may be slow, but I come around eventually," she said lightly, and he kissed her again.

* * * * *

Throughout the next couple of weeks, Macy spent a great deal of time at Jayson and Elizabeth's home while Aaron was gone with work and school. Prior to losing the baby, Macy had been in the process of looking for a new job after she'd been laid off, which she now considered a blessing. She was glad for some time to recuperate, emotionally as well as physically. And since they were living with Aaron's family, rent money was not an issue.

Because Jayson worked at home and he considered himself mostly retired, he enjoyed having Macy around. They did some things together and had long talks that helped both of them come to terms with the loss of Macy's baby. Neither of them believed the grief would completely go away until another baby came, but they felt hope and peace, and they had each other. Jayson was inexpressibly grateful for his daughter. They'd been through a great deal together, but they were close because of it, and he loved her dearly.

Two weeks after the miscarriage, Macy said, "I should probably call Debbie and tell her . . . before she calls with some of her ridiculous jokes about becoming a grandmother."

Jayson groaned as he usually did at the mention of his ex-wife. Macy had taken to calling her by her given name since she'd started calling Elizabeth her mother. In Debbie's presence, Macy would call her Mom, but only to avoid an argument. Debbie was worldly, selfish, and belligerent. She hadn't been that way when Jayson had married her. But Jayson's phenomenal success in the music industry had lured Debbie into a questionable lifestyle that she had easily embraced. While Jayson had worked hard to remain aloof from the unseemly behaviors of the social circles associated with his career, Debbie had gravitated to them. Jayson had left her when he'd discovered she'd been sleeping with some sleazy punk star. And it had all gone downhill from there. Elizabeth had saved both Jayson and Macy from drowning in the destructive aftermath, and then the gospel had fully changed their lives. Now Debbie had become an inconvenience that had to be dealt with occasionally due to her blood relationship with Macy. But Jayson knew that Macy was better at having a good attitude toward Debbie than he was. He had way too much experience with how hurtful she could be, and he knew that no amount of effort on his behalf would ever make her change her destructive ways. Macy had visited her mother a few times in LA, and they kept in touch. He knew that Macy and Aaron both believed they could eventually help Debbie find a better life. Jayson admired them for their love and concern, but he feared they would be disappointed.

"I suppose you should," he said.

"I don't want to tell her. You know she'll freak out and say something stupid that will make me cry."

"Yeah, she probably will," Jayson agreed.

"So, you'll call her for me, right?"

"Me?" Jayson protested. "I don't want to talk to her."

"But you'll do it for me, right?" She stuck her bottom lip out in an exaggerated pout. He sighed and she added, "You're the one who married her. If you'd married Elizabeth to begin with, this wouldn't have been a—"

"I asked Elizabeth, remember? She told me no."

"Well, I wasn't there, but that's what I've heard. You *will* call Debbie for me, won't you?"

Jayson sighed again. "Okay, but you owe me. Or we could just change all of our phone numbers and never talk to her again."

"That's tempting," Macy said. "Very tempting. You choose. Either call her, or change the numbers."

"Okay, I'll call her. But I'm not going to talk to her while you're listening."

"So, you're going to talk about me?"

"Obviously. But if you're listening, you'll cry anyway. So my calling her would be pointless. I'll call her later."

"Fair enough," she said.

"Anything else I can do for you?"

"You're already the best dad on the planet."

"I'd do just about anything if it could make you happy."

"I *am* happy, Dad," she said and got contradictory tears in her eyes. "I mean . . . I want a baby, but I believe it will happen. I love Aaron and he loves me. We have the gospel."

"Yes, we have that. How are things going living with Aaron's family? Any better?"

"Well, I spend a lot of time here, as you well know. I love them; I love them all. They're a great family. Layla is so good to me, but it's just so crazy with all the kids, and . . . I hope we can get an apartment soon. If I'd get a job it would help move that along."

"Any luck yet?"

"Not really, but I'm still trying."

"If you need help with the money, baby, all you have to do is—"

"We are *not* having this conversation again."

"It's been *months* since we had this conversation."

"And the answer is still the same, Dad. I know you made millions and most of it's still in the bank. But we need to make it on our own. You know why that's important."

"I know," he said. "I just don't want to see you go without."

"All of our needs are being met, Dad." She took his hand. "I promise if we really need something, I won't be too proud to ask."

"Okay, baby," he said, and almost bit his tongue from saying what else he was thinking, mostly because they'd had *this* conversation many times before, as well. But he just had to say it. "You know you and Aaron could live here."

"Dad, we—"

"Now, hear me out. I know we've talked about it before, but maybe you feel different now. The two of you could have more of your own space and privacy. I know the apartment's not big, but it's adequate, and it's private." He was referring to the little apartment they had built onto the back of the house the previous year. The plan had been to add a large living room on the main floor that moved back off the dining room. They wanted space for comfortable gatherings with family and friends, and plenty of room for kids to play near the kitchen. Prior to their building it, there had only been the front room, which was barely big enough for the grand piano and a couple of couches. They jokingly called it the "home teaching room," since its only purpose was to receive company or play the piano. The family room was in the basement, and with a toddler in the house, he was always playing under Elizabeth's feet in the kitchen or in the little office she had near the kitchen where she was often busy. After having a second baby, they'd decided to build the living room. It was spacious and comfortable and meant for exactly what they'd named it—living. It was the room where everyone felt comfortable, and they spent a great deal of time there in the evenings and on Sundays. The large deck that had originally been behind the dining area had been rebuilt at the back of the living room, with sliding glass doors that opened onto it.

The living room was usually cluttered with toys and other evidence of being well used by the children nearly every hour of every day, which meant it was serving its purpose. But it had been necessary to build something on the basement level, since the design of the house required a room beneath the living room for proper structure. They'd come up with the idea to build an apartment with an outside entrance, which could serve many purposes. If friends or family came from out of town, they could comfortably stay there. It would also prove useful when someone occasionally came to do business with Jayson, or to record in the music studio that was a part of the house. The apartment had an outside entrance, but it also connected into the basement family room. It was small but had kitchen facilities, a bedroom-living area that was a fairly good-sized room, and a nice bathroom. Jayson knew that at Layla's home, Macy and Aaron only had a small bedroom and had to share a bathroom with a couple of Aaron's siblings. The apartment was sitting empty, and Macy was frustrated with the lack of privacy and crowded situation at her mother-in-law's home. And he was quick to point that out.

"I know you prayed about this before," he went on, "but maybe the answer is different now."

"It's not, Dad," she said and got teary. "We prayed about it again, just a few days ago. Because I *want* to be here. Obviously, Aaron is the one gone most of the time with work and school, and I would be more comfortable living with *my* family. He agrees with that, and he wouldn't have a problem with it. But we both got a very firm answer. We are supposed to be there. I don't know why; we just need to have faith."

"Yeah," Jayson said, inspired by his daughter's faith, especially when he felt so disappointed himself. He pushed his concerns and desires aside and lightened his voice. "Okay, then . . . if you won't live under my roof or take my money, what can I do for you?"

"You can play me a song."

"A song?"

"You sound like you don't know what I'm talking about." She laughed softly. "You're a rock star, Dad. You haven't forgotten, have you?"

"Retired rock star," he said.

"And you've forgotten how to play a song for your daughter?"

"Just haven't been practicing much lately."

"You don't need practice." She made an exaggerated scoffing noise. "It's like breathing. Come on." She stood up and held out her hand. "Play me a song. Maybe two."

"Deal," he said, and they went through the living room to the home studio that Jayson had supervised the building of a few years earlier. Another advantage of building onto the house had been making a more feasible entrance to the studio from the living room. Previously, they'd had to go through the garage. The studio had a grand piano, several guitars, drums, a few other instruments, and all the recording equipment necessary in the separate sound booth to record anything that Jayson might come up with. He could do almost all of it on his own, except that he needed his older brother Drew to play the drums when it came to serious percussion. He could only pull off a basic, simple rhythm. Elizabeth had done many vocals and had played the violin and flute on several of his recordings, and even on stage.

Music had been Jayson's life for all of his life. But it had taken a back burner since he'd released his solo album and settled more deeply into family life. Now he considered himself a good old Mormon boy with a family to care for and enough free time on his hands to do a great deal of temple work and service wherever it might be needed in his ward and neighborhood. Music was now more a pastime, a hobby, something that he enjoyed indulging in on a more casual basis. He'd been working slowly on some recordings of hymns that he would like to eventually see released, but he was content to take his time with it. He even had some original compositions that were purely of a spiritual nature, and would be perfect for an LDS audience. He'd also done unique things with some Christmas music, but that too was a slow and passive project. Occasionally he performed for a charity benefit concert, and he played the piano for the ward choir. He did firesides on a regular basis where he played some spiritual music and told his conversion story. He loved being able to share his testimony and felt that he was using his gifts to help build the kingdom. That was good enough for him. Music had greatly blessed his life, and now he was taking advantage of all his blessings.

Once in the studio, he asked his daughter, "What do you want to hear?"

"Anything."

"That's a little broad. Guitar or piano?"

"Oh, I think I'm in a guitar mood," she said. "I know. Play that one you wrote for me; the one I heard on the radio that made me decide to come home."

"It's been a long time," he said, "but I'll give it a shot."

Jayson sat on a stool and settled an acoustic guitar on his thigh. The guitar had been a gift from Elizabeth's father when he'd graduated from high school. It was one of his most treasured possessions. He'd never performed with this guitar. He played it for pleasure, or when he was writing music. It took him a minute to remember the chords enough to pull the song together, but he saw Macy smile when it started to sound like the song she'd requested. He fumbled a little over the lyrics of the first verse, but that made her laugh. By the time he got to the chorus, he was back in time and knew every note, every word. *"Only my baby knows . . . how the love inside me grows . . . each time I hold her on my knee . . . and looking at her I see . . . the stars in baby's eyes. Only my baby knows . . . how my heart has opened wide . . . since I held her at my side . . . in the hour that she was born . . . and looking at her I see . . . the stars in baby's eyes. 'Cause only my baby knows."* Jayson really messed up the second verse and made up something silly as he went along, which really made Macy laugh. Then he got the chorus right again, and before he finished he saw tears in her eyes.

"It wasn't *that* bad," he said.

"It's beautiful," she said and sniffled. "I love that song."

"Now it's your turn," he said and motioned her toward the piano. She was hesitant, but they sat side by side on the bench and he reminded her of some of the things he had taught her. In a short while he had her playing a song called *Harmony,* written by Elton John—the song his mother had made him learn before she would buy him a guitar; the song after which he and Elizabeth had named their youngest daughter. This song had a lot of history for him, and he loved it.

"That was beautiful," Elizabeth said when Macy finished, and Jayson and Macy both turned to see that Elizabeth had come into the room.

"She's brilliant," Jayson said, and Macy snorted a laugh.

"No one can feel too brilliant with music when Jayson Wolfe is around," Macy said.

"That *is* a fact," Elizabeth said with a smile and a wink.

"She's brilliant," Jayson said again.

Macy's cell phone rang, and she took it from her pocket on her way out of the room. It was obvious from the way she answered that it was Aaron. When she was gone, Elizabeth sat on the bench beside Jayson and took his hand. "It's good to hear you playing. I miss it when you don't." She smiled at him, but he saw something in her eyes that made him suspicious. She had something she wanted to say. "A man with such a gift should not be squandering it."

"I'm not *squandering* it. I use my gift all the time."

Elizabeth smiled with something close to mischief in her eyes and he looked at her sideways. "But you're not using it the way you're capable of using it."

"Oh, no," he said. "No, no. No, no, no, no, no!"

"That's a lot of *no* when you don't even know what I was going to say."

He stood up. "I know very well what you're going to say. You think I need a project, something to occupy my time and give me some focus."

"That's not at *all* what I was going to say," she said. "I was going to say that you need a project because the world needs what you have to offer."

He scowled at her, then turned away. "I've given the world what I have to offer. I made a difference with my music. I did. Now I . . ."

"What? Want to sit in a rocking chair with a guitar for the rest of your life?"

"No, of course not, but . . ."

"But what? You're still young. You have so much music left inside of you, and—"

"I haven't had anything new come up—at all—for . . . a long time. I can't remember how long. What brought this up, anyway?"

"Rick called," she said, and he made a disgusted noise.

"He's a good guy."

"I'm not saying anything against Rick. He *is* a good guy, and I'm grateful for him. But his regularly calling me to nag about doing another album is getting on my nerves. Now he's . . . what? Resorted to calling my wife to get her to nag me?"

"That's exactly what he said. He said, 'I need you to nag him for me.' But you should know me better than to think that I would speak on his behalf if I didn't agree with him."

Jayson looked at her hard. "You really think I should do another album?"

"I do."

"You want me to be obsessed with writing, practicing, recording; then go on tour? And you'd have to come with me, you know. I need you on stage with me. Our lives would be insane!"

"You talk as if I've never been exposed to this kind of thing before. I was there last time, remember? We managed fine. We recovered. It was great . . . most of it, anyway. Nothing good happens without glitches, but we can handle glitches."

"I do *not* want to do another album, Lady."

"Well, maybe it's not about what *you* want."

"But I'm working on some Christmas stuff, and some spiritual stuff that would be great for an LDS album. And I've been recording hymns, and—"

"Yes, and all of that is good, but . . . I just don't know if this is the season in your life to do those things. I mean . . . they're kind of dragging, right? It's not really going anywhere at the moment."

Jayson didn't want to admit she was right on that count, so he said nothing.

"Have you prayed about it?" she asked.

Jayson hated the question because he didn't have an answer. Or rather, the answer was no. He didn't want to pray about it.

"Are you afraid God will tell you to do it, so you're just not going to ask?"

"How do you do that?" he asked.

"Read your mind, you mean?" She laughed softly. "I just know you. I know you've been avoiding this. If you pray about it and the answer is that God wants you to be retired, you can keep being the neighborhood Good Samaritan and tell Rick no, once and for all. And if the answer is yes, you can get to work and produce some great music. But at least you'll know, and you can stop living with that quiet nagging you're trying to ignore."

"How do you know there's quiet nagging? Maybe there's nothing."

"Maybe you aren't listening."

Jayson sighed and pushed a hand through his hair, which reminded him that what had always been brown was starting to show some vague hints of graying at the temples. As if that might make a difference he said, "I'm getting too old to be a rock star."

"Do you want me to start naming the musicians who are still recording and touring who are ten, fifteen, twenty years older than you?"

"No, I do not!"

"So, pray about it," she said and left the room.

CHAPTER 2

Jayson resisted cursing, knowing it was against his religion. But Elizabeth's challenge *did* create a quiet nagging. Or perhaps only enhanced it. Although, by the next day it was getting pretty loud. He began a fast and went to the temple. He prayed and attempted to do it with humility and an open mind, even though he made no bones about telling God this was not what he wanted to do. He pulled weeds in the flower beds around the house, and spent long hours in the vegetable garden in the backyard. And he made certain Addie and Trevin put in a reasonable amount of time helping him. He walked Mozie, the family dog, and he helped Elizabeth in the kitchen. He certainly didn't have any trouble keeping busy, and he felt sure that his time was better spent contributing to home and family than to throwing himself into the obsessiveness that came with the creation and production of music.

He knew that most other men had to make a living and didn't have the choices he had. Money was not an issue for him, and he was grateful for that. But he'd worked hard to get where he'd gotten, and the price had been high. He consciously used his time and his money to serve his family and others in need. He also knew that most other men were not faced with the all-consuming intensity in their work that he knew was inevitable for him. A part of him missed it; a part of him was terrified to step back into that territory that had brought such a polarity of grief and joy into his life.

He pondered and prayed and went to the temple again. The ten-minute drive from the temple to the house cemented in his mind the answer he'd been given, and he pulled into the garage feeling stunned by the intensity and clarity of that answer. He sat for a couple of minutes in one of the two SUVs they owned that met the needs of a busy family. He liked the life he'd settled into as a full-time family man. But hadn't he heard once that comfort zones were not a place where God allowed His children to camp?

"What?" Elizabeth asked when he walked into the kitchen, removing his tie. She was busy shoveling baby food into Harmony's mouth while Derek was more dumping out toys than playing with them in the living room nearby.

Jayson yanked off the tie and sat down. "I'm supposed to do another album."

Elizabeth just smiled and said, "I know."

"If you know, then why did you—"

"You could never do it if you didn't get the answer for yourself," she said and reached for his hand.

Jayson sighed and took in what she'd said. He knew it was true. But he was having a hard time settling with this, perhaps mostly because he was still stuck on what *he* wanted as opposed to what he knew *God* wanted for him. He was also troubled by another point.

"Have I been that stubborn and oblivious?" he asked his wife.

"You are neither stubborn *nor* oblivious," she said. "This is just . . . hard for you, I know."

"But if you knew it was right, why didn't I?"

"I can't answer that, Jayson. The important thing now is that you've come to an answer; you know what to do, and you're going to do it." She looked momentarily panicked. "You *are* going to do it, aren't you?"

"Of course I'm going to do it," he said. "It's just that . . . it's never come in this order before. I've always had more music to produce than I knew what to do with. But the good stuff has already been given to the public. I feel blank. Do you have any idea of how much material I need to come up with?"

"Yes." She laughed softly. "I do. And I know you can do it."

"At least one of us has faith in me."

"God has faith in you," she said. "Remember, with God nothing is impossible."

He stood up, then bent to kiss her. "You keep reminding me," he said just before Harmony decided she was done eating and abruptly knocked the spoon from Elizabeth's hand, spraying Gerber plums all over Jayson's white shirt.

"Oh, thank you very much, little lady," he said with a chuckle, and Elizabeth started to laugh. "Go ahead and laugh," he said to her. "You won't think it's funny when you have to get the stains out."

"Oh, it's funny," Elizabeth said, and Harmony started to giggle, which made them both laugh harder.

Elizabeth worked on cleaning up the baby while Jayson took his shirt straight to the laundry room. After he'd changed his clothes, he found Harmony in the bathtub and Elizabeth sudsing up her curly blonde hair. "There was too much lunch in her hair to handle with a washcloth," Elizabeth said, and immediately added, "You'd better call Rick."

"I suppose I should."

"And you'd better get writing."

"Well, that's easier said than done. If God wants me to write ten or twelve songs, He's going to have to send some help. The muse has apparently been asleep for a very long time."

"It will happen," she said with such perfect confidence that he believed her.

He became distracted by Harmony's antics and sat on the edge of the tub to make funny noises at his littlest daughter. She giggled, and he took the washcloth from Elizabeth. "I'll bathe Harmony," he said. "You go write a song that'll be a big hit. Let me know when it's ready."

"Funny. Very funny," she said. "I'll do laundry while you bathe Harmony, and *then* you can write a song."

"Funny. Very funny," he said, even though he didn't think it was. But Harmony giggled.

A few minutes later Elizabeth brought Jayson the phone. "It's your son," she said. He knew Trevin was at school, so he wasn't surprised to hear Aaron's voice.

"What's up, kid?" Jayson asked.

"I've been meaning to call you and it's just been so crazy, with work and school and all."

"I know how busy you are. Don't worry about that. What can I do for you?"

"I just wanted to thank you," Aaron said. "I've been thinking about your being there when Macy lost the baby, and you're there for her a lot when I can't be. And I just didn't want my appreciation to go unspoken. So, thank you. That's all, I guess."

"We're glad to do anything we can to help," Jayson said. "You're a great guy and I know you take good care of her."

"Well, I try, but . . . I know it's hard on her being at my mom's place, especially with me gone so much, but . . ."

"Apparently it's the right thing," Jayson said. "I'm sure you'll manage."

"I'm sure we will, but . . . I wanted to also thank you for giving us the option of staying with you. Macy told me everything you said. We both know we're supposed to be here, even if we don't know why exactly. But I still wanted to thank you for giving us an option. It's nice to know we have family."

"We'll always be here," Jayson said, then tried to steer the topic elsewhere. "So, how's school?"

Aaron talked a little about his classes and his job, and they had a nice chat. It had been several weeks since the two of them had just been able to talk, and Jayson told him it was good to talk to him. He hung up the phone, grateful once again for knowing his daughter had such a fine young man in her life.

* * * * *

Jayson decided to wait until morning to call Rick, but he knew he couldn't put off calling Debbie any longer. Macy told him that her mother had called her cell phone, but she'd purposely let it go to voice mail because she didn't want to talk to Debbie until she knew that Macy wasn't pregnant anymore. Jayson dialed the number, disappointed when he had to leave a message. Now that he'd talked himself into doing it, he wanted to get it over with. Debbie called back late that evening. The kids were in bed, and he and Elizabeth were snuggling on the couch in the living room, watching a movie.

"Oh, great," he said with sarcasm as he glanced at the caller ID and pushed Pause on the remote.

"You called?" Debbie said without a hello.

"I did," he said. "I'll get right to the point." They'd long ago stopped trying to pretend they enjoyed talking to each other with senseless small talk. "Macy had a miscarriage."

"Is she okay?" Debbie asked, showing a rare glimpse of motherly concern.

"Physically she's fine. But it's been hard. She was about halfway along."

"It's probably just as well," Debbie said. "She should know by now that kids aren't all they're cracked up to be."

Jayson always believed she couldn't surprise him with her warped ideas and delusions, but she always managed to say something that made him wonder where the woman he'd once been married to had gone. "Yeah," he said with sarcasm, "we sure would have been better off if we hadn't had Macy."

Elizabeth shot him an astonished glare. Debbie said nothing. He loved it when he shut her up. It gave him the opportunity to say, "I just wanted you to know. When you talk to her, try not to be *too* insensitive. In spite of the way *you* feel about having kids, she really wants one. Have a nice night." He hung up the phone before she could say anything else.

"You're going to have to explain that one," Elizabeth said.

"You *and* Debbie should both know me well enough to recognize sarcasm when you hear it," he said. "She told me that Macy should know kids aren't all they're cracked up to be." Elizabeth gasped. "I can only imagine how great it will be when Debbie calls to offer some perspective to Macy by letting her know that it's not really such a bad thing to have gotten out of actually having the kid. This from a woman who got her tubes tied without telling her husband."

"At least you got Macy first," Elizabeth said.

"Yes," he muttered and put his arm around her, "she's probably the only good thing that ever came from Debbie."

"She came from you, too," Elizabeth said and kissed him. "She has an amazing father who more than makes up for having a lousy mother. I have a lousy mother, remember?"

"Yes, she does call often enough to remind us that she's still around. But Macy has a *wonderful* mother. She has you." He returned her kiss. "You've been there for her in ways I never could have."

"Then I guess it just worked out all nice and cozy, didn't it."

"Yes," he chuckled, "it certainly did."

* * * * *

Jayson's phone call with Rick, his rep at the record company, left him feeling a little better about the firm decision he'd made to produce a new album. Still, if it weren't for absolutely knowing it was what God wanted him to do, he doubted he could find any positive aspect to it at all. He simply didn't *want* to do it. And he certainly wasn't getting any inspiration.

On the weekend he spent less time worrying about it, since he wouldn't have been working anyway. The whole family, including Macy and Aaron, went to the zoo on Saturday, an excursion that was made most enjoyable by seeing Derek and Harmony watch the animals. Aaron lifted Derek up on his shoulders so that he could see better, and Derek squealed with excitement each time he saw a new one. He jabbered about them in a language that only he could understand, but Aaron talked to him as if he'd understood every word. Harmony just stared in silence at each new creature until she fell asleep in Jayson's arms.

Sunday morning brought its typical chaos of trying to get the entire family to church early enough to settle into a reverent mode before the meeting began. Elizabeth was grateful, as always, for Addie's helpfulness. She was ready early and kept Harmony and Derek occupied while Elizabeth finished getting ready herself. She walked into the master bathroom where Jayson was combing his hair in front of the long mirror, and turned her back to him, lifting her hair as she said, "Would you zip me up, please?"

"I would love to," he said and kissed the back of her neck before he did the task.

He went back to fixing his hair, which included a little more hair wax than the average man his age would ever use. But Elizabeth liked it; it went so well with the way he dressed. There was no man on earth who dressed like Jayson Wolfe. He'd been compulsively drawn to dressing in a noncon-formist way for as long as she'd known him, and long before that. He was perfectly respectful in dressing appropriately for church, but unless he was attending the temple or participating in a priesthood ordinance, he rarely wore a white shirt. Today his shirt was dark burgundy, and his tie was black with tiny silver stripes, which went well with his black slacks. The real uniqueness showed up in the vest. He collected vests. He loved vests. He wore them to church, with jeans, to clean the garage. He wore them over dress shirts, T-shirts, and anything in between. Today his vest had silky black fabric in the back, and the front was a rich brocade print fabric of black and burgundy, like a tapestry that might be hanging in a castle. Macy had given it to him for his birthday, and he loved it.

"I think I need a haircut," he said while she was applying as much mascara as she could get on in thirty seconds.

Elizabeth paused to take hold of the hair hanging over the top of his collar. "I don't know," she said. "I kind of like it. I miss the ponytail some-times." He'd worn one when she met him at the age of sixteen, and he'd worn it until the day of his baptism soon after they'd been married a few years ago. She'd told him then that he could be a good member of the Church with a ponytail, and she knew that he knew that. But he'd been ready for dramatic changes in his life and that was how he'd wanted to do it. "I don't know," she said, "maybe you should just let it grow. Since you're going to be doing another album, maybe you should go for that rock star look again."

"There are a lot of rock stars with short hair," he argued. "And I'm more concerned about keeping the image of a good Mormon boy."

"Maybe some people need to see that you can be a good Mormon boy and look different. Wearing your hair a little long is not a sin. You have the countenance of a good Mormon boy. Perhaps there are some callings that might require a clean-cut example, but right now . . . well, I think you should let it go for a while. You can always cut it off if you get so you don't like it."

"Apparently I'd need your permission first," he said. "Come on. We're going to be late."

Arriving at the church building, the standard unspoken procedure ensued. Trevin got Derek out of his seat, while Addie got Harmony out of hers. Jayson walked around the car and opened Elizabeth's door for her, holding her hand as she got out. She knew better than to get out on her own, no matter how late they were. He wouldn't stand for it. Jayson and Elizabeth each carried a shoulder bag that was a combination diaper/book bag and followed the children into the chapel, arriving at five minutes before the hour to sit on their usual bench in the center and three rows from the back.

As they got settled in and tried to get the children into a reverent frame of mind, Elizabeth glanced around and realized that she still only knew about half of the people in the ward since they'd been part of a ward division that had happened about six months earlier. It had been a challenging change for many people, but a part of the culture of the Church that couldn't be helped when the area was growing so fast. She noticed, not for the first time, a few discreet glances toward her family, but she knew the reason and it made her smile. Being married to Jayson Wolfe had come with a great amount of attention from others, even though that had never been his intention with making and selling music, *or* in the way he dressed. But it happened, nevertheless. The fact that he was a very nice-looking man, combined with the way he dressed, often provoked curious glances. Or perhaps people were thinking that he looked familiar, but they couldn't quite place him. The fact that he'd been on magazine covers and on television often had that effect, even if people had no idea of his profession. And she suspected that many of these people didn't.

She had no idea what most of the men in the ward did for a living. While Jayson's career had brought him great fame, it was only among a certain audience, and he hadn't done anything active with his career since the ward change had taken place. She knew Jayson was fine with that, and she was too. Their church attendance had nothing to do with any of the worldly aspects of their lives. They came to worship. But the social aspects couldn't help but go along with their associations there, and she wished that she could get to know people better. And perhaps if people knew their family better, they would come to understand why Jayson Wolfe stood out in a crowd.

As usual, Jayson and Elizabeth sat at the end of the bench, and Trevin and Addie sat on the other side of Derek and Harmony to keep them corralled in between. Jayson only had to take Derek out once during the first part of the meeting. Then he went to the front with the choir to play the piano for the special musical number they had rehearsed the last few Sundays.

When the meeting was over and they were hurrying to gather everything up, Elizabeth noticed a sister in the ward approaching her husband. She'd met this sister once or twice, but couldn't recall her name. Elizabeth purposely hovered close by out of curiosity. "Brother Wolfe?" the woman said. "Is that right? That's what it said in the program."

"That's right," he said. "And you are?"

"Alisha Randall," she said. "I just have to tell you that your accompaniment was beautiful. I *love* the piano, but I haven't heard it played that well since . . ." she laughed softly, "probably since the last time you played for the choir, but I didn't get a chance to talk to you then."

"It's a pleasure to meet you, Sister Randall," he said. "And I'm glad you enjoy the piano. It is an amazing instrument."

Elizabeth smiled as he deftly steered compliments away from his talent or himself.

"I heard someone say," Sister Randall added, "that you're a professional musician. Is that true?"

"I'm afraid it is."

"What do you do, exactly?"

"A little piano. A little guitar. It was nice meeting you. I'd better get my son to nursery."

Jayson smiled at her and hurried away with Elizabeth at his side. She whispered with a hint of amusement, "A little piano? A little guitar?"

"What was I supposed to say? I never know what to say when people ask that question . . . especially at church."

"Oh, you could say, 'I've been on the cover of *Rolling Stone Magazine* and I've won a few Grammys.'"

"Oh, and then she could say, 'I thought you were a *real* professional musician. Can you play Mozart?'"

"And you could say that your middle name *is* Amadeus, but you play screaming guitars."

"Very funny," he said, not thinking it was. But she laughed anyway. They exchanged a quick kiss in the hall before she took Derek to his nursery class, then she went off to teach her Sunday School class of fourteen-year-olds.

Jayson went to the Gospel Doctrine class, which he doubted he'd be able to sit through with Harmony's antics, but he always made a good effort.

They proceeded through the rest of their Sunday routine as usual. They all worked together to fix a nice dinner, they ate it, then they all worked together to clean it up. Then they either did something together as a family, or took naps, or read, or studied. Jayson usually had choir practice in the middle of the afternoon, and they liked to have dinner over and cleaned up by then. On that particular evening, Jayson had a fireside to do, and there was nearly an hour's drive to get there. Trevin was left in charge of the kids, since he'd heard the presentation enough times now that it was getting old. Elizabeth almost always went with him, mostly because she was on the program. The couple of times she hadn't been able to make it, he'd managed to fill in, but he preferred having her be a part of it. He enjoyed the opportunity to share his conversion experience and his personal tragedies that had been integrated with the ugliness of the music industry. He enjoyed playing a few songs that were spiritual and appropriate, and he loved to have Elizabeth join him with violin and backing vocals. She also usually spent a few minutes at the pulpit sharing some of her own experiences and perspective. The bottom line was that they both had the opportunity to bear their testimonies of the truthfulness of the gospel and the healing power of the Atonement. Afterward, there was always a long line of people who wanted to meet Jayson and Elizabeth and shake their hands. It could be tiring, but they knew it was where the Lord wanted them to be, and if only one person present would make positive life changes, it was worth the time and effort.

The fireside went well, but it was late when they got home. The children were all in bed except for Trevin, who was reading his scriptures. They quickly checked on everyone and went to bed as well. Jayson fell asleep praying that inspiration would come. Now that he'd made a commitment to the record company, he needed some really great music to give them. He hoped that his diligent obedience to the Sabbath would count in his favor.

School started that week, and the household became more structured. Jayson went to his studio each morning after the children left, coming out only for lunch, and staying there until they came home. Trevin came in more than an hour before Addie, the same way he left more than an hour earlier in the morning. Jayson always made it a point to spend some time with each of them when they came in from school, then he went back to work until supper. He figured if he was actually in the room with the instruments, and even playing them, he would be more likely to get something. But he was blank. Hopelessly and utterly blank. After seemingly countless hours in front of the piano and toying with the guitars, he was still blank. He discussed it with Elizabeth, committed himself to praying harder for the inspiration he needed, and again he fasted and went to the temple.

Macy often came to visit, which Jayson appreciated, even though he knew her being there wasn't likely to get his creative juices flowing. She was gifted at rubbing his neck and shoulders, however, which helped him feel less tense. She reported that she had handled the phone call with Debbie rather well once her mother had finally called, and she was starting to feel a little better. She still hadn't found a job, but she'd been doing some projects around her mother-in-law's home that had helped the family and had made Macy feel better.

More than two weeks after Jayson had made the decision to get back to work, he still felt dried up creatively.

"Maybe I got the wrong answer," he told Elizabeth. "Maybe it just isn't going to work."

"Be patient with yourself, and keep at it," she said. "It'll come."

"I'm glad somebody believes that," he said.

"Maybe that's the problem." He scowled at her, and she added, "Go . . . back to the piano." She shooed him with her hand. "Go. Go. I'll put the kids to bed."

"Yes, ma'am," he said with sarcasm. "But you'd better bring them in for a hug before you do."

"I promise," she said, and he sulked off to the studio.

* * * * *

Long after the kids were all asleep, Elizabeth sat in bed reading, or more accurately, pondering the situation with her husband while a book lay open on her lap. She prayed as she had countless times that the inspiration would come to him. He needed his confidence in his gift reaffirmed. She had seen him do marvelous things with his music, and because of his fame, the influence of his beliefs had accomplished a great deal of good. She knew he could do it again, and she knew that God knew it. She just prayed that it would happen soon. She could sense his growing discouragement and didn't want it to *keep* growing. She finally set the book aside and turned off the lamp, but it still took her a long while to relax. The fact that he hadn't come to bed seemed like a good sign. She hoped so.

Elizabeth was nearly asleep when she heard Jayson come quietly into the room and close the door behind him. She expected him to go into the bathroom and get ready for bed, but he lay down beside her and whispered, "Are you asleep?"

"Yes," she said, and he chuckled.

"Did I wake you?"

"No, but . . . I was *almost* asleep."

"I'm sorry."

"It's okay." She rolled toward him. "What do you need?"

"A kiss . . . for inspiration."

"It's not going well?"

"Much worse than that."

"Then why don't you just come to bed and get some sleep?"

"I can't sleep. My brain is wired. At least I feel like maybe I'm *close* to coming up with something. I'm just not quite figuring it out. It's like . . . there . . . but in a haze. Just give me a kiss."

She did, then said, "And you expect me to believe that you came here intending to stop with a kiss?"

"Maybe," he said and kissed her again. "You *are* my inspiration."

"I don't know about that," she said and kissed him.

"You're like . . . the stars that brighten the heavens . . . hey, that's good. Kiss me again."

She did. "You're talking like a songwriter."

"I hope so," he said and kissed her.

"You always did, you know. Even when we were in high school. You wooed me with that songwriter talk . . . and you didn't even realize you were doing it."

Jayson was apparently oblivious to what she was saying. "The stars that brighten the heavens," he repeated. Another kiss.

"Yeah, like that," she said, but he didn't hear her.

"The moon illuminating the nighttime sky. Oh, that's good, too." Another kiss. "Oh." He sat up. "No, it's skies, not sky. The nighttime skies. And . . . the sun in all her radiant glory."

"Hey, that's good," she said.

"It's a start."

"It's also a lovely description of the bodies of light in the sky that—"

"I've got it," he said. "'The stars that brighten the heavens, the moon illuminating the nighttime skies, the sun in all her radiant glory, can't hold a candle to your eyes.'" He laughed. "Great chorus. I can hear the music." He kissed her again and jumped off the bed. "Thank you. I knew a kiss would do it."

"Glad I could help," Elizabeth said after he'd left the room. She laughed softly, said a little prayer expressing gratitude that his inspiration had gotten started, and another that his inspiration would continue, and she went to sleep.

* * * * *

The next morning Elizabeth got a call from her mother. She knew it was her before she answered the phone, thanks to the caller ID, and she steeled herself to be kind and polite, but not to get caught up in any of her mother's typical critical behavior. Elizabeth was pleasantly surprised to hear her mother simply ask how everyone was doing, and then she asked many questions about the children and what they were specifically up to these days. When Elizabeth hung up the phone, she wondered if she'd ever talked to her mother without feeling some kind of anxiety. But it had actually been a pleasant conversation. She wondered what might be behind such a change, and hoped it didn't have some ulterior motive. Beyond that she didn't give it another thought except for mentioning it to Jayson. He sounded suspicious, but then her mother had never given either of them any reason *not* to be suspicious.

Elizabeth forgot all about her mother while she sat in the studio listening to Jayson pick out a melody on the piano, then on the guitar, then back to the piano. Two days later he played the song for her on the piano, singing the lyrics fluidly. It was a beautiful love song that showed off the incredible range and clear quality of his voice. Elizabeth felt near tears to be the first to hear his new creation. It was a privilege she didn't take for granted. Then he told her where she would be playing the violin, and what he could hear. At one time she'd resisted recording with him, because it also meant going on tour with him. But she had long ago taken that issue to the Lord, and she knew that her place was with Jayson, both in the home and with his music. Their family had fared just fine the last time they'd done this; they would surely be able to survive it again.

With one song completed, Elizabeth expected the doors of Jayson's creativity to open wide. But he quickly regressed into his creative dearth. He started making jokes about the muse being on vacation, or spending time with some up-and-rising musician who was going to take the world by storm. Elizabeth just kept encouraging him, certain it would come when the time was right. She prayed that it would come soon.

* * * * *

After Trevin and Addie were off to school, Jayson took Mozie for a walk, then he spent some time playing with his babies while Elizabeth was busy cleaning something somewhere in the house. He'd decided that the studio had become old and he wasn't getting any inspiration there. He needed stimulation and interaction. While he was lying on the living room floor with the babies crawling over him repeatedly, his eye was drawn to what Macy had dubbed *The Career Wall*. He'd become accustomed to having it there; he passed it multiple times each day. But he hadn't really looked at it for a while.

During the last tour they'd done when Derek was a baby, Macy had gone along as the tour nanny, and she'd thoroughly enjoyed it. She'd taken along a camera and had kind of accidentally become the band historian. She'd come up with some really great photos, and the results had become addictive for her. When they'd returned, she had methodically gone through old scrapbooks and folders of everything Elizabeth had kept through the years of his career. There were reviews and magazine articles interspersed with the photographs. She'd scanned, copied, enlarged, cropped, and framed bits and pieces of the musical history of Jayson's career. Elizabeth was there with him at the beginning, in the band they'd been in with her brother and his in high school. Then there were the years of his hugely successful band, Gray Wolf. Then the history merged into his solo album and the tour he'd done with Elizabeth by his side again.

The visual history seemed to inadvertently capture the history of his relationship with Elizabeth as well. The framed pieces were hung close together and arranged artistically across the wall, with much space yet to fill, an indication that there would be more. At first Jayson hadn't been certain he'd wanted that much of his fame spread out on a wall in his house where people would come and go and see it. But he'd found over time that it had helped him find an abstract sense of fulfillment that he'd not felt before. Having the career wall in the living room seemed the perfect merging of his two worlds. Here he found that the evidence of each side of his life gave perspective to the other. He'd come to see, as Macy had suggested, that it was not a bragging wall; rather, it was a reminder of all he'd struggled through and survived.

When the babies became occupied with toys, Jayson stood up and slowly walked the length of the wall, feeling happiness and sorrow over certain memories, marveling that it had all really happened. He felt a more tangible hope that he really could do another album, even though the lack of inspiration made it difficult to comprehend at the moment. After he'd perused the length of the wall, he turned to face the glass cabinet that housed some things that were very precious to him. His Grammy awards were in there. But more importantly, there was a pair of red shoes that had belonged to Elizabeth in high school and that had deep significance. And there was a silly hat that had belonged to Derek. It had a propeller on top of it, and Derek had worn it—or something equally silly—during many performances. Jayson really missed him, and he considered that hat one of his most precious possessions.

"Admiring the Grammys?" Elizabeth asked, coming into the room.

"No, the hat," he said. "And I remember how great you looked in those shoes."

"It all seems like a dream," she said, sitting on the long couch beneath the career wall.

"I was thinking exactly the same thing."

"Getting any inspiration?" she asked.

"No," he said, not wanting it brought up.

"What can I do to help?"

"What *don't* you do?" he asked, tossing her a fond glance. "You take such good care of me—and everyone else around here—that sometimes I almost feel guilty."

"Guilty?" She sounded astonished.

Jayson sat on the couch beside her and took her hand. "I feel so blessed, that sometimes I wonder why. And you're at the center of everything for me, Elizabeth." He kissed her. "I'm just trying to tell you that you are a great blessing to me in more ways than I can count."

"You can say things like that to me anytime you want, Jayson Wolfe. But feeling guilty doesn't fit in there in any way. You have a good life because you've always tried to make good choices. And you've given *us* a good life. It hasn't been easy, and it will probably be hard again. But we're in it together. There is nothing I do for you that is any kind of sacrifice. *You* are a tremendous blessing in *my* life. I wonder every day how I ever lived without you."

He smiled and kissed her again. "I wonder that, too. Because you're so amazing."

She made a facetious scoffing noise and stood up. "Write a song about it, Jayson. Or tend the kids while I do something amazing like . . . the laundry. I'd swear I have a bushel of baby socks to fold."

CHAPTER 3

Jayson watched Elizabeth leave the room and chuckled to himself. The words he'd said to his wife warmed his heart again as he considered all the ways she blessed his life. She truly *was* amazing. During the many years that their relationship had mostly been a long-distance friendship, more like a brother and sister, he'd had little opportunity to see all that she was capable of. But now that he'd been married to her for a few years, he'd grown to appreciate all she did. She was often complaining about how parts of the house were cluttered and disorganized, and how she wished she was better at cooking or actually enjoyed spending time in the kitchen. Her father was a great cook, and she commented frequently how she missed having him around so they could all eat better. While Elizabeth seemed able to only see all that she didn't do— and that she would like to do, Jayson could see all that she did. She kept the household running, overseeing every aspect of it with efficiency. On top of that, she more or less worked as his manager. Right now, while there was little going on, it didn't amount to much, but he'd seen her manage many of his business affairs efficiently while he'd been consumed with the musical aspects of his career. He knew that she was well aware that if he was going to do another album, she would become very busy with many related arrangements. They'd both agreed a long time ago that if it ever got to be too much for her, he'd hire someone. But she'd assured him that for the most part she enjoyed the involvement, and he would certainly rather have her do it than someone who didn't know him as well as she did.

The most amazing thing about Elizabeth, however, was her capacity to love. She lived the gospel to its fullest, and she was such a good wife and mother that Jayson was often left in awe. The personal relationships she shared with each member of their household—as well as Macy and her husband—were exactly what he believed was exemplary. She was keenly in tune with each child's mood and needs, and they were her highest priority. She'd told Jayson more than once that she put the kids' needs above his, because he was a grown-up and he could be patient enough to wait for her attention. And he was more than all right with that. He was grateful every day to have this incredible woman as the love of his life. He wondered if his years without her had made him more aware of his gratitude for having her there now. Whatever the reason, just having her in his life day in and day out was a blessing he didn't take for granted. The fact that she had found this great religion, and that it was through her family that he had come into the Church only added to his convictions. He'd spent too many years living in hell to ever take living in heaven for granted.

A fight between the babies brought him out of his reverie, but he broke it up, changed a diaper, picked up the toys, fed the kids lunch, and fixed a sandwich for Elizabeth and one for himself. While they were eating together after he'd gotten the kids down for naps, she said, "You know, babe, I really like having you take such good care of me and the kids, but it's not what you're supposed to be doing. You're the genius songwriter in this house. *Anyone* can change a diaper and fix a sandwich."

"Not anyone can be their daddy—or your husband."

"That's true." She pointed comically at him. "You've got me there. However . . . you can still get some of that in every day and be a genius songwriter."

"I'm not feeling very genius at the moment."

"It'll come," she said. "But I'm not sure it'll come while you're finding ways to avoid it."

Jayson knew she was probably right, and the following morning he began another long day in the studio, but not because anything was happening musically. He talked to his brother on the phone, and he talked to Rick. Neither of them seemed as concerned as Jayson felt. They both appeared to be conspiring with Elizabeth on the notion that it would come and there was nothing to worry about. But Jayson was worried. He'd been praying hard and struggling to do everything he knew to get the creative juices flowing. But they just seemed to have dried up.

That evening at dinner, Macy and Aaron were there, and he was glad to see her doing well—as long as nothing about babies came up. He wasn't thinking at all about music when the conversation at the dinner table became suddenly distant, and other sounds consumed his mind. Something familiar, but different. Strangely comfortable, but unexplainably strange. He listened. He waited. He listened again, and it came more clearly.

"Oh!" he said, startling everyone at the table and putting an abrupt halt to whatever Elizabeth had been saying. "Oh!" he said again, mostly oblivious to anything but the notes playing in his head, over and over, louder and louder. "Excuse me." He slid his chair back and stood up. "Oh!"

Elizabeth watched Jayson leave, hurrying toward the studio. She chuckled and broke the silence that had fallen over the table. "Apparently he's been inspired."

"Apparently," Macy said. Aaron looked baffled but amused. Trevin gave up a subtle smirk. The other children didn't care. And they went on with dinner.

When the meal was over and long since cleaned up, Elizabeth went to check on Jayson but found the door to the studio locked, even though the recording light was not on. She knew that knocking wouldn't do any good when there were two doors with space in between for a sound barrier, and for that same reason she couldn't hear whether or not he was actually playing something. She waited a few minutes and called his cell phone.

Jayson felt his phone vibrate on his belt and glanced at it before he answered. He didn't want to talk to anybody except Elizabeth; thankfully, it was her.

"Were you worried about me?" he asked without any other greeting.

"Not worried, exactly. Just . . . wondering . . . what great thing is going on in there. And your daughter is leaving soon. You should probably say good-bye."

"Yes, I should. Thank you. I'll be out in a minute."

"Why did you lock the door?" she asked.

"I don't know," he said almost absently. "I guess I just . . . wanted to be . . . alone."

"So, it's a *secret* composition?"

"Maybe," Jayson said and chuckled. "But I assure you that when it's unveiled, you'll be the first to hear it."

"Ooh, I can't wait."

Jayson hung up the phone, hurried to write down a couple more notes, then he left the studio to find most of the family in the dining room while Elizabeth was putting some cookies on a plate to send with Macy and Aaron to share with Aaron's family.

Macy teased him about ignoring her, but he knew she understood, and she finally admitted that she was excited to think of such inspiration coming. She couldn't wait to hear the results. Jayson felt so anxious to get back to the piano he could hardly breathe. Once Macy and Aaron were off, Elizabeth gave him a tight hug, saying, "I can't wait either."

"Neither can I." He chuckled.

"Why don't you go spend one minute with each of your children, and then I'll keep the home fires burning while you burn on that piano. Or is it the guitar?"

"No, it's the piano." He chuckled again, a delighted little laugh, as if the creative energy might burst out of him if he didn't give it an outlet. "Very good advice, Mrs. Wolfe," he said and went in search of each of the children. He spent more than a minute with each of them, then he found Elizabeth again, and spent more than a minute with her before she sent him back to the studio with a warm, passionate kiss for luck.

Elizabeth was astonished over the next few days at how much time Jayson spent in the studio. He came out for meals, but only with strong urging. And she had to do the urging by calling him on his cell phone because he was keeping the door to the studio locked. He didn't go back to the studio in the evenings after supper until the children had gone to bed and he'd spent some quiet time with her, but she knew he was distracted by the music in his head. She knew that look well. She'd first seen it when they'd been teenagers and he'd been drawn away from the present as if he were hearing ghosts calling him from another dimension.

He was as kind and concerned for his family as he had always been, in spite of a certain soberness about him that left Elizabeth more intrigued than worried. She wondered what manner of creation he was absorbed in, and what the results might be. She encouraged him to work every minute that he could, but they both agreed that he needed to remain disciplined about spending time with his family and his Church responsibilities, and that he would surely be blessed for doing so. Still, he was in the studio early and late every day, although he didn't spend a minute there on Sunday. He never had. Since he'd joined the Church, he had honored the Sabbath with conscious respect to the commandment. He'd admitted more than once that keeping the law had likely kept him from burning out during creative periods, the way he'd seen other musicians do. But Elizabeth knew it wasn't easy for him. She knew the music in his head didn't stop Saturday night at midnight, and it took a great deal of faith for him to believe that it would still be there enough for him to write it down come Monday morning.

She noted that he was up *very* early Monday morning, in the studio with the door locked. He ate a quick breakfast with the kids and was back at it. Elizabeth took him some lunch, but he met her at the door to get it, greeted her with a smile, a kiss, and an expression of deep gratitude. And then he was back to work.

On Tuesday he asked her if she could pick up some more staff paper for him when it was convenient. She knew he'd had a great deal of it on hand, and she wondered what kind of music he'd been pouring onto the blank music sheets. Or perhaps he'd been throwing a lot of it away due to trial and error. She didn't ask and he didn't tell her, but she knew when he was ready that he would tell her everything. Even better, she knew she would be his first audience. Sometimes she got butterflies thinking of what it would be like when that moment came.

More than a week after Jayson's big epiphany at the dinner table, he climbed into bed, and Elizabeth stirred from her relaxed state to glance at the clock. 12:42. "Good morning," she muttered through the darkness and eased close to him.

"I tried not to wake you."

"I wasn't asleep; if I had been, you wouldn't have wakened me." She settled her head onto his shoulder and luxuriated in his arm coming around her. "How's it going?"

"Good . . . I think." He chuckled comfortably. "I do believe I've nearly got it all dumped out of my head enough that I can actually think straight again."

"Ooh, when do I get to hear it?"

"It needs a little more practice and organization before I come out of the closet."

"Okay. By *it*, you mean an album?"

"No, just one song."

Elizabeth leaned on her elbow. "One song? You've been working this long on one song?" She didn't mean to sound so astonished, and hurried to add, "It's just that . . . usually a song comes together more quickly than that."

"I know," he said and chuckled again, "but this is different. Be patient just a little longer."

"It's okay, Jayson. I knew this was part of the bargain when I married you."

Jayson leaned on his elbow as well so that he could kiss her. "You're very good to me. I know it isn't easy living with someone like me. I want you to know that I'm grateful."

"I understand."

"Yes, I know you do."

"It's not so terribly difficult, you know. I don't feel like I'm making any great sacrifice, Jayson. You take very good care of us. Besides, I know the source of your inspiration, and I'm not going to quibble over that."

Jayson rolled onto his back and sighed. "Yes, I know its source too, Elizabeth." He sighed again. "It's incredible. Sometimes I . . . I can't believe it. Even while it's pouring through my head, I marvel at how quickly and clearly it comes. It's not humanly possible for me to do what I'm doing. It feels so . . . utterly spiritual, so remarkable. Before I learned the gospel and learned how the Spirit works, I just took the gift for granted, just knew that when the muse put ideas into my head, I had to bring them to life. But now I see how the gift is inseparable from my spiritual knowledge. What I'm trying to say is . . . that I know it's true. Every good gift *does* come from Christ. I know it's true, Elizabeth. And I know that God is with me in this. I just hope that I can do it the way He wants me to do it, and not let Him down. If nothing else, it makes me very aware of just how human I am; how powerless. Without the gift from Him, my abilities are nothing."

Elizabeth smiled in the darkness but knew he felt the glow of her smile by the way he chuckled. "I love you, Jayson Wolfe," she said and kissed him.

"I love you, too . . . Mrs. Wolfe," he said, and they kissed again.

The following morning when Elizabeth woke up, Jayson was already in the studio. After the older children were off to school and the little ones occupied, she called his cell phone to urge him to come and get some breakfast, but he didn't answer. She went to the door, knowing it was a long shot that he might hear her knock, but she was going to try anyway. She was surprised to try the knob and find it unlocked. She held her breath and went quietly through the door, and then through the second door that was wide open. At first she heard nothing, then she heard a tinkling sound on the piano that quickened her heart. It had a classical sound to it, very different from anything she'd ever heard him do—except the couple of times he'd proved to her that he could play Mozart. That was it, she thought. It sounded like Mozart, or at least his style. Was this the song he'd been working on, or was he just taking a break and messing around? She listened for only a minute before she felt guilty for eavesdropping when he'd made it clear he wanted privacy. She cleared her throat ridiculously loud. He stopped playing and turned abruptly.

"Sorry," she said. "The door was unlocked."

"Was it?" he asked, not sounding at all like it mattered. "How careless of me." He removed the glasses he'd come to need for any close-up work. She'd teased him about how it was a good thing he always memorized music before he performed it. She doubted the glasses would go well with his rock star image. He'd just told her that he would get contacts if he needed to, but she'd assured him that was not the point. The fact that he was wearing glasses now meant that he'd been working on either writing music down, or playing from written music. Eventually he would put all of the music he wrote by hand into a computer program so that it could be printed out.

"Freudian slip, perhaps?" she asked, wondering if he was ready to share his secret.

"Perhaps," he said with a smile and rose to greet her with a kiss. Then Elizabeth's eyes were drawn to the sheets of music scattered over the top of the piano, all covered with the scribbling of hand-written music notes. She was surprised at how many there were, and the chaotic look of them, especially when he said he'd been working on just one song. She wanted to ask but didn't want to pry.

"Um," he drawled, sounding uncharacteristically shy, perhaps a little sheepish. "This is, uh . . ." he chuckled, "my new song."

"If you're not ready to tell me, then—"

"No, it's okay." He picked up a few of the sheets and glanced at them as he handed them to her one at a time. "Um . . . these are the . . . violins, and . . ." He picked up more and sorted through them, handing them to her as he looked them over. "These are the cellos. And the horns. The flutes here. I think that's all . . . except the piano. I don't have the piano all written down yet, but I can play a somewhat tolerable version of it."

"Jayson," Elizabeth said, shuffling through the papers, taking in the evidence of what she was seeing, "this is . . . what? Orchestration? You're composing for an orchestra?"

"Well, not a *whole* orchestra," he said as if he were apologizing. "Only, say . . . twelve or so."

"Jayson," she said again and let out an astonished burst of laughter. "This is incredible. I mean . . . you don't know how to do this."

He chuckled and stuffed his hands into the pockets of his jeans. "I don't know if that was a compliment or an insult."

"A compliment, of course. What I mean is . . . you were never trained for this; you've never done it before."

"I think that's why it's called a gift," he said matter-of-factly. Their eyes met as if he were seeking some kind of approval. He smiled as if he'd found it and sat again on the piano bench. But he just sat there.

"Will you play it for me?" she asked.

"Oh, I can't play it yet," he insisted. "I need more practice. The piano is pretty complicated, different from anything I've ever done. But I'm getting it."

"I'll look forward to it," she said. "So . . . tell me about it. Tell me what you hear."

He urged her to sit on the piano bench beside him and took the pages from her. He responded eagerly to her request, and his eyes lit up as he explained how the idea had come into his mind suddenly and forcefully, every instrument at once. He'd been able to hear the completed piece, and he'd been working hard to pick it apart and put down notes for the separate instruments. He became animated with excitement as he shared a very clear vision of how it would be performed in the middle of a concert, and how vital orchestration would be to the entire concert, even if the music was considered rock and roll. She realized as he talked that he had found the theme for the album and the title track, but he was holding out on her as to what that was exactly. Then he started talking about Mozart, about listening to his mother's Mozart records as a child, how his mother had made him learn to play some Mozart in order to earn privileges. She'd known all of this, but it was evident he was now seeing these facts as seeds to something bigger, as opposed to simply tidbits of his childhood. She actually got a chill as she thought of something else about him just a moment before he smiled and spoke the same thought aloud. "And, of course, my middle name *is* Amadeus. So, it stands to reason that I should write a tribute to Mozart."

"Is *that* what you've done?"

"In a roundabout way, yes." He leaned toward her, and his eyes sparkled with a faraway look. "That's how the idea came to me, Elizabeth. I could hear Mozart's music in my head, or . . . at least bits and pieces of it, all put together in a new and unique way. It's like . . . well, you know how the definition of creation is not making something out of nothing, but in bringing other matter together to make something new and original. It's like . . . the seeds were planted by Mozart, and somehow they just blossomed and went out of control in me."

"So, tell me if I understand this. The song you're writing is in a style that's more . . . classical."

"Yes."

"It's like . . . a medley perhaps . . . that's based on . . . or inspired by . . . different pieces by Mozart."

"Yes."

"So, what's the title?" she asked.

He smiled. "I'll tell you later."

"And you will play the piano accompanied by several other musicians."

"Yes."

"Wow!" She let out a delighted laugh. "That's so cool."

"Yes," he said again and laughed the same way, taking her hand.

"But it's . . . so *un* rock and roll."

"Yes and no," he said. "Remember how my classic favorite of all time by Elton John—'Funeral for a Friend'—is completely instrumental, very unusual, then it merges into the next song which is purely rock. Technically it's two songs, but they are hooked together."

"Yes," she drawled.

"The first part of this song will be like a classical tribute to Mozart, inspired by his music and style. The second part is the rock and roll." His eyes took on a more faraway look. "I can hear it . . . and see it. The classical part ends on two strong notes, then there's one beat of silence and the drums come in really big, then the guitars, then the piano again with the same melody but in rock style. And the lyrics."

"You have the lyrics?"

He chuckled. "I do, but I'm not telling you yet. After I practice some more, I'll just do the song for you—as much as I can by myself."

"Of course. I'm used to that step."

"Yes, so am I . . . except that it sounds more hollow than usual to me when I can hear the orchestration in my head."

Elizabeth squeezed his hand. "You are so amazing."

"Hey, I didn't ask for this gift. I'm just trying to do what I'm told. Sometimes it feels as if I will shrivel up and die if I don't get the music out of my head."

Elizabeth took a deep breath to try to absorb the musician—and the man—all over again. He never ceased to amaze her, both by his gifts and his humility in using them. "I should go and let you practice, because I can't wait to hear the results." She stood up. "I also need to check on your babies, and *you* should come and eat some breakfast."

"Yes, I should," he said and stood up as well.

During the remainder of the day, Elizabeth couldn't stop thinking about Jayson's new project. She felt so excited about it she was nearly giddy. And if anyone could pull off presenting classical music to a rock-and-roll audience, it was Jayson Wolfe. His fans would love it. She knew without even hearing the song, because she knew that part of his gift was a deep and finely tuned instinct to what his fans wanted to hear. It was easy to imagine his vision of performing the song on stage with thousands of screaming fans and the full effect of the lights, the orchestra, the drums, and the guitars. And she couldn't wait! She felt privileged to be the person who was privy to each step of the process more than anyone else in his life. And even more so, she felt privileged to be the woman he loved.

The next morning, Jayson was still asleep when Elizabeth got up with the children, and she left him to rest. He didn't waken until late morning, then he ate, spent some time with her and the little ones, then went back to bed with a headache coming on. Elizabeth recognized the signs of creative letdown. Although he'd not admitted it, she suspected he had finished whatever had been in his head, and now the adrenaline was no longer there to push him through tireless hours of song writing. He mostly slept that day, aided by the pill he'd taken for a migraine. It wasn't until the next morning after breakfast when the older kids were off to school that he said, "You want to hear my song?"

"Do I *want* to?" She laughed. "Is that what you asked?"

"Well?"

"I've been dying to hear it! Is it ready?"

"As ready as it's going to get without a dozen or so other musicians."

"Okay, I'm ready to hear it." She checked on the children and knew they were playing in a baby-proofed area and would be fine for a little while. She also had a baby monitor with her so she could hear them.

They went into the studio and she sat in the chair she typically used for such moments. Jayson sat at the piano bench and did a comical display of stretching his fingers, then he abruptly ruffled his own hair which made her laugh. Without a word the gesture implied some effort to make himself look more like a slightly mad—or at least very eccentric—eighteenth-century composer.

"The song," he said, more serious now, "will be the title track of the album. And the title is . . ." He hesitated and chuckled at her expectancy. Then he said it, "The Heart of Mozart."

Elizabeth felt chills. "Oh, wow!" she said. "I love it!"

"Here goes," he said and didn't wait another second before his hands came down on the keys with a series of chords that were so fast and so strong that his hands were almost a blur. While he played he would say things like, "Violins are strong here," or "the horns come in here . . . big, then softer," and, "flutes here." The speed and strength of the piece merged into a slow, softer interim, then the piano built back up to an amazing pace while he described all of the instruments coming together for the powerful finish. Elizabeth was so stunned she could hardly breathe. She'd been in awe of his gift from the first time she'd heard him play, back in high school. She'd been amazed over and over at the intensity and skill he possessed. But she'd never imagined anything like this. He completely surpassed anything he'd ever done before. She had hardly taken it in when he paused for just a second, saying, "The drums start here, with electric guitar. The rhythm changes, but the melody is the same." He started playing the rock version of the classical-sounding piece he'd just played. And then he started to sing. And Elizabeth felt as if she'd melt into the chair.

"Hear the beat, beat, beat of my heart, heart, heart. Feel it stop, oh, then feel it start. Who's that calling, who's that there? The sound is inside me, it's everywhere! The muse is amusing, it's magic and maze. The muse is confusing, it's blindness and craze. The muse is a monster, it eats me alive. It drives in high gear till there's nothing to drive."

The music changed, and Elizabeth recognized the merging of verse to chorus. *"But sanity comes at the edge of reason. The muse is a voice without limits or season. From the end of the world, right back to its start. It's been speaking and singing to the mind and the heart, Of madmen like me with the heart of Mozart."*

With that last line Elizabeth couldn't hold her emotion inside any longer. Tears burned into her eyes and trickled over her face. But Jayson was oblivious. He could only feel the song. She could see it in his countenance. He was in his element, filled with a gift that was too unearthly to describe. He played an intricate bridge and went on to the second verse.

"Is this madness or magic? Am I lucid or lame? Will the noises inside me bring fury or fame? The muse is colossus, it gnaws from inside, Till there's nothing to spare, and nothing to hide. It haunts and it blesses, it curses then cries. It bleeds and it heals, it sings and it sighs. But how can I doubt it when I know life without it, Is colorless, noiseless, and turned out inside."

And the chorus again, but this time with more fervency. *"But sanity comes at the edge of reason. The muse is a voice without limits or season. From the end of the world, right back to its start. It's been speaking and singing to the mind and the heart, Of madmen like me with the heart of Mozart."*

Following another bridge that was more embellished, his voice seemed to reach deeper from his soul, and the song finished with an air of personal triumph, and a sense of soaring straight from his heart into the open. *"Oh, bring on the madness! And help me to soar! Let the angels in heaven grant me more, more, and more. May the music inside me, let it always abide me. Let the muse ever guide me, the light never hide me. Oh, hear the beat, beat, beat of the heart, heart, heart . . . The heart of Mozart, yeah, the heart of Mozart."*

He finished playing after a powerful series of chords that brought the song back to its classical sound. The moment it was done he spun on the piano bench with an elaborate flourish and a little laugh. Then he saw Elizabeth crying, and his countenance fell.

"What's wrong?" he demanded.

"Wrong?" she blubbered. "It's the most amazing thing I've ever heard. I can't believe it. I mean . . . I can . . . because I know you better than anyone, but . . . Jayson. It's incredible!"

"You really think so?" he asked. "I mean . . . really?"

"Are you kidding? It's the best work you've ever done." She stood up, and he did the same just as she threw herself into his arms. She hugged him tightly, then she took his face into her hands. "I'm so proud of you, Jayson. If no one but me ever heard this song, it would be remarkable. But the world is going to hear it. This song will lift spirits and inspire hearts everywhere. People will listen to it on their stereos over and over and over. This is the kind of music you were born to write . . . and perform. It will be marvelous!"

Elizabeth saw tears in his eyes before he wrapped her in his arms and pressed his face into her hair. She knew he was crying, but then he laughed and picked her up, turning her around a couple of times before he set her back down.

"The music is great, Jayson," she said, still trying to take it all in. "But the lyrics are incredible, too. You must have spent hours piecing the words together that way."

He chuckled and looked down. "Actually, the lyrics were the easy part. They just came." Elizabeth knew what that meant. She'd seen things just *come* to him for years, but she was still surprised when he added, "About twenty minutes."

"That's it?"

"That's it. Now, you and I both know that it's not humanly possible to write such complex lyrics with meaning that quickly. I've had such experiences many times, but now I know that all things are created spiritually before they are created in reality."

"So . . . how do you think that works?" Elizabeth asked, pondering the implications. "Obviously you've thought about it."

"Yes, I certainly have. Sometimes I wonder if someone on the other side of the veil has created it first, and then given it to me . . . like the ministering angels that Mormon talks about."

"Ooh, what a delightful thought!"

"Or maybe *I* created it before I was born, and the Spirit just helped me remember it."

"Ooh, that's a delightful thought, too. Which do you think it is?"

"Obviously I don't really *know,* and it really doesn't matter *how* it happened as much as I need to remember that all good things come through the light of Christ, and it is God who deserves the credit for whatever I might create. Still, I think that both principles apply to my gift, and maybe there are other principles as well that we simply cannot begin to grasp or understand from our mortal perspective. I figure that as long as I keep listening and doing the best I can, I'll be able to face God with a clear conscience, knowing I did my best to use the talent He gave me to help build the kingdom here on the earth."

"Amen!" Elizabeth said with exaggerated delight, followed by a joyful laugh. She felt giddy and ecstatic over the song, and she couldn't wait to see where it would take him.

CHAPTER 4

With Jayson's permission, Elizabeth invited her father and stepmother, as well as Macy and Aaron, over for dinner that night to unveil the new song. Family was always Jayson's first audience, and he felt ready to let them have it. Dinner wasn't ready when everyone arrived, so Elizabeth coaxed Jayson into doing the song first, which suited him fine.

"Then I can get it over with," he said.

"Are you nervous?" Macy asked him as they all went in a small herd to the studio and crowded in.

"Maybe," he said. "I've never done anything like this before, and I can't make it sound the way I hear it in my head . . . not by myself at least."

Will gave Jayson a playful slap on the back and said, "I remember the first time you played one of your originals for me. You remember that?"

"How could I ever forget?" Jayson said. "I was terrified. I was afraid you were going to think all that time we'd been spending in the basement making music had been a waste. You'd been feeding me, and you were so nice to me, and I was afraid it was all going to end."

"We were all having fun," Will said. "Even if it had been lousy music, we wouldn't have wanted the fun to stop."

"He's told me this story a dozen times," Marilyn said. "He's no more proud of you now than he was then."

"Well, I was wondering," Jayson chuckled. "After we'd played he didn't say a word."

"I was speechless," Will said. "It was incredible! I was expecting to have to humor you a little, but . . ." he chuckled, "it was amazing."

"Well, be prepared to be speechless again," Elizabeth said, and they all got comfortable in chairs and on the floor. Addie was keeping her baby sister happy with some quiet toys. As always, the child's maternal instincts were a great blessing to Elizabeth. And Macy was holding Derek on her lap, whispering something to him that was keeping him still—at least for the moment. Trevin sat close to Elizabeth, his eyes eager with anticipation. He too loved music and was learning from Jayson. He took great pride in his stepfather's music, and the unveiling of a new creation was no small thing.

Elizabeth watched Jayson get comfortable at the piano. His little adjustments of the way he sat and positioning his feet at the pedals were very familiar to her, and it almost seemed to make him one with the instrument. It was all so natural and artless for him. He was wearing very old blue jeans, white running shoes, and a dark green vest unbuttoned over a cream-colored polo shirt. She noticed his hair was now hanging down the back of his neck, and she liked it. He'd told her he didn't know if he wanted to grow it out or not, but he felt too lazy to get a haircut, which had been the deciding factor—for the time being at least.

He set his fingers lightly on the keys, breathed deeply, and began. Elizabeth felt the thrill all over again. She thought that he did even better than he had earlier in the day. Everyone was mesmerized. Even the little ones held almost completely still throughout the entire number, which was nearly ten minutes. When Jayson was finished, there was a long moment of silence, followed by cheers and applause sufficient to have been caused by three times that many people. Aaron and Trevin were comically cheering as if they were at a football game, behaving as any brothers would who were egging each other on. Elizabeth noticed that her father had tears in his eyes. So did Macy. They knew Jayson's gift and understood it deeply.

Jayson took in the compliments from his loved ones in a way that was more reticent than in the past. She sensed that the difference in this piece, and the new heights it had taken him to, had left him a little in awe himself. She'd often heard him say that he was okay with people being in awe of his gift—his music—because he was in awe of it, too. But he didn't want people to be in awe of him, because he was only an ordinary man simply blessed with the privilege of having such a gift, and he genuinely wanted to use it to make the world a better place. He'd certainly done that! And he was doing it again.

Jayson was relieved to have the unveiling over and get on with dinner. Sharing a meal with everyone this way was one of his favorite things. He became caught up in Will's reminiscing over the days when Jayson and Elizabeth had been in high school, and his son Derek had been alive. And they'd all been playing music together, along with Jayson's brother, Drew, who had always been an incredible drummer. Derek's sudden death in their senior year had been a nightmare for all of them. But time had passed, wounds had healed, and they could now talk about him and the times they'd shared without feeling the intense heartache.

During the conversation, however, Jayson noticed that Macy seemed despondent. He wondered what might be wrong and started watching her closely. She barely managed a smile when something funny was said, and she was clearly distracted by her own thoughts. While dinner was being cleaned up, Jayson whispered to Elizabeth that he needed to talk to Macy. She nodded in agreement, as if she'd sensed something amiss too. Since Will and Marilyn were doing the dishes, having enlisted the help of Trevin and Addie, and Aaron was playing with the babies, everything appeared to be under control.

Jayson took hold of Macy's arm and gently guided her to the front room where they could have some privacy. They sat on the couch near the grand piano there, and Jayson took her hand. Before he could speak, she looked up at the large framed photo on the end wall and said, "That is a really great picture . . . if I say so myself."

"Yes, it is," Jayson said, glancing at it himself. The enlarged photo in an expensive frame was something Macy had given to him and Elizabeth as a Christmas gift the previous year. She'd told them that of all the pictures she'd taken, this was her favorite, and she felt like it captured something important about the life and the love they shared. She called it "The Missing Ingredient," which was the title of a song Jayson had written when he'd been trying to talk Elizabeth into having more active involvement in his music. The photo was of him and Elizabeth onstage, both singing into the same microphone. He had his guitar on his back. She was holding the violin and bow passively in her hands. Most importantly, the photo had captured a loving gaze between them. The stage lights behind them gave it an ethereal effect.

There were three walls in the front room, where the piano and two comfortable couches were the only pieces of furniture. On one was a magnificent print of an artist's interpretation of the Savior. Jayson had been deeply drawn to it when he'd first come to stay with Elizabeth and her father, and its presence had had a great impact on him. On the wall opposite the Savior was a large family portrait. It had been taken on the temple steps the day that Jayson and Elizabeth had been sealed, and all of the children had been sealed to them. They were all dressed in white. Derek had been a baby at the time, so Harmony wasn't in that picture, but to the side there was a smaller framed picture of her on the day she'd been blessed.

Jayson liked the way the pictures of the family and the Savior faced each other, and he'd made a point to use it as a metaphor in teaching his family about how these two pictures represented everything that really mattered. Macy understood his reasoning, and she had made a point of telling him that a picture representing his music and the part Elizabeth played in it was perfect for the third wall. It too was also a huge part of his life; for him, the three were inseparable.

He took in the three pictures, then said, "You're trying to distract me. What's wrong?"

She pretended to be surprised by the question for only a moment before she started to cry. Jayson wrapped his arms around her and let her get it out of her system before she finally admitted, "Everything!" She went on to tell him how hard it was living under the same roof with her mother-in-law and Aaron's younger siblings, and that despite all of her efforts she hadn't been able to find a job that would make it possible for them to get into an apartment that was decent. She clarified that she really loved Layla, and they got along well. They were just different in the ways they wanted things done around the house, and since it was Layla's house, Macy felt a little lost there. And worst of all was simply the fact that she wanted a baby and couldn't help counting how far along she would have been by now if she hadn't miscarried. Jayson listened, offered compassion, and asked if there was anything he could do. Inwardly he was desperately wanting to just buy his daughter and her husband a home and see them settled comfortably. Or at the very least, have them live under his roof where they could have more space and privacy. He knew what the answer had been the last time he'd brought it up, but he wondered if it had been a matter of timing. Maybe it was right to help her now. Still, he bit his tongue instead of bringing it up again. Macy knew it was an open offer, and if her own conviction on the matter had changed, she wouldn't be afraid to let him know. She thanked him for listening and told him she just needed to get a grip and have some faith. Then Aaron came looking for her and they were soon on their way home.

After Will and Marilyn had gone as well, Jayson and Trevin jammed together with guitars for a while. He'd found that the boy learned best when they played together, and it was something they did often. Elizabeth helped Addie with some homework, then she and Jayson got the little ones bathed and put to bed. Once they were alone, Elizabeth, was quick to ask, "What's going on with Macy?"

"Same old stuff," he said and filled her in on the details, which led him to say, "I really don't think it would be such a bad thing to just help them get a place to live."

Elizabeth rubbed lotion into her hands, sitting on the edge of the bed beside him. "It's probably *not* a bad thing. It's hard to make ends meet on minimum-wage jobs while you're going to school. I feel the way I've always felt. If we can pray about it and both agree that helping her is the right thing to do, then we should do it. Otherwise . . . we need to step back and allow them to learn whatever it is that God wants them to learn. If we step in when we're not supposed to, then we might be denying them the opportunity to learn something that's more important."

"I never looked at it that way," he said. "I just hate to see her struggling so much."

"As any parent would. The difference is that a lot of parents aren't in a position to help, even if they want to." She took his hand and squeezed it. "We'll pray about it. Maybe the time is right."

"Thank you," he said and kissed her.

"For what?"

"For understanding me; believing in me. For knowing me well enough that it's easy to tell you how I feel . . . because you can practically read my mind."

"That works both ways," she said, and they knelt together to pray.

They were about to get into bed when the phone rang. Jayson answered and was asked by the executive secretary in the ward if he and Elizabeth could meet with the bishop the following evening. After the appointment was set up, Jayson crawled into bed next to his wife and wondered what new adventure might be awaiting him. By the way the phone conversation had been worded, he felt relatively certain that this was a change for him, and Elizabeth was just being asked to come along for support. He loved playing the piano for the choir, but it was terribly easy for him, and he couldn't deny that a challenge might be good. He just hoped it wasn't *too* challenging.

Jayson woke up in the dark feeling alarmed but not certain why. His mind was focused intently on one of the ugliest memories of his past, even though he couldn't recall dreaming about it, and he certainly hadn't thought about it for a long time. But the despair and hopelessness he'd felt at a time that had eventually convinced him to take his own life felt close and familiar. He closed his eyes and focused his mind on fervent prayer until peace and calm replaced his anxiety, but he lay there for a long while pondering the possible source of such feelings. Was it simply some kind of opposition? Or a form of forewarning that the goodness of his life might only be temporary? Such a thought only prompted him back to the feelings he'd awakened with, and again he prayed his way out of them, although it took more effort the second time. He went into the bathroom where he wouldn't disturb Elizabeth and prayed aloud, asking with the confidence of a righteous man for his dark feelings to depart by the power of the Savior. He finally returned to bed where he prayed himself back to sleep and woke up in the morning with nothing more than a mildly uneasy memory of the internal drama that had taken place during the night.

Before the time for the appointment arrived, Jayson and Elizabeth had both come to separate conclusions that it was not right to help Macy and Aaron with their finances; at least not at this time. Driving to the church together while Trevin was left in charge of the children, they talked and agreed that they could pray for them and offer love and support, but they needed to step back and allow them to grow from these challenges in their lives. Jayson had heard that being a parent to adult children was a great course in empathy for how our Heavenly Father must feel to allow His children their free agency, their consequences, and their growth. He was at least grateful to know that Macy and Aaron were righteous people. At least they weren't doing stupid things that caused concern. Jayson had experienced that agony when Macy had gone through those difficult years in her youth. At least they were beyond that now, and he could count that as a huge blessing.

Stepping into the office of Bishop Bingham, they were met by a warm smile and friendly handshakes. Since the ward was fairly new, they didn't know Bishop Bingham very well. He'd not been in the same ward when Jayson and Elizabeth had been married and Jayson had been baptized. Their only personal encounters with the bishop were when Elizabeth had been called to teach Sunday School, and Jayson had been called as the choir pianist. They'd shared some conversation, which had included questions about the family and the work they did. He knew Jayson was a professional musician, and that he and Elizabeth had worked together. But that was all he knew.

Following these same kinds of questions, which made it evident the bishop was trying to get to know the members of his ward better, he asked Jayson if he would be willing to serve as a counselor to the Young Men president, and to be released as the choir pianist—which he lightly said would give someone else the opportunity to hone their musical skills. Jayson felt the rightness of the calling immediately, and he was glad to take it on. Since Trevin was active in the Young Men program, it would give him an opportunity to spend more time with his son, and also to get to know the other boys Trevin's age. He'd never done anything like it, but that's what excited him. On the way home, he admitted to Elizabeth that he was very pleased and couldn't wait to get involved.

On Sunday Jayson was sustained in sacrament meeting, and later that day he was set apart for the calling. The counselor to the bishop who actually spoke the blessing was also someone Jayson hadn't known prior to the ward boundary changes. But unlike his experience with the bishop, he'd never had any personal conversation whatsoever with this man. He knew practically nothing about Jayson's life or career, which made the content of his blessing all the more remarkable. In it he was told of the great influence for good that he could have on the young men in his stewardship, and how his unique gifts would have a positive impact on some in particular. He was admonished to be patient with himself and with others, not to judge, and to trust in the Lord. He was also told to remember that God loved all of His children. Then the blessing became more personal as Jayson was told that the path he was taking in his career was pleasing to his Father in Heaven and that he would be richly blessed as he diligently pursued that course. He was told that God was pleased with the way Jayson had used his gifts, and that he would continue to receive guidance so long as he sought it and kept his covenants.

Jayson said, "Wow," in the car five or six times on the way home. And nothing else. Elizabeth just laughed softly and held his hand. As he pulled the car into the garage and the door closed behind them, he turned the key and just sat there, trying to take it all in. He knew Elizabeth sensed his need to do so by the way she just sat there with him. He finally had to say, "How long has it been since I found out you'd become a Mormon and I wasn't happy about it?"

"Not so many years," she said and touched his face.

"Feels like a lifetime ago."

"In a way it was. We were living a different life. You were like a brother to me."

He snorted a laugh. "It feels impossible to imagine now. I can't imagine living any other life. I remember how it used to be, but it's still incomprehensible." He shook his head. "I think of the day that you drove me to drug rehab. Macy had been gone for so long that I'd begun to wonder if she was dead. It was hard to come up with something to live for."

"Which would explain the suicide attempt," she said, and he looked at her sharply. "What? You'd forgotten?"

"I guess I had," he said, not wanting to mention how vividly it had come to his mind in the night, which made her bringing it up now feel a little eery. "I mean . . . not really. But when you say it like that . . . I just can't imagine. I'm so happy now that . . . I don't know how I could have ever been so . . . *un*happy."

"Those were tough years . . . for both of us . . . but especially for you."

"The gospel has a marvelous way of changing lives."

"Yes, it does," she said, "but don't lose perspective here, Jayson. You were *always* a good man. The drug addiction was more accidental than anything. Your music was always good. Your intentions were always good . . . long before you had the gospel."

"I owe that to my mother, I think."

"She was a good woman. But you still made the choice to live by her teachings. You *deserve* to be happy, Jayson. You've earned it."

He smiled at her. "I am certainly blessed; that's for sure."

"So am I," she said and kissed him.

"How is that?"

"I have everything a woman could ever want."

They went into the house to find everything reasonably under control, but the remainder of the evening was crazy with homework, phone calls, and two toddlers who were spinning out of control. Macy showed up just as Jayson was getting the kids out of the bathtub while Elizabeth was reading with Addie. Macy joked with him and helped by getting Harmony into her pajamas while he did the same with Derek. But he could tell she wanted to talk, and he wondered what was wrong. Was it the *same old stuff*, or something more?

Once the children were in bed, Jayson didn't even have to ask before Macy said, "Can I talk to you and Mom?"

"Sure," he said. "I'll get her."

The three of them sat together in the front room, and Elizabeth said gently, "What's going on, Macy? You know you can talk to us about anything."

"I know," she said. "And I would have talked to you about this a long time ago, but Layla didn't want anyone to know."

"Know what?" Jayson asked when she hesitated too long.

"She's sick; she has been for a long time, but she kept saying she could handle it . . . that it was nothing serious; just stress, she would say. I've really tried to help ease her stress. Aaron and I have both wondered if that's why we're supposed to be there. I've helped with the house and the kids, but . . . apparently it's a lot more than stress."

"What do you mean, honey?" Elizabeth asked while sharing a panicked glance with Jayson.

"She's in the hospital."

"What happened?" Jayson asked.

"She just got so weak that she could barely get to the bathroom and back to bed, so Aaron took her to the hospital. They did some tests and wouldn't let her go home. Apparently there're some pretty serious symptoms, but they don't know the cause."

"*What* symptoms?" Elizabeth asked, as if she might be able to figure it out herself. Or at least she would have liked to.

"Different stuff; weird stuff. Things that don't seem like they could be connected. She's tired all the time, and weak. She has stomach aches and bathroom problems. She says her muscles hurt like she's had a big workout, but she hasn't done anything. She's told me that some of it's been bothering her off and on for years, but it's getting worse. She thinks the different symptoms are just coincidence, but how could they be? How can a person have more than one thing wrong and have it be a coincidence?" Macy started to cry.

"Well, it doesn't seem very likely," Jayson said.

"So, what now?" Elizabeth asked.

"We don't know how long she'll be in the hospital. She has some pretty good benefits with her job, so her income is okay for a while. But . . ." Macy's tears increased, "what if it's serious?"

"I don't think you can worry about that until you know whether or not it is," Elizabeth said. "I think you should just face what's in front of you right now. What can we do to help?"

Macy took a deep, sustaining breath, as if to draw in Elizabeth's calm advice. "I think we'll be okay. I have to admit that for the first time in weeks I'm actually glad I don't have a job. If I can help the family, that's a good thing."

"It *is* a good thing," Elizabeth said, "but it can also be stressful. You need to know it's the right thing, and you need to figure out how to handle it so that you don't burn out."

"I know. I appreciate your saying it, but I have thought it through, and Aaron and I have talked about it. The kids are all in school, so I can get them off in the morning, and be there when they get home. Aaron will help me most evenings. And the Relief Society president already called me. They're going to bring in meals so I don't have to worry about that. It'll be okay. I just . . ." She sobbed.

"What, baby?" Jayson asked.

"I almost feel guilty about . . . complaining so much. I know now that I'm supposed to be there. She told me today that she didn't know what she would have done without my help these past few weeks because it's been worse. And now . . . now . . . we're just scared. The kids are scared. Aaron's holding it together. But he's scared, too. And I feel like I have to be strong for him, for them, and . . ."

"What can we do to help?" Elizabeth asked again.

"The best thing you can do is help hold me together so I can be strong for them."

"We can do that," Jayson said, "and if you think of anything else, let us know. We mean it."

"I know you do," Macy said and sniffled. "You're the greatest parents on the planet."

"We have a great daughter," Elizabeth said. "And there's certainly no reason for you to feel guilty. No one would dispute that your circumstances are a challenge. I think you're doing just fine. I can understand why Layla is so grateful for you and your help. Maybe this is the way it needed to be."

Jayson gave Elizabeth a startled glance that Macy missed. But he knew his wife was thinking the same thing. If Jayson had stepped in and helped Macy and Aaron get a place to live, they wouldn't have been under the same roof with Aaron's family to be able to help with the present situation. And while the situation was obviously challenging for Macy, it was a great opportunity to grow and to serve. When she *did* get a family of her own, she was going to have a great deal of training on how to manage a household.

Macy finally pulled herself together, thanked them for listening, and went home. Layla was in the hospital for four days while the doctors ran many tests, but nothing was conclusive. They knew that it wasn't cancer, and they'd ruled out a number of other possibilities. But they didn't know exactly what was causing this variety of strange symptoms. Once at home, Layla managed to care for herself for the most part, but she was too weak to do anything around the house. Still, her presence in the home helped a great deal with the children coming and going, and Macy was able to step back and just help with chores that Layla couldn't do. The two of them got along well, and the system was working. They all just wanted to figure out what was wrong and fix it.

* * * * *

Jayson's first introduction into working in the Young Men program was to attend a meeting with all of the other leaders. A guy named Roger was the president, and Jayson liked him right off. They'd already spoken on the phone a couple of times, and they seemed to click well in the way they felt about the calling, and in being able to communicate. At the meeting, Jayson met the other leaders, only one of whom had been in the ward prior to the boundary change. Since Jayson was one of three men who were new to the organization, Roger asked that they go around the room and have everybody introduce themselves and their calling, and then tell a little about their family, and something about their profession. Jayson enjoyed listening to the others, but he dreaded his turn. He certainly wasn't ashamed of his career; quite the opposite, in fact. But in a culture where meekness and humility were encouraged, he didn't know how to talk about what he did—even in the humblest possible way—and not have it sound awkward. His profession brought with it a lot of attention and curiosity, and he was used to it. But in a situation such as this, he wasn't sure what to say or how to say it. He considered some possibilities. *I mostly work at home, except when I'm on tour.* Or he could tell them, *I'm available to help as much as you need because I don't actually have to work, and I can determine my own hours.*

He heard the other men talk about their professions, all of which had been preceded by college degrees. Roger was an attorney. Among the others there was a CPA, a retail manager, a physical therapist, a construction contractor, and a computer technician. They talked about their work comfortably, then Jayson's turn came last of all. After introducing himself and explaining his new calling, he said, "I haven't been a member of the Church for very many years. I was baptized right after I married my wife, Elizabeth. I have a daughter, Macy, from my first marriage. We have Trevin and Addie, who are from my wife's first marriage. Together we have Derek and Harmony. If you've lived around here very long, you probably know about Robert and Bradley Aragon, who were killed in a drowning accident at a Scout camp some years back." They all nodded or made noises to indicate they'd heard about it. "That was my wife's first husband and their son," he said and stopped, hoping the meeting would move on.

"And what do you do?" Roger asked him.

Jayson stated the answer as simply as possible. "I'm a professional musician. I have a studio at home where I work most of the time, so I'm usually available any time of day."

"Really?" Roger was the first to say. "What do you play?"

Jayson gave his standard answer. "A little piano. A little guitar."

They were all looking very impressed, but Jayson wanted to move on.

"What kind of music?" one of them asked.

Jayson let out an embarrassed chuckle. "Why don't we talk about what kind of law Roger does?"

"Because that's boring," Roger said. "We want to know what kind of professional musician we have among us."

"Okay," Jayson said. "I play rock and roll."

"No way!" one of them said with glee. "Really?"

"Are you famous?" another asked. Jayson couldn't keep track of their names at this point.

Jayson chuckled again. "I'll give you the scoop on one condition."

"Anything!" Roger said with a little laugh.

"Whatever you may learn about me and my profession will not come up with the boys we work with. I would really like to get to know them on a personal level, not because of what I do."

"We can do that," Roger said, his eyes eager. The others all agreed, but they were like a bunch of kids waiting for some great surprise, and Jayson knew he just had to get it over with.

"Okay, guys. If you learn this about me and you still want me here, then we're good."

"Hey, the Lord put you here," one of them said. "We just have to cope with the fact that you're obviously the most cool of all of us."

"Yeah, we're boring," another said.

Jayson shook his head and chuckled. Not having had much socializing on a personal level since he'd joined the Church, this all felt a little strange. He put his hands in the air and said, "Okay. Have any of you guys ever heard of Gray Wolf? The band was pretty hot several years ago, and—"

"Oh, yeah," one said, and others quickly agreed. A couple of them hadn't heard of it, but they were listening to the others talking about songs they liked. One of them had seen Gray Wolf in concert.

It was Roger who asked, "So, you played with Gray Wolf?"

"Yeah," Jayson said. "Definitely."

"Oh, my heck!" one of them said and laughed. Since he was the one who had been to the concert, Jayson knew he'd figured it out. "Jayson Wolfe?" He laughed. "You were like . . . the main man!"

"You *are* famous!" another said.

"I'm afraid so," Jayson said, as if it were a curse. At the moment it felt like one.

"*How* famous?" Roger asked. "Come on. Out with it. We're your buddies now."

"Okay," Jayson said, "but what happens at presidency meeting stays at presidency meeting."

"Your secret is safe with us," Roger said. "Although, if you're famous, it can't be much of a secret."

"So just Google me later and let's get on with the meeting."

They all laughed, but Jayson lost that awkward feeling as he stopped long enough to realize they were genuinely interested in him and they *did* feel like his buddies. They were a wonderful group of men. They shared his convictions and beliefs and standards, and they were all part of a team put in place to help the young men in the ward thrive in the gospel.

"Just get on with it," Roger said. "We haven't got all night."

"Hey, we could call his wife."

"Yeah, let's call his wife."

Jayson laughed. "Did you guys get called to this job because you act like teenagers?"

"Yes!" several of them said at the same time.

"Well, my wife would tell you that I've won some Grammys and I've been on the cover of *Rolling Stone*. Can we get on with the meeting now?"

They were all pleasantly astonished, but in a fun, easygoing way. "So, you work at home?" someone asked more seriously.

"Most of the time, yes," Jayson said. "I'm working on my second solo album. I'll probably be going on tour next summer."

"That is so cool!" Roger said. "Okay, now we can get on with the meeting."

"Remember," Jayson said, "it's a secret with the boys . . . at least until they get to know *me*. Fair enough?"

They all wholeheartedly agreed, then the meeting calmed down and became serious as they talked through plans and assignments for Sunday lessons and Wednesday night activities. The meeting was long, but these men didn't behave any differently toward Jayson. He had a strong sense of such things, and he was glad to know that they could all see him as just one of the guys. He had a feeling he was really going to like this calling.

CHAPTER 5

Jayson quickly became involved in the Young Men program, and he loved it. Occasionally among the other leaders the subject of his career came up with a simple question here or there, which was typical with people who knew *about* him, but didn't really *know* him. He was always glad to answer their questions and satisfy their curiosity. He'd learned a long time ago that his musical career naturally caused a bit of a stir, and people were interested. And he was okay with that. It was rare that anyone who talked to him more than a minute was ever in awe of his fame. He considered himself skilled at quickly making it clear that he was an ordinary person, and he owed the credit for his gift to God. Before the change in ward boundaries, he'd given up on remaining incognito. He'd known that most members of the ward knew who he was and what he did, but they also knew him as just another ward member and neighbor; a guy with an eccentric job. And that's the way he liked it. Now, he was starting over in that regard, but his association with the men he worked with had made it less awkward.

Whenever the subject came up, Jayson took the opportunity to reemphasize to the other leaders his desire for them to steer the interest of the young men away from Jayson's work, at least until he'd had a chance to get to know them. He wanted to connect with the boys in a personal way, not because of his fame. They were all fine with that, although Roger pointed out that they had a few boys who were interested in music in various ways and Jayson might be able to help them. Jayson liked that idea, and they agreed to just give it some time and let it evolve.

All in all, Jayson considered life to be good. He kept close track of Macy and her other family, and kept working on his music while taking care of his own family. The music was starting to move steadily along, and he was pulling pieces together. He found joy in every day, and prayed it would remain that way.

* * * * *

Folding laundry that was spread all over her bed, Elizabeth reached for the phone without glancing at the caller ID. Then she wished she had either ignored the call or had some kind of warning when her mother said, "Hello, dear."

"Hello, Mother," Elizabeth said, not trying to sound falsely cheerful, but considering it good that she didn't sound distressed. She reminded herself that their last phone call had been pleasant, but that just heightened her suspicion. Beyond that last call, she hadn't heard from her in months, so she naturally said, "This is quite an occasion."

"An occasion?" Meredith Greer asked.

"Hearing from you twice in so short a time. Did you miss me all of a sudden, or did you have some exciting news or something?" Elizabeth hoped her mother didn't detect that barest hint of sarcasm in Elizabeth's voice. She'd never been close to her mother, had never liked her mother, and had never enjoyed her mother's company—on the phone or other-wise. She knew her father had similar sentiments toward his ex-wife—or at least he'd not liked her or enjoyed her company for many, many years. But Will had reminded her many times that she deserved Elizabeth's respect, simply for the fact that she was Elizabeth's mother. And of course, Elizabeth sincerely wanted to be a charitable person. It would never be her intention to be otherwise with anyone—not even her mother. Given her mother's history, she'd found that she could be charitable, but she could never trust her, or open herself up to being candid and companionable. Such efforts in the past had *always* resulted in Elizabeth getting hurt in one way or another.

"Both, I would say," Meredith answered. "I have been missing you . . . but not all of a sudden. And I hope you'll consider my news exciting. I want to come and visit you and spend some time with your family. The sooner the better."

Elizabeth sank onto the edge of the bed, having to recall the words to make certain she'd heard them correctly. Then she had to consciously will herself to keep from saying something unkind. She wanted to snap at her and say, *You haven't come to visit me through the births of all of my children and the funerals of my husband and son. You couldn't make it to my wedding to*

Jayson. And you're coming now? Elizabeth wondered what she meant by *the sooner the better.*

Elizabeth told herself to be gracious, but she did *not* want her mother coming to visit. She simply said, "It would be great to see you, Mom, but things are kind of crazy here. Jayson is recording a new album, and the kids are—"

"Oh, I figured you would all be busy. I'm sure there's hardly a time when you aren't. I won't get in the way, I promise. And I promise to behave myself."

What does that mean? Elizabeth wanted to scream. She suspected it was more a manipulative tactic than any effort to admit that she *rarely* behaved herself. "Maybe I can help out a little. If it's not too much trouble, I'd like to be able to stay at your place. That way I can see the kids more."

Elizabeth bit her tongue to keep from saying, *You think you can just drop in on us like this and expect life to go on as usual?*

When Elizabeth said nothing for several seconds, attempting to find some sane and reasonable response to the situation, Meredith said, "I'm going to be frank, dear. I wouldn't blame you at all if you didn't want me to come, and you have the option to say no. I know I haven't been a very good mother or grandmother. I would really like to make up for that . . . just a little bit. I want to see you and the kids. If you don't have space at the house, I can get a hotel. Maybe you could suggest some that aren't too far away."

Again Elizabeth was stunned into silence. How could she argue with what her mother had just said? How could a Christian woman respond to such a declaration with a refusal to see her? And if she suggested a hotel, her mother would quickly realize once she was in their home that they had a couple of spare bedrooms, plus the apartment. It would be ridiculous to expect her to stay elsewhere, and Elizabeth could never live with telling her she couldn't come.

"Elizabeth?" Meredith said.

"Sorry, Mom. I'm just . . . a little overwhelmed."

"I can understand that, and I hope you'll be completely honest with me."

"Okay," she said, "if I'm going to be completely honest about being honest, I have to say that being honest with my feelings in our relationship has not generally worked out well."

"We could try to work on that."

"Okay, why? Why do you want to work on that? Why do you want to come and visit now when you haven't *ever* been to this home where I've lived for years? And I know you can afford to travel."

Silence preceded Meredith saying quietly, "I've had a change of priorities. I'm not getting any younger."

Again Elizabeth couldn't argue or come up with a response that wasn't unkind. Wanting to avoid any further discussion of honest feelings, Elizabeth asked, "So, when were you planning on making this grand sojourn?"

"How about Thursday?"

Elizabeth almost choked. She resisted the urge to shriek, *This* Thursday? She frantically tried to search for any honest reason why this would be impossible, but she couldn't think of one. Jayson was busy, but there wasn't anything else going on beyond the usual family life. She finally resorted to a quick, silent prayer that didn't consist of anything more than, *Please God, help me.* A few seconds later she found the ability to say, "Thursday would be fine, but you can't expect anything to be any different around here than it always is."

"Oh, of course not!" Meredith said, sounding both thrilled and pleased. Elizabeth couldn't recall hearing her mother use that tone of voice *ever*. "You just go ahead and do everything you usually do. I'm coming with no expectations . . . honestly."

Elizabeth couldn't bring herself to believe *that*, even with the declaration of "honestly" at the end. Still, she had to take this on as best she could and make the most of it.

"Can you give me some suggestions for a hotel that's not too far from your home?"

"There's no need for that, Mom," she said. "We have a small apartment attached to the house. You're welcome to stay there."

"Oh, that's wonderful!" Meredith said. "Are you sure it's okay? I know I'm being presumptuous here, but . . ."

Elizabeth wanted to scream, *Yes you are! And no, it's not okay!* But she asked herself what Jesus would do and said, "It's fine." Needing some kind of disclaimer, she said, "I just have to say that . . . if you're going to be in my home, I need you to respect me, my family, my methods; everything. If we start having problems—at all—I will ask you to leave."

"That's more than fair," Meredith said, whereas Elizabeth had expected an argument. The Meredith Greer she knew would have given her one. Maybe she *had* changed her priorities. The question was whether or not she'd truly had a change of heart. If this was sincerely an effort to renew relationships with family because she'd come to a place of regret, Elizabeth could live with that. In fact, the idea was appealing. It just seemed too good to be true.

"Okay, then," Meredith said, "I'll get a flight for Thursday. I know your address so I'm sure I can get a cab and—"

"There's no need for that either, Mom," Elizabeth said, wondering who this was speaking out of her own mouth. "As long as your flight comes in after I get the kids off to school, I can come and get you. Just let me know what time and which airline."

"Oh, that would be wonderful!" she said. "I'll be looking forward to it."

They said good-bye, and Elizabeth turned off the phone before she looked at it as if it were some alien device that had just beamed her into some science fiction realm.

Glad that the babies were napping, she hurried to the studio and flung open the door, interrupting Jayson. The piano stopped abruptly. "I don't care how busy you are," she said, "or what kind of inspiration I'm inhibiting. I need you!"

"Okay," he said, turning on the bench. "You should know you're always more important than whatever is going on in here."

"I do know. That's why I'm here." She sat down on the bench beside him and initiated a tight hug.

"Elizabeth, what's wrong?" His concern was evident.

"My mother just called," she said.

"What did she say *this* time?" he snarled. "Why can't she call and just be nice?"

"She *was* nice! That's the problem."

Jayson eased back to look at her. "She was *nice?*"

"Yes, and . . ." Elizabeth groaned, and her shoulders slumped, "she's coming to visit. She'll be staying with us."

Jayson was so astonished he laughed.

"This is not funny!" she said as if she might hit him.

"Sorry," he said. "Why? Why would she come and see you after all this time?"

"Us. She's coming to see *us*. And I don't know. She said she wasn't getting any younger, she's changed her priorities, and she wants to spend time with her grandchildren."

"Wow!" Jayson said. "That's a good thing, isn't it?"

"We can hope so," she said and went on to repeat the gist of the entire conversation. Jayson just listened until the estimated time of arrival came up.

"*This* Thursday?" Jayson said and laughed again.

"Go ahead and laugh. You can just go on working and hide in here. I have to deal with her all day every day."

"Or you could . . . go to the temple more often. That's one place she can't go with you if you need a break."

"That's true. Okay, I like that idea. How about every day?"

"Wouldn't hurt," Jayson said. "Maybe Grandma will babysit. I bet that won't last long."

"No, but Grandpa is usually willing. Oh," she groaned, "I'm not sure we should let them be in the same room together. I'm so nervous."

"Why? You don't have to impress her, and you told her everything was going to go on as normal. Will can handle her whenever he happens to show up. What have you got to be nervous about?"

"I don't know. I just . . . have so much to do."

"What do you have to do?"

"Forget it, Jayson. You wouldn't understand." She headed for the door. "Thanks for listening."

When Jayson took a break a while later, he found Elizabeth in the laundry room, cleaning vigorously. "What *are* you doing?"

"I'm cleaning," she said.

"Because your mother is coming?"

"Exactly."

"The *laundry* room? Do you think she'll inspect it?"

"Probably."

"So, what if she does? This is *our* home. No one's standards matter but yours and mine, and I think the house is perfect just the way it is." She only glared at him and he said, "Clean if you want to clean, Elizabeth, but do it for yourself. Don't do it for your mother. What she thinks just doesn't matter."

Elizabeth tried to tell herself that while she spent the next twenty-four hours doing little *but* clean. Jayson gave her his lecture again, but she told him he wouldn't understand. Macy showed up after breakfast, asking if she could play with the babies. Elizabeth was thrilled to have someone watch out for them so she could get more done. Then it occurred to her that Jayson had probably asked her to come with the hope of keeping her from getting so stressed out. She felt tempted to be angry with him, then realized he was being thoughtful and she shouldn't let her own embarrassment over this sudden obsession make her angry with her husband for trying to be good to her. She questioned Macy, who admitted that her father had bribed her, but she was more than glad to do it. When the kids went down for their naps, Macy said, "I'm your slave while they're sleeping. What do you want me to do?"

"You do *not* have to do this," Elizabeth insisted while she was scrubbing the front of cupboard doors in the kitchen.

"Listen," Macy said, moving closer, "I've cleaned and organized like crazy at my *other* house. I'm pretty good at it. Besides, I owe you."

"You don't owe me anything!" Elizabeth protested.

"You got on a plane and flew to California to rescue me when I was pregnant and terrified. And you weren't even my mother yet."

"I was glad to do it. I promised your father. That's irrelevant. You don't have to—"

"I want to help," Macy said.

Elizabeth sighed. "Your father thinks I'm crazy."

"Because you want the house clean when your mother comes? Men don't understand. I agree with him on the point that if you want to clean, do it for yourself, not for her. But if you're going to feel more comfortable with it clean, then let's clean."

"Okay," Elizabeth said, and told Macy some things she could do to help. She stayed until dinnertime, helping with the kids again after they woke up. Jayson came out of his studio early to order pizza, then he told Elizabeth he would take care of the kids for the evening. He also assigned Trevin and Addie a couple of extra chores and made sure they did them. After the kids were in bed, Elizabeth found him straightening and dusting in the bedroom, and putting things away that had been piling up.

"Why are you being so helpful?" she asked.

"Because you need help," he said.

"But you don't agree with my reasons for needing help," she said.

He just smiled and said, "'Are we not all beggars?'" She hugged him, and he tossed the dust rag to the floor. "I'm sure I'll get even—if I haven't already. Just wait, I'll freak out over something and you'll have to help me—even if you think it's silly."

"You think this is silly?"

He took her shoulders into his hands. "I want you to feel comfortable with your mother here, and if this helps you feel more comfortable, that's fine. I don't want you to think you have to be pretentious with her. Our home is wonderful, Elizabeth. It's well kept and clean and comfortable. There's no bacteria growing anywhere, and our kids can bring their friends here without being embarrassed. Nothing else matters. What Meredith thinks of your housekeeping skills just doesn't matter."

She started to cry and felt embarrassed. But hiding her face against his shoulder wasn't going to hide the fact that she was crying.

"What did I say?" he asked.

"You said everything just right. I . . . don't understand why I feel this way."

"What way?" he asked, urging her to the edge of the bed where they sat close together.

"All these years, and the thought of seeing my mother makes me regress right back to high school when she was still living under the same roof, looking at my life through a microscope even though she had no involvement whatsoever. I had to be perfect at everything I did, and I had to do it all. I thought I'd grown beyond her. Now, look at me . . . exhausting myself because I'm afraid she'll think . . ."

"What?" Jayson asked, stroking the back of her head while she cried against his shoulder. By the way she cried, he realized she'd been holding a great deal of emotion inside since her mother's call, and it was probably good for her to get it out. While he patiently held her and waited, he was surprised at how clearly he recalled one of his few encounters with Meredith Greer. He'd been at the house celebrating the news that their band had gotten its first job, playing at a dance hall in Portland on Saturday nights. Will was almost excited as the rest of them.

They all sat around the kitchen table eating Oreos after Jayson had called his mother to let her know where he and Drew were and to tell her the good news.

Mrs. Greer came home, and the laughter quieted immediately when she entered the room.

"Isn't this fun?" she said with obvious sarcasm, and he wondered what made this woman so miserable.

"It is actually," Will said. "Why don't you join us?"

Jayson noticed that there was no kind of greeting between them as husband and wife; no kiss, no hello, nothing.

"No, thank you, I'm tired," she said. "I'd appreciate it if you'd keep the noise down."

"Meredith," Will said as she started to leave the room, and Jayson realized he'd never known her first name. "Remember that dance hall in Portland we used to go to occasionally? The one that's been there for years?"

"Yes," she said, her tone bored.

"Our children just got a job there, playing live every Saturday night."

"You're kidding," she said with such astonishment that it was evident she'd never imagined they were actually doing anything productive in the basement.

"They're amazing," Will said. "You've got to hear them play."

"One of these days," she said, and Jayson heard Elizabeth sigh loudly. He felt sure her mother would never make the effort to hear them play.

Meredith Greer stood there for a long moment in silence as if she were trying to digest what she'd just learned. Then she said in a voice of astonishment, "Wait a minute. Did you say children?" She turned to Elizabeth, looking at her as if she'd broken out in polka-dots. "You too?" she asked, her tone and expression implying that Elizabeth had just taken a job as a cocktail waitress. Jayson also felt she was implying that she expected Derek to do something stupid, but not Elizabeth. Jayson wondered how Derek must feel to know that his mother saw him as an inferior underachiever next to his sister.

"Me too," Elizabeth said with pride.

"School will be starting soon. How can you possibly do something like this and keep up with everything else you'll be doing?"

"It really won't take that much time," Elizabeth said. "But the only thing I have to work around is orchestra. That's like a few concerts through the whole school year. It's not a big deal."

"What about chorus?" Meredith demanded, apparently oblivious to the fact that others were present. "What about student government?"

"The officers were elected in the spring, Mom. I'm not in student government anymore."

"You didn't run for office?" Meredith countered hotly.

"I would have thought you'd noticed that months ago," Elizabeth said, her voice rising. "No, I didn't run for office, and I didn't try out for chorus, and I'm not doing any plays this year. I am, however, taking AP classes and getting college credits, and I will do my best to keep pulling straight As, the way I always have. Not that you would notice. Maybe you would notice if I got crappy grades and did nothing."

"Nope, that doesn't work," Derek said.

Meredith looked at her son as if she would like to slap him, good and hard. Before she got another word out, Will said with firm resolve, "Meredith, I don't think this is a good time to get into it. Derek's grades were improving on the last report card, and I've encouraged Elizabeth to back off a little and not exhaust herself so much."

Meredith's angry glare turned to her husband. "Well, you would do that, wouldn't you. If you were—"

"Meredith," he interrupted, still completely calm, "this is not a good time." He glanced discreetly at Jayson and Drew.

Meredith made a disgusted noise and hurried from the room. All was silent until they heard a door slam from somewhere upstairs. "Guess I'll be sleeping in the guest room tonight," Will said in a voice that attempted to sound light.

"More peaceful that way, I'd bet," Derek said, and Will made no comment. "Sorry about that," he finally said, glancing again at Drew and Jayson.

"Not a problem," Jayson said. "It was much worse when our dad showed up." Drew made a noise of agreement. "But maybe next time we should just . . . quietly leave and—"

"Oh, no," Derek said. "Your being here kept it from getting ugly. I think you should be here all the time." To his father he added, "Why do you put up with it? She's been like this ever since she got her degree and started working."

"No," Elizabeth corrected, "she keeps getting worse."

Will said, "I put up with it because I married her for better or worse, and marriage isn't something I take lightly. I have every hope that one day the woman I married will emerge again. She's just got some issues she needs to work through. We need to be patient with her."

"Yeah, well," Derek said, "I'm not going to hold my breath until she comes around."

The conversation lightened up again when Will started talking about how proud he would be when they got their first record deal.

"I'm such a mess," Elizabeth said, bringing Jayson back to the present.

"If my dad was coming to stay, I'd be a mess."

"Since he's been dead for years, I think we'd all be a little unnerved."

"You know what I mean."

"Yes, I know what you mean."

"But listen to me, Elizabeth, you don't have to prove anything to her."

"I understand that, but . . . I'm still trying to do it . . . like some sick compulsion."

"So, let's talk about it. Why? Why do you think everything needs to look perfect when she comes? Obviously it's not going to stay perfect, unless you're going to lock up the kids. And she did say she was coming to see them, right?"

"Yeah," Elizabeth chuckled, "I don't think we can lock up the kids."

"So, talk to me. What is it that's bugging you . . . specifically?"

"My mother always expected me to excel, so I tried to excel at everything. Then I just got tired. You knew all of that."

"Yes, but tell me what it has to do with the present?"

"She knows I'm a full-time homemaker. So, what kind of homemaker is she going to think I am if everything isn't perfect?"

Jayson looked at her hard. "If she says a word—one word—I want you to tell her that you're a *homemaker,* not a housekeeper. Your homemaking skills *are* perfect, Elizabeth. The spirit of love and respect in our home is a result of everything you do for me and the kids. It has nothing to do with how clean the laundry room is."

Elizabeth started to cry again, but these were happier tears. "Oh, you're right," she said. "How do you always say the right thing?"

"Just lucky," he said.

"I don't believe in luck."

"Okay, inspired. I was praying."

"I can live with that."

They sat for a long while and talked through a plan for how to deal with Meredith's possible reactions to situations that they knew from experience could likely bring out her negative, critical personality. They decided firmly on rules that they both agreed to keep. They could be kind and respectful to her without letting her intimidate or talk down to them or the kids.

That night as Elizabeth lay in bed, she felt inexpressibly grateful for Jayson's understanding and support—and for his perspective. He too had grown up with a severely dysfunctional parent. Their problems had been in entirely different realms, but the damage had been a common bond between them. Elizabeth would never forget the night her mother had announced that she was leaving her marriage and children. Jayson had been in the house that night, and the divorce his family had survived had helped give them all perspective. Will had become the father that Jayson had never had, and Jayson's mother, Leslie, had become like a mother to Elizabeth. But Leslie had passed away years ago, and Elizabeth's relationship with her mother had always been vaguely present, but never real. Exchanging phone calls, emails, and occasional photographs hardly counted for a real relationship—especially when even those had often been laced with a standoffish criticism that Elizabeth had difficulty contending with.

Memories of ugly encounters with her mother marched through her mind, while she could find little if anything positive to balance them out. The worst of all those memories, beyond her mother's actual declaration of abandoning her family, came to the forefront. It was the day of Derek's funeral when family and friends were gathered at the house afterward. Losing her brother had been one of the worst things she'd ever been through. And as if the events surrounding that weren't bad enough, her mother had added gasoline to the fire. She and Jayson had been dating a long while before Derek's death, and Meredith just happened to walk into the backyard at the right moment to see Jayson and Elizabeth kissing.

"Oh great," Elizabeth muttered under her breath and tried to ease away, but Jayson kept his arm firmly around her to prevent her from moving.

Meredith closed the door behind her and said, "I had no idea the two of you were . . . romantically involved."

"We've been dating for several months, Mother; since last fall."

"I see," Meredith said and glanced down. She looked up again and said, "I would really like to hear your band play. When will your next performance be?"

"There won't be any more performances, Mother," Elizabeth said, unable to keep from sounding terse.

"Why not?" she asked, sounding astonished.

"Our bass player is dead," Jayson said with blatant anger.

"But surely you can—"

"One plus three does not add up to four," Jayson interjected.

"As usual, Mother, you're a little late to catch the performance."

Elizabeth felt sure her mother would erupt with anger, but before she had a chance, the back door came open and her father called, "Hey, Jayson. Could you come here a minute? There's someone I want you to meet."

Jayson cast a cautious glance toward Elizabeth, not wanting to leave her alone, but she nodded subtly. "Excuse me," he said and went into the house.

"So," Meredith said with no apparent sign of anger, "how old is your boyfriend?"

Attempting to be civil, she answered, "He's eighteen; the same as me."

Meredith's surprise was evident. "Really? He looks and acts much older, but then you do as well, I suppose."

"Mom, he's Derek's best friend. How much older did you think he would be? Actually, Jayson is between us in age."

"I see," Meredith said. "And did I hear him say the two of you are getting married?"

"It was a joke, Mother," she said, glad Jayson wasn't here. He likely wouldn't agree.

"Well, I'm glad to hear that. He seems like a very nice young man, but you're much too young to be getting married."

"You think I don't know that? I'm going to Boston. I have a scholarship."

"Really?" Meredith sounded extremely impressed, but Elizabeth had to resist the temptation to point out how ridiculous her ignorance was in relation to her children's lives. "Well, I hope you have the good sense to follow through and get a degree. Don't be doing anything to blow your chances for some real success."

"I have no intention of messing up my life, Mother, but I'm certain our definitions of success are entirely different. My goals would likely not impress you."

"What are your goals?" she asked in a tone that implied she would like to hear them if only to discredit them.

"It really doesn't matter; I don't want to talk about it."

"And what of Jayson?" she asked as if she were cross-examining a witness in the courtroom. "Is he going to college?"

"No, actually. Jayson is one of those rare individuals who has the potential to make millions with very little education. And I'm certain he will."

"What do you mean?"

"You heard him play . . . and sing. He's brilliant. And you haven't heard the half of it. He's going to LA and he's going to be world renowned."

"LA is a long ways from Boston."

"Yes, it is. But that's just temporary."

"You're in love with him," she stated as if it were a criminal action.

"Would I be dating him this long if I weren't?"

Meredith folded her arms and looked at her daughter hard. "Are you using birth control?"

It took Elizabeth several seconds to convince herself that she'd not misheard the question, and then the fury she felt erupted out of her mouth with a sharp, "What?"

"You heard me. You're old enough to talk frankly with your mother. I know how kids are these days."

"You know nothing! Absolutely nothing inappropriate has ever happened between us, not that it's any of your business. He is a gentleman in the truest sense."

"Men are all alike, Elizabeth. Just give him half a chance and he'll have you pregnant, and your life will be shot. Trust your mother on this."

"Why should I trust you on anything? You've never given me one lousy reason to trust you. And obviously you don't trust me."

Meredith sighed as if she were exercising great patience. "I truly did leave you far too much in your father's care. If he—"

"My father is the most amazing man in the world, and you have no idea what you're talking about. If you—"

Elizabeth's words were interrupted by her own scream when her mother slapped her hard across the face. She was amazed at how badly it hurt, and she couldn't even think how to respond. She was relieved beyond words when the door came open and Jayson demanded, "Are you okay?" With her hand pressed over her face, she could only stare at him. She saw his eyes go to her mother as he closed the door and said firmly, "I heard you scream. Are you okay?"

Elizabeth wondered if that meant everyone else in the house had heard her as well, or if Jayson's ears were simply more tuned in to her. "No," she admitted with a shaky voice, "I don't think I am."

As he moved toward her, Meredith said, "This is between me and my daughter, and you'd do well to—"

"What?" Jayson interrupted, standing directly in front of Meredith. "Tell me what you'll do Ms. Greer. Will you hit me, too? I've got scars to prove I can survive much worse than you. I know how people like you work. You're just like my father. But at least he had an excuse. At least he was drunk when he started hitting the people he was supposed to love."

"This is none of your business," she growled. "And you'd do well to—"

"Elizabeth is a lot more my business than yours. You have no business calling yourself a mother. All they ever wanted was your approval, but you couldn't give even that. Now Derek's dead, and you have the nerve to actually hit your own daughter."

"With that kind of belligerence, any parent would have done the same," she countered as if she were in a courtroom.

"Belligerence?" Jayson gave a scoffing laugh. "We're not talking about the same person. She is wonderful and brilliant and kind and good; clearly nothing like you. You're nothing but an overgrown bully in a skirt. And if you ever—ever—hurt her again, I will have you slapped with domestic violence charges so fast you won't know what hit you. I might be just a kid to you, but I have a lot of experience with that. I wonder how that would reflect on your brilliant attorney reputation. And don't think I wouldn't do it."

Meredith's expression softened slightly, as if she knew he had her. In a terse voice she said to Elizabeth, "Your boyfriend is charming. It's no wonder the two of you get along so well. But don't be thinking that—"

The door came open and Will demanded, "What's going on?"

Jayson waited for one of the women to speak. When they didn't, he clearly took great pleasure in tattling. "Your ex-wife just hit your daughter."

Will closed the door with a studied fury showing in his face. In a voice that was barely calm, he said to Meredith, "I don't want to know why; I don't want any excuses or rationalizations. There is no justifiable cause for hitting a child."

"She's no child," Meredith snapped. "She's a woman, full grown."

"You bet she is," Will said. "And a fine one, at that—in spite of growing up with a lousy mother. Now get out. You are no longer welcome here—ever."

"Will you cause a scene at our son's funeral?" she snapped.

"You bet I will," he said firmly. "So you can graciously walk out and get in your car and drive away, or I will escort you out by any means necessary."

Meredith looked hard at Will, then at Jayson, who looked as if he'd like to tear her to pieces. "Fine," she said. "I'm leaving. Now I don't have to wonder why I left this wretched place to begin with."

Meredith gave Elizabeth a harsh glare, then went through the house to leave. Will followed her to make certain she did. The moment her mother was absent, Elizabeth allowed her composure to falter. She was grateful to feel Jayson's arms come around her, giving her perfect love and acceptance as well as a firm shoulder to cry on.

Now, all these years later, Jayson was still there for her. She prayed that her mother's visit wouldn't end up a disaster, and that somehow Meredith truly had changed her priorities. For a long moment she allowed herself to indulge in fantasizing over such a possibility. But it seemed so difficult to believe that she felt certain the indulgence would only futilely get her hopes up. Instead she just kept praying.

CHAPTER 6

Jayson awakened, expecting Elizabeth to be up and getting a little more cleaning done before she went to the airport to get her mother. But she was huddled in the bed, not looking very well.

"What's wrong?" he asked. "Are you sick?"

"It's not contagious," she snarled. "That time of the month hit in the night in all its glory." Her sarcasm sounded close to breaking into tears. "If I'm done having children, why do I still have to go through this?"

"I don't have the answer to that question," Jayson said.

"And why today?"

"I can't answer that question, either," he said. "Do you want me to go with you to the airport?"

"You have work to do."

"It can wait. A few hours isn't going to make that much difference. I was going to take some time off to watch the kids anyway, remember?"

"Oh, yeah. My brain is foggy. But if you go with me we either have to take the kids or have Dad come and watch them. We already talked about this. That's *why* you were going to watch the kids, so my mother's ex-husband and his new wife wouldn't be here when she arrives."

"Okay then," he sighed, "it seems that it would behoove me to go and get your mother and leave you to rest . . . although that's not going to be easy with the little maniacs running around."

"Behoove?" she said and laughed. "Are you starting to talk like Mozart?"

"No, it just sounded like the right word to fit the situation. To tell you the truth, I intended to offer to go get your mother right off. I just wanted you to appreciate the sacrifice I'm making."

"Oh, I do," she said. "But since this ailment I've got made it possible for me to give you children, I think you should keep perspective on sacrifice."

"Okay, point taken," he said and set to work getting the babies dressed and fed.

When it was time for him to go, the house was in good order except for a few toys in the living room, and the babies were contentedly playing there. Elizabeth had showered and was lying on the living room couch. "Be careful," she said when he kissed her good-bye. "And don't let her throw any of her attorney courtroom tactics at you."

"I think I can handle her," he said and kissed her again.

Elizabeth sighed deeply after he left. As much as she felt lousy and wanted to be at her best, she was grateful not to have to go and get her mother. She said a prayer and counted blessings and enjoyed watching her children play.

* * * * *

Jayson parked the car and went into the airport to hover in the baggage claim area, as opposed to just picking Meredith up at the curb, since she wasn't familiar with the airport. He thought it strange to think of her as his mother-in-law, when he had no relationship with her at all. Beyond their few distasteful encounters in his teen years, he'd only spoken to her on the phone for a total of about five minutes in as many years since he'd come back into Elizabeth's life. He'd come to think of Marilyn as his mother-in-law. She was married to Elizabeth's father, and they were both actively involved with the family on a regular basis. Jayson knew that even when Will had lived in Oregon and Elizabeth had lived in Arizona with her husband and children, Will had flown out a couple of times a year to spend time with the family. He'd not allowed miles to inhibit his relationships. For Meredith, it had been the opposite. Miles had been a good excuse to keep the distance she had always kept before. Jayson didn't feel as traumatized by Meredith's visit as Elizabeth did, but he still had to admit that he wasn't looking forward to it, and he prayed that everything would go well.

He was surprised at how easily he recognized her, even though her hair had gone completely gray; however, it was stylish and attractive. She looked as good as she ever had with the exception of being perhaps a little too thin. She was dressed fashionably and looked all confidence and coolness. He saw her stop and scan the area, obviously searching for her daughter. He approached and said, "Hello, Meredith."

"Jayson," she said with a little laugh. "It's been years."

"Yes, it has," he said.

She looked around. "Where's my daughter?"

"She's home, actually. She's not feeling well, so I offered to come and get you."

"Is she ill?" Meredith asked.

"Feminine stuff," he said nonchalantly. "She just didn't feel up to making the drive. She's looking forward to seeing you."

"Now you're placating me, Jayson," she said, taking him off guard. But she didn't say it with defensive accusation. It was somewhere between teasing and being appropriately straightforward. She looked away as she added, "I'm well aware that my daughter is *not* looking forward to my visit, and I don't blame her at all. She is being very gracious; I'll give her that." She looked at Jayson. "And so are you."

Jayson didn't know what to say. But since she was carrying only a purse, he knew they needed to wait for the luggage to arrive on the carousel, and they weren't in any hurry. He was relieved when she filled in the silence. "It's been a long time. I think the last time I actually saw you was at Derek's funeral; or rather, after it."

"Yeah, that would be it," he said, knowing she could never forget what had happened any more than he could.

"You played beautifully at the funeral," she said. "And you sang with Elizabeth. It was amazing." She laughed softly and added, "No pun intended." He felt confused until she said, "The two of you sang 'Amazing Grace.'"

"Ah," he said, getting it now. "So we did."

"How old were you?"

"Eighteen," he said, but she would have known that. He'd been the same age as Derek.

"And now you have a grown daughter of your own."

"Yes, I do," he said with pride.

"How is she? Macy, isn't it?"

"That's right. She's fine."

"Isn't she married?"

"Yes, she is. They live close by; I'm sure you'll get to meet them."

"I'll look forward to it," Meredith said. "Will and Marilyn live close by as well, don't they." It wasn't a question.

"They do."

"You see them often?"

"Yes, we do. But I'm sure if you want to avoid them, it can be arranged."

"On the contrary," she said, "I'd very much like to meet Marilyn, and to see Will again. Elizabeth has told me they're very happy. That's good."

"Yes, it's good," Jayson said, beginning to believe that this woman truly *had* experienced some miraculous change. He hoped that it would last and that it wasn't just a temporary pretense that would lead to eventual dramatics.

She excused herself to find a ladies' room while they were waiting, and Jayson called Elizabeth. "Okay," he said, "I've found her. She's in the ladies' room, and she is *not* acting like the woman that I know gave birth to you."

"So, she's being nice to you, too?"

"Can you believe it? And I'm the guy who got you pregnant."

She giggled. "Not until after you married me."

"Imagine that," he said with mild sarcasm.

"Are you okay?"

"I'm fine. Are *you* okay?"

"I'm fine. I'm just glad I'm not standing in an airport."

"See you soon," he said. "I love you."

"Love you too. Drive carefully."

Meredith was in the ladies' room for a long time, and Jayson began to wonder if she might be ill. But she came out looking fine and smiled at him.

"I called Elizabeth," he said, "to let her know I found you."

"I can't wait to see her," Meredith said.

They moved closer to the carousel when it began to move and luggage started emerging.

"I have two bags," she said. "Kind of large; they're shocking purple. You can't miss them. That's why I bought them, so I'd never have trouble finding my luggage at airports."

"Very wise," he said and saw the bags a moment later. He got them for her, glad they had wheels since they were both on the heavy side. She pulled one, and he pulled the other as they left the airport to find where he'd parked the car.

"So, I understand you're very busy these days. Elizabeth told me you're recording a new album."

"That's right," he said.

"Forgive me if I'm being too nosy, Jayson, but is this a guaranteed deal or . . ." She stopped when he shot her a questioning glance. Then she said, "I'm sorry. That *was* too nosy."

"I guess that all depends on your reasons for asking," he said. "If you're wondering whether or not my being busy is just a waste of time and will come to nothing, then yes, it's nosy. If you're genuinely interested in what I'm doing and why, then you can ask me anything you want."

"I don't blame you for being defensive, Jayson. You and I have never had a cordial word in the past, and I know that was my fault. I'm just hoping we can start over."

Jayson stopped walking to look at her, and she did the same. "You're serious."

"Don't I look serious?" she asked.

"You do. I just . . ."

"Don't trust me?" Meredith said. "I don't blame you for that, either."

Jayson couldn't comment. He just walked on and said, "The record company that did my solo album has been asking me to do another one ever since the last tour ended. I wasn't sure I wanted to. But we finally made the decision to do it. The record company is pleased and waiting impatiently."

"So it is a guaranteed deal."

"I'm sure if I gave them a load of horrid music they'd have no trouble throwing it out. But I'm not worried about that."

"No, I wouldn't think you'd have to be worried about that."

"That doesn't mean I'm not worried about coming up with good music; it just means that I wouldn't give it to them if I didn't know it was good."

"And is it?" she asked.

"I've got a few good pieces so far."

"And you're still enjoying it?" she asked. "I mean . . . it hasn't become tedious for you?"

"Most of the time I enjoy it," he said, and they arrived at the car. He put the luggage in the back, opened the door for her, which seemed to surprise her, and then they were headed toward the freeway.

"How long is the drive?" she asked.

"About forty-five minutes," he said.

"Oh, we don't have too far, then." She seemed pleased, or anxious. "The mountains are beautiful!" she said. "I've never been to this area before."

"They *are* beautiful," he said. "If marrying Elizabeth hadn't made me stay in Utah, I might have stayed anyway—if only for the mountains. I love them."

"So, tell me about yourself, Jayson; not the kind of stuff I can read in entertainment magazines."

"You read that stuff?"

"Only the reputable stuff," she said. Still, Jayson wondered what she'd read about him in magazines. "I'd like to hear the other stuff."

"Why don't you tell me what you know—or have read—and I'll tell you whether or not it's true."

"Okay," she said, and Jayson felt like he was in some kind of time warp. It really was Meredith Greer sitting there. But the resemblance was only physical. This woman had nothing in common with the Meredith Greer he'd known all these years.

"I'm ashamed to say I know more about you from things I've read than from what I ever learned because of your association with my family. I've read that you came from a difficult home, that your parents were divorced, that your father was an alcoholic, that there was just you and your brother, and you were both very musically inclined from a young age."

"That's all true," he said. "I would add that my mother was incredible. She was the rock in my life."

"I read that too," she said and laughed softly. "I was getting to that. I met your mother once. It was at Derek's funeral. She was very kind. I know she couldn't have heard anything good about me, but she was still very kind."

"She was like that," Jayson said, always missing her when her name came up like this.

"She's not with you anymore."

"We lost her to cancer."

"How long has it been?"

"It was . . . before Elizabeth lost Robert and Bradley."

"Years, then."

"Yes."

Silence made it evident she was sniffling, then she was digging into her purse for a tissue. Jayson was wondering whether he should pretend he hadn't noticed, or whether he should say something. He finally couldn't bear the tension and asked, "You okay?"

"I'm sorry," she said, and he could see that she'd been crying more than he'd realized. "It's just . . . I've had a lot of regrets lately, but . . . one of the biggest is . . ." It took her a couple of minutes to compose herself enough to speak, and Jayson just allowed her to do so. "I'm sorry," she said again.

"It's okay. I cry more than any man on the planet. I cry when the dog begs for table scraps."

"You have a dog?" she asked in a voice that he couldn't distinguish between alarm or excitement.

"We do," he said. "Is that a problem? You're not allergic, are you?"

"No," she said. "I just . . . didn't know you had a dog. We had dogs when I was a little girl, and I have fond memories of that. I just never wanted to deal with one after I had babies. What's his name? Is it a he?"

"It is a he, and his name is Mozie—sort of short for Mozart. Elizabeth named him long before I came on board, which means Mozie has more seniority in the house than I do."

Meredith laughed. "Tell me about Mozie."

"He's fat and lazy and he eats a lot, but I make him take a walk with me every morning anyway. He's a yellow lab, and he's very friendly."

"I can't wait to meet him," Meredith said, and he wondered if she would get back to her biggest regret. Perhaps it was better if she didn't.

Jayson started telling her a little bit about some points of geographical or historical interest as they were driving, which kept the conversation from getting too personal. He was continually amazed at the seeming changes in her, and prayed that her kindness would hold out through the length of her visit.

* * * * *

Elizabeth heard the garage door and glanced at the clock. Right on time. She felt physically better now that she'd had a little rest, and the medication she'd taken earlier had kicked in. The babies were in good moods and playing contentedly. The timing couldn't be better, all things considered. But she felt horribly nervous. She reminded herself of everything that she and Jayson had talked about and put herself into the proper frame of mind.

When Jayson and her mother walked into the living room, Elizabeth stood up and was immediately struck by both the obvious and subtle changes. Her mother had aged, but there was something warm and open in her countenance that Elizabeth had only vague, obscure memories of from her early childhood. "Hi, Mom," she said.

Meredith smiled. "Hello, Elizabeth." She set her purse at her feet and opened her arms. "Do you have a hug for your mother?"

Elizabeth swallowed carefully and felt emotional. She stepped forward and accepted her mother's embrace, fighting to hold back tears. She refused to start crying now when they'd only been together about twenty seconds. She realized the attempt was futile the same moment her mother drew back and caught Elizabeth with tears.

"Sorry," Elizabeth said and hurried to wipe them away. "It's just been . . . a really long time since I got a hug from my mother." She couldn't admit in that moment how desperately she'd wanted all through her teen years to just get a hug from her mother—any sign of affection or approval. But it had never happened.

"Far too long," Meredith said, sounding a little emotional herself. "And I'm sorry about that."

While her mother looked around, taking in her surroundings, Elizabeth exchanged a discreet glance of astonishment with Jayson She couldn't wait to be alone with him and hear how the drive from the airport had gone.

"Oh, your home is lovely!" Meredith said just before the dog approached her, sniffing curiously. Elizabeth moved to pull him back but her mother said, "Oh, he's fine." She ruffled the dog's ears and laughed when Mozie licked her hands. "Jayson told me all about him." Once her greeting with the dog was complete, her eyes then went to the children playing on the floor. "And there are my little darlings," she said and laughed softly, moving closer carefully as if they might be wild animals who would run away if she startled them.

"They don't bite, Mother," Elizabeth said, then she chuckled. "Actually they *do,* but not very often, and only when they're fighting over the same toy."

"Oh, they're adorable!" Meredith said. Of course, the children were too young to have any understanding of this woman telling them that she was their Grandma Meredith, but they were always interested in someone who wanted to play with them. "You've sent me lots of pictures . . . and I'm so glad for those, but pictures just aren't the same, are they."

"No, they're certainly not," Jayson said and moved closer to Elizabeth. They both watched in amazement as Meredith got down on the floor with the children and started talking to them. Her awkwardness made it evident she'd had little to no interaction with young children in a very long time; probably since Elizabeth and Derek had been toddlers.

"I can't believe it," Elizabeth whispered, knowing her mother couldn't hear, especially with the noise the children were making.

"That makes two of us," Jayson said. "You want to hear my theory?"

"On what?" she asked, looking at him.

"The big change?"

"What *is* your theory?"

"I think she's sick," he said, and Elizabeth chuckled, certain he was teasing. Then she saw his eyes and realized he wasn't. He lowered his voice even further and said, "She's trying very hard to cover it, but when I helped her in and out of the car, I could tell she was in some kind of pain. She looks too thin. She's mildly shaky. And sometimes her response in conversation is a little slow."

"Meaning?"

"She's taking pain killers."

"And you're a detective now?"

"No, I just know pain and drugs."

Elizabeth took in what he was saying instead of trying to discredit it. The theory would certainly explain a lot, but Elizabeth wasn't certain she could contend with the deeper implications. While she was trying to think of any other feasible reason for such a visit and such dramatically different attitudes in her mother, Jayson whispered, "Watch her, Lady; watch her when she moves." Elizabeth did, and as she watched, she saw the evidence of Jayson's theory about her mother. She moved slowly, carefully. A discreet grimace. A very soft sharp intake of breath. Jayson added, "I think she's putting everything she's got into appearing as normal as possible, and I'd wager it won't be long before she's needing to rest."

"Are the other children in school?" Meredith asked, turning her attention back to Elizabeth and Jayson without getting up off the floor.

"They are," Elizabeth said. "Are you hungry?"

"No, no. It's not nearly lunchtime yet, is it?"

"No, but if you're hungry—"

"I'm fine," Meredith said, "but I did have to get up early to make my flight. Would it be all right if I rest for a while before lunch?'

"Of course," Elizabeth said, glancing at Jayson.

Meredith turned carefully and took hold of the couch to stand up. Jayson hurried to her side, taking hold of her arm to help her. She leaned on him far too much for a woman her age, although she laughed it off, saying, "Thank you. I'm getting too old to play on the floor."

"I'll take your luggage downstairs," he said. "Elizabeth can make sure you have what you need."

Meredith became distracted by the career wall and perused it for a few minutes, asking a few questions and commenting on the photos of Elizabeth and Derek when they were younger. Elizabeth's attempt to quickly show her mother where to find the things she might need turned into a leisurely tour of the house, ending at the family entrance to the little apartment where she would be staying. "Oh, it's lovely," she said when she walked in to see her luggage on the couch, ready to be opened.

"I hope you'll be comfortable here," Elizabeth said. "I'm usually not too hard to find if you need anything, but . . ." she considered the possibility of what Jayson had said being true and added, "if you need anything, you can use your cell phone to call the house phone. I almost always have a cordless phone with me. Then you don't have to go looking for me. I assume you have the number in the memory."

"I do, yes. Thank you. Everything is perfect."

Elizabeth wanted to demand right this minute to know the reasons for her visit—and her change of heart. But she couldn't bring the words to her lips, and could only smile and say, "I'll come and get you for lunch, then."

"Elizabeth," Meredith said before she could close the door. "Thank you. It was very kind of you to let me come and stay on such short notice. You and Jayson have both been very kind. So . . . thank you."

"It's not a problem, Mom," Elizabeth said. "Let me know if you need anything."

Elizabeth hurried to close the door before tears came again. By the time she found Jayson in the living room with the kids, she was practically sobbing. "Hey, hey," Jayson said as she pressed herself into his arms and cried. "What is it? What's wrong?"

"Did you hear what she said? Did you see what she did?"

"I think so."

"A hug, Jayson," she said. "A genuine hug. And then she said, 'Your home is lovely.' And she meant it. She wasn't being phony. I can tell when she's phony."

"Yes, I caught that."

"And just now . . . she thanked me for being so kind, for allowing her to come. That's all I ever needed from her, Jayson. Just a little bit of affection and approval. A little bit of appreciation. That's all I ever wanted."

Jayson held her closer. "And now you have it."

"Yes, now I have it," she said and cried harder, grateful the kids were absorbed in the PBS program Jayson had turned on. She was finally able to say, "I get a moment . . . one moment of . . . my mother is finally everything I ever needed her to be, and . . . she's sick."

"That's just my opinion," Jayson said. "It could just be—"

"No, I think you're right," she said and sniffled. "It makes perfect sense. But for her to have changed *so much,* I'm afraid she must be *really* sick. Do I finally get my mother back, only to lose her?"

"I doubt it's that serious."

"I doubt anything less serious would bring about such drastic changes. You do remember what she was like, right?"

"Oh, I remember! I remember threatening her with domestic violence charges after she slapped you."

Elizabeth let out a soft laugh. "You called her a bully in a skirt." She tightened her arms around him. "You were my hero that day. You still are."

They talked for a long while, sharing feelings and speculations, and Jayson told her all about their conversation at the airport and on the way home. They only had to interrupt the conversation three times for a diaper change, a fight over Spongebob, and the need for snacks.

When Elizabeth realized it was nearing time for lunch, they took their conversation to the kitchen while Jayson helped her pull things out to make the fixings of nice sandwiches. He put the babies in their highchairs to give them lunch while Elizabeth went downstairs to get her mother. She knocked lightly at the door, wondering if she was asleep, but Meredith answered the door, looking chipper.

"Lunch is ready," she said, "whenever you are."

"I'm ready," Meredith said, and they went up the stairs together. Elizabeth noticed that she did move a little slowly; not enough to be hugely noticeable, but she knew her mother had always been in a hurry. She'd always walked faster than the average person.

"It's just sandwiches," Elizabeth said. "I'm not much of a cook."

"You got that from me," Meredith said lightly. "Anything is fine. Don't you worry about me."

"Well, I *am* going to cook some dinner . . . only because I fixed it yesterday and I can just stick it in the oven. But that won't happen every day."

"The house and children must keep you very busy," Meredith said in a way that felt utterly validating to Elizabeth—the exact opposite of the subtle critical jabs she'd been expecting. "Who has time to cook when there are so many other good things you can do with your time?"

"My thoughts exactly," Elizabeth said, wondering when her mother had magically transformed into a woman who could think the same way she did.

Jayson offered a blessing on the food before they made sandwiches and ate them. Meredith made no comment on the prayer, but Elizabeth wondered what she thought. No prayer had ever been spoken in Elizabeth's home during her growing-up years. Even though she'd been the first one to find the Church and be baptized, Jayson had been more prone to spirituality when they'd been dating. Meredith mostly asked questions about each of the children, their interests, their friends—anything and everything. She kept watching Derek and Harmony, commenting and laughing over their antics. She said, "I considered bringing gifts for the children . . . something to bribe them with." She laughed softly. "But I knew that you could buy them whatever they wanted, and it would be better if I just came to get to know them."

"An excellent plan, Mother," Elizabeth said. "Trevin and Addie are pretty sharp. I think they could see through the gifts."

Jayson helped clean up lunch, then announced that he had to get some work done. While Meredith was preoccupied with the babies, Elizabeth said to Jayson by way of warning, "I might bring Mom into the studio. She was asking about it."

Since Jayson had gotten past any concern that Meredith might be trying to find something wrong with him, he had no problem with that. He'd long ago gotten over any shyness with having people hear him rehearse—once a song was past a certain stage, anyway. "Fine," he said, "bring her into the sound booth after the babies go down for their naps, and you can help me record."

"You're still working on the same piece?"

"Yes, and I need to do the voice again. I don't like it."

"Okay, I'll be there; *we'll* be there."

About half an hour later Elizabeth had the babies down for their naps. She found her mother in the living room and said, "I need to help Jayson record something. Do you want to come along?"

"Oh, I'd love to!" Meredith said, setting aside her magazine. Elizabeth led her through the first door into the tiny area that created a sound barrier. The door in front of them led into the studio. The door to their right led into the sound booth, and that's where they went. From there they could see Jayson through the soundproof glass, wearing headphones and singing into the microphone. Elizabeth sensed a certain awe in her mother, but she didn't comment. Realizing it probably sounded strange to only be able to hear what Jayson was singing and nothing else, Elizabeth explained. "Most of the other tracks have been recorded, so he's singing along to what he can hear in the headphones."

"Oh, I see," Meredith said, and Elizabeth handed her a set of headphones. "Oh!" she said with delighted surprise and put them on, immediately smiling.

"It's okay for us to talk in here," Elizabeth said, "even when we're recording." The volume in the headphones was low enough that they could hear each other. "The equipment only picks up noise from the studio."

"Incredible!" Meredith said, taking in the complicated equipment in front of them.

Elizabeth put on her own headphones and listened and watched. Since Jayson had his eyes closed, he didn't know they were there. She loved watching him sing like this. When he wasn't concentrating on playing an instrument as well, he put all of his focus and energy just into singing. She was continually amazed at how he could sing so naturally, as if it took no more effort than breathing. He could open his mouth as if to casually speak, and rich, beautiful sounds came out. It was rare, if ever, that he sang in public without also playing the guitar or piano. It was only when he was recording his voice that he *only* sang. And he usually closed his eyes. It was just him, the music he could hear in the headphones, and the sound coming out of his mouth. She could watch him and feel how he became a part of the music. Without an instrument to keep his hands occupied, they were usually out to his sides, moving with the music as if he were gliding and they helped him keep balance. Now, like a thousand other times in her life, she felt deeply privileged to be the woman who had claimed the heart of Jayson Wolfe.

CHAPTER 7

When Jayson finished the song, Elizabeth flipped a switch so he could hear her, and she said, "We're here, babe."

He turned and waved. Elizabeth blew a kiss, and Meredith waved with such beaming enthusiasm that Elizabeth couldn't hold back a chuckle.

"Okay," Jayson said. "It's all set. You know what to do. I'm just doing it straight through."

"Here goes," Elizabeth said, and the music began again. She exchanged a smile with Jayson before he eased himself into the music, closed his eyes, and began to sing.

"His voice is remarkable," Meredith said.

"Yes, it is!" Elizabeth agreed with enthusiasm.

"So . . . were all of the instruments recorded this way . . . one at a time?"

"That's right," Elizabeth said.

"And who is playing?"

"Well, that's me on the violin," Elizabeth said, mocking excessive pride. "The rest is Jayson."

"The rest?"

"Yeah. In this case, acoustic guitar, piano, bass guitar, and drums. Well, as you can hear the drum beat is just a simple sequence to give the song a foundation. His brother will come and record the *real* drums; the fancy stuff. No one can play the drums like Drew."

Meredith shook her head. "I had no idea Jayson was so talented."

"You heard him play and sing when we were eighteen."

"Yes, at my son's funeral. I remember being impressed, but I really didn't know he was so . . . diversified and . . . gifted."

Elizabeth chuckled. "You thought all the awards and success were just . . . accidental?" Her mother scowled slightly, and Elizabeth added, "I'm not making fun of you. I'm just . . . wondering."

"I never paid attention to that kind of music. I suppose I assumed that it didn't take that much talent. I guess I was wrong."

Elizabeth sighed and smiled to herself, watching her mother watch Jayson sing. "Yes," she said, "he is certainly gifted."

When he was done he reached for a bottle of water and drank some before he said, "How did it sound to you?"

"You're asking *me?*" Elizabeth asked. *"You're* the perfectionist. I thought it sounded great."

"Me too," Meredith said, and Jayson smiled.

"Let's take it from the top," he said, and they did it three more times.

Elizabeth thought her mother would get bored, but she sat there like a child at a circus, asking an occasional question and just taking it all in.

The remainder of the day went well, although Elizabeth became keenly aware of the evidence to which Jayson had drawn her attention. Meredith was in pain and working very hard to conceal it. She was excited when the little ones woke up, and while Harmony was still sleepy she was willing to snuggle on her grandmother's lap for a few minutes. It was such a sweet moment that Elizabeth grabbed her camera and took a picture. She decided that her mother's visit probably warranted a great many pictures. She considered the possibility that it might be her last, and she couldn't even entertain the thought for more than a moment. It was just too impossible to comprehend or accept.

In response to her father's request, Macy stopped by to meet Elizabeth's mother. He came out of the studio while she was there, since she couldn't stay long. Meredith showed genuine interest in her and wanted to hear about her life and her interests. When Macy had to go, Meredith hugged her and thanked her for making the effort to come by. After Macy left, Jayson went back to the studio, and Elizabeth continued to visit with her mother.

When Trevin came home, Meredith was excited to see him. He showed more enthusiasm than most teenaged boys might to see a grandmother he'd only seen a couple of times—one that he barely remembered. Meredith showed genuine interest in him, and asked him to sit and tell her about himself. Before he went off to do homework, she made him promise to play the guitar for her later. Then Addie came home and quickly warmed up to her grandmother, even though she didn't remember her at all. They'd both been forewarned of their grandmother's visit, and it all went rather well.

While Elizabeth was changing a diaper, she pretended not to notice how her mother said softly to Addie, "Do you think you could go downstairs and get Grandma's purse for me, honey? There's some medicine in there I need to take."

Addie followed the instructions and came back with the purse while Elizabeth was disposing of the diaper. While she was washing her hands, Addie came to the kitchen and said, "Grandma needs a glass of water."

"That's very nice of you to be so helpful," Elizabeth said, then she discreetly peered around the corner to see her mother open a pill container and dump a variety of pills, five or six in different colors, into her hand, then swallow them. Elizabeth told herself not to mar these pleasant moments by jumping to fearful conclusions.

When Addie went off to play with friends, and Jayson was still busy in the studio, Meredith asked Elizabeth, "Do you think it would be possible to see your father and meet Marilyn?"

Elizabeth looked at her mother squarely. "You're serious."

"Yes, I'm serious."

"I thought the two of you had some kind of unspoken pact to never see each other again."

"Any such pact, unspoken or otherwise, should be dissolved. I would just like to see him, but I don't want to cause any problems. If you think that Marilyn would be upset by my visit, or—"

"No, she wouldn't be upset."

"Does he know I was coming?"

"No, actually. I haven't talked to him for a couple of days. Truthfully, I was just hoping he wouldn't stop by before I had a chance to talk to him."

"Well, maybe you should warn him," Meredith said. "If it was the other way around, I think I would appreciate a warning."

"Right. Okay," she said and stood up. "You hang out here and keep an eye on the kids. I'm going to call my dad."

Elizabeth went to her bedroom and closed the door. She tried to take in the emotional overload of spending the day with her altered mother, and the possible reasons for it. Thankfully she was mostly in shock, and was caught up enough in the pleasantry of the moment that she could ignore any fears or concerns. Then she had to gear herself up to call her father. She dialed his number, and he answered after the first ring.

"Hi," she said. "How are you?"

"I'm good. How are you?"

"I'm fine. We haven't talked for a few days."

"No," he said, sounding mildly suspicious. "I called a day or two ago, and Trevin said you were busy cleaning the entire house."

"Sorry, he didn't give me the message that you'd called. I *was* kind of trying to clean the whole house."

"Special occasion?"

"You might say that," she said. "My mother is here."

"Oh, really," he said through a laugh. "Are you having a delightful time?" His sarcasm was evident.

"Yes, we are actually . . . and yes, I really mean that."

"You're serious."

"She's being so kind and appropriate that it's like . . . well, it's weird. But it's a good weird."

"Why?"

"Why what? Why is it weird, or why is—"

"Why is she there?"

"She just called a couple of days ago and asked if she could come. She promised to be nice. What could I say? She told me she wanted to spend some time with her grandchildren."

"Is she *sick?*" Will asked, and she knew he didn't mean it literally, but she found it difficult not to cry.

Thinking it would be better if she didn't share her suspicions with her father at this point, she just said, "She said she'd like to see you, and to meet Marilyn. Her intentions appear to be honorable, but if you don't want to—"

"I'd love to see her again," he said, "especially if she's being nice. And Marilyn's said a hundred times that she wished she could meet Meredith."

"Okay, then . . . well . . . how about if you come over for dessert later? I'd invite you to dinner, but quite frankly, I didn't make enough."

"No worries. Dessert would be fine. Can we bring anything?"

"Just your cheerful and charming selves."

"Are you okay?" Will asked.

"I am; really. We'll see you about seven-thirty. Trevin promised Grandma he'd play the guitar for her."

"Ooh, I can't wait," Will said and ended the call.

Elizabeth returned to the living room and announced to her mother, "They're coming over for dessert at seven-thirty."

"Oh, wonderful!" Meredith said, then immediately started telling Elizabeth about something funny Derek had just done. She commented on how wonderful it was that she had a grandson with the name of her son, and she said how she'd never stopped missing Derek. Elizabeth sat nearby and mostly listened. It was almost as if her mother hadn't had anybody to really talk to for years, and now she couldn't stop.

Elizabeth took a break to put the Parmesan chicken in the oven. She had prepared it the previous day, and she had salad in the fridge and dessert prepared, so she assigned Addie to set the table and Trevin to make some Kool-Aid. For once, Addie did what she was asked without complaining, and Elizabeth returned to the living room to visit with her mother, feeling as if it was all some magical dream that would inevitably come to an end.

"Honey, I'm home," Jayson said facetiously when he came out of the studio just a few minutes before dinner was ready. He laid on the floor and played with the kids until it was time to put them in their high chairs and eat. The meal was pleasant, but Elizabeth couldn't help noticing that her mother wasn't eating much, and she definitely looked uncomfortable, no matter how prudently she was handling it.

Because they had visited so much over the dinner table, Elizabeth was surprised to note that it was almost seven-thirty when they barely had the kitchen in order. Her father was nothing if not punctual, and she was just hanging up the dishtowel when she heard him come in the door. She greeted him with a hug, and hurried to intercept him before he got to the living room.

"Everything okay?" he whispered.

"Yeah," she said and smiled at him. "How about you?"

"I'm great."

"Hello, dear," Marilyn said, hugging her as well.

"You ready for this?" she asked Marilyn.

"Ready and eager," Marilyn said with a sly smile.

They all stepped into the living room where Meredith was sitting on the couch, leaning forward to see what the kids were doing on the floor. Will immediately said, "This is certainly unexpected."

Meredith looked up, smiled, and came slowly to her feet. "William!" she said, stepping forward to give him a hug. Jayson and Elizabeth exchanged one of those astonished glances. Marilyn seemed nothing but pleased.

"How are you?" Will asked when the hug was done.

"I'm very much enjoying my grandchildren. And you?"

"I'm great." He motioned to his wife. "This is Marilyn; Marilyn, Meredith. I doubt the two of you need any more introduction than that."

"It's a pleasure to finally meet you," Marilyn said, eagerly taking Meredith's hand.

"And you," Meredith said.

They all sat down and chatted comfortably for more than half an hour before Will said, "I heard a rumor that Trevin was going to play for us."

"Oh, yes!" Meredith said with enthusiasm.

Trevin was a little shy as he said, "Only if Dad plays with me." He'd never had a problem playing for anyone else on his own, so Elizabeth assumed the presence of someone who didn't fall into his comfortable family category made him feel more reserved. He'd not yet taken his talents outside of the family circle.

"You don't need me," Jayson said, but Trevin tossed him a subtle scowl. "But I would love to play with you if that's what you want to do."

Trevin left and came back with two acoustic guitars. He handed Jayson his most prized instrument, the one that Will had given him as a gift for high-school graduation. Trevin sat down beside Jayson and settled his own guitar onto his thigh. He looked directly at Meredith, and with a maturity that contradicted the shyness he'd just displayed about playing alone, he said gently to his grandmother, "This guitar means a great deal to me. I thought you should know . . . it was Derek's guitar."

Meredith daintily put her fingers over her mouth for a few seconds before she said with a cracking voice, "Oh, that's wonderful!" She turned to Will. "Did you give it to him?"

"No," he said, "I gave it to Jayson after Derek died; I gave him pretty much everything. They were partners in music. It felt like the right thing to do." Will smiled. "Jayson gave Trevin two of Derek's guitars after Robert and Bradley died. I do believe the music has helped heal this young man."

Trevin ignored the way he was being talked about beyond muttering a quiet, "Amen."

"He's got a gift," Jayson said, then to Trevin, "What are we playing?"

"The one you wrote for your grandmother," Trevin said. "I've been practicing that one."

"Doesn't it have a title?" Will asked.

"Actually," Jayson chuckled, "it doesn't. I only sang it publicly at the concert she attended—and at her funeral. I never gave it a title."

"Oh, just play it," Elizabeth said.

"This isn't fair," Jayson said, humorously whining like a child. "We're supposed to be hearing Trevin play the guitar, but I have to sing. I'm not singing unless he does the backing vocals."

"Fine," Trevin said with equally exaggerated humor. He and Jayson exchanged a nod that started a silent count, and the song began. The intricate guitars that they each played were not the same, but they harmonized beautifully. Elizabeth felt proud to see how well her son was doing. In addition to his readily evident skill, he had become composed and relaxed when he played. Jayson's tutelage was coming through very well.

Following a lengthy musical intro, Jayson began to sing, *"Wrapped up in my child's bed, I heard voices in my head, singing, always singing. Drowning out the voices I heard down the hall, through the wall, shouting, always shouting. Raging with hot-blooded youth, the voices sang to me of truth, luring me, assuring me, curing me of every pain, wooing me into the rain that bathed my aching soul. The voices singing in my mind; they call to me, call to me. From another place and time they seem to say, 'One day you'll see . . . some day you'll see . . . that true love lasts forever, that no heart beats alone, that a mother's care reaches out across the sea and sky and brings the wanderer home, brings the wanderer home. The voices calling in my mind; they sing to me, sing to me . . . that music flows like water . . . turned to wine . . . in perfect rhyme with seasons gone before me and seasons yet to cross.*

"In the wavering sands of manhood I hear the voices in my head, they sing to me, sing to me, luring me, assuring me, curing me of every pain. The hands of time hold me securely . . . as surely . . . as darkness turns to light, daylight turns to night and reaches out toward another dawn. And reaching to the east I feel your hand in mine, finding me, reminding me . . . that true love lasts forever, that no heart beats alone, that a mother's care reaches out across the sea and sky and brings the wanderer home, brings the wanderer home. The voices calling in my mind; they sing to me, sing to me . . . that music flows like water . . . turned to wine . . . in perfect rhyme with seasons gone before me and seasons yet to cross."

Several bars of the beautiful guitar duet continued while Jayson and Trevin smiled at each other a couple of times. After the final strum, everyone applauded, and Elizabeth noticed her mother discreetly drying tears.

"Okay," Jayson said to Trevin, setting his own guitar aside, "now you can play that other one you've been working on—all by yourself."

"Okay, fine," Trevin said with mock chagrin, then he played a beautiful guitar version of his favorite song from Primary, "A Child's Prayer."

After he'd played it through once and received generous applause, Will said, "Now I think you should do it again, and your mother and sister can sing it."

"This was not meant to turn into a concert," Elizabeth said.

"No, it's family singing time," Will said. "We're waiting. Addie wants to sing it, don't you, Addie?" Addie nodded, and Elizabeth sighed, wondering if she felt more self-conscious with her mother around, the same way Trevin had.

Trevin started the song again, and Addie came in right on cue, singing sweetly, *"Heavenly Father, are you really there? And do you hear and answer ev-'ry child's prayer? Some say that heaven is far away, But I feel it close around me as I pray. Heavenly Father, I remember now Something that Jesus told disciples long ago: 'Suffer the children to come to me;' Father, in prayer I'm coming now to thee.'"*

Elizabeth then sang, *"Pray, He is there; Speak, He is lis-t'ning. You are His child; His love now surrounds you. He hears your prayer; He loves the children. Of such is the kingdom, the kingdom of heav'n.'"*

Then the two of them sang both parts together, as it had been intended by its composer. The effect was deeply stirring. The three grandparents all got a little teary, and Jayson felt hard-pressed not to join them. He would never forget the way Elizabeth had sung that song to him while he'd been in rehab, completely falling apart. Its principles and message had warmed him and given him hope. Now he knew the absolute truth of them, and he wondered how he'd ever coped without that knowledge.

"Singing time is over," Elizabeth announced and got Jayson to help her serve the brownies with ice cream and hot fudge. In the kitchen she said softly to him, "This is so weird I can hardly stand it. *My* parents—and the new wife—having a marvelous time together."

"They have a lot in common."

"They do?"

"All they talk about is those adorable grandkids." Jayson kissed her. "That's our fault, you know—that they have something in common."

"It's just so weird."

"I hear you," he said. "I was there in the good old days, remember?"

"It's just so weird."

"You said that already. Is the fudge hot yet, because I'm having a chocolate fit here."

"You think chocolate will make all of this easier to accept as reality?"

"Exactly," Jayson said, then he called everyone to the dining room for dessert.

While they were gathered around the table, Elizabeth noticed that her mother didn't look well. She asked for only a tiny piece of brownie, but she only picked at that. With a seeming burst of energy she stood up and said, "I hate to be party pooper, but my day started early and I think I'd better get some rest." She thanked everyone and told them all how good it was to see them and to be together. She hugged every single person and thanked them for their kindness. She lingered a little with each of the children, as if she didn't want the day to end.

As Meredith headed toward the stairs, Elizabeth followed her, saying, "Do you need anything, Mom?"

"No, thank you. I have everything I need. You've been so gracious." She stopped and looked directly at Elizabeth. "You have a wonderful family, my dear, and you are clearly such a good wife and mother—and a good daughter, to both me and your father. Thank you for everything." She took Elizabeth's hand and squeezed it. "I'll see you in the morning."

"Sleep as late as you want," Elizabeth said. "We can visit whenever you're up to it. And remember, you can call me on the phone if you need something."

"I'll be fine," she said and went down the stairs.

Elizabeth took a deep breath to try to take in the day and all she was feeling. She returned to the dining room to find dessert being cleaned up, mostly by Will and Marilyn, with a little help from Addie. Trevin had gone to start on his homework. Jayson had taken Derek and Harmony to start the evening bath. Elizabeth sent Addie to get ready for bed and do her reading. While she was alone in the kitchen with her father and stepmother, Will asked, "Are you okay? You look a little . . . dazed."

"I *am* dazed. Aren't you?"

"A little, yes," Will said. "I've prayed for her every night and day since I learned how to pray."

"So have I," Elizabeth admitted.

"And now we have seen the answer to prayers. Our family is being healed, Elizabeth. That's a good thing."

"It's a *very* good thing, and I'm grateful. It's just that . . ." She wondered whether or not to say anything about her suspicions, but decided that she couldn't hold them inside. And perhaps they needed to know. "I wonder *why*. Why such a dramatic change? Why so quickly?"

"Maybe it hasn't been quickly. You've shared nothing but occasional short phone conversations with her for years. How do you know what's been going on in her life, or how many years this has been in the making?"

"That's true, but . . ."

"But what?" Will asked.

"Is something wrong, dear?" Marilyn asked, and Elizabeth started to cry.

"I think she's sick," Elizabeth admitted, and went on to tell her what she and Jayson had observed throughout the day.

"Your concerns sound well-founded," Will said, "but until you talk to her about it and know what's really going on, you're just going on speculation. She could have arthritis, or something. She could be taking medications for any number of things. Health problems plus change of heart do not automatically equal the possibility that she's dying."

"Okay, you're right," Elizabeth said. "Do you think I should just ask her?"

"Tactfully and carefully, yes," Will said. "That's my opinion. You should make it a matter of prayer." He kissed her cheek. "Thanks for a nice evening. You call me if you need anything."

"Thank you, Dad," she said and hugged him. She hugged Marilyn as well before they found Jayson and the kids to tell them all good night.

Elizabeth felt consumed with exhaustion when she finally crawled into bed next to her husband. She put her head on his shoulder and recounted her feelings regarding such a red-letter day. She drifted off to sleep with his arm around her, praying for the words to be able to speak frankly and appropriately with her mother. Now that she finally had a good relationship with her mother, she wanted it to last, and she wanted to make the most of it.

Long after Jayson knew that Elizabeth was asleep, his mind wandered through memories of his own parents. He'd lost his mother to cancer, and everything associated with that was still difficult to think about. But the relationship they'd shared had been as good as a mother and son could share. They'd shared love, respect, and commitment. They had taken care of each other, and he had no regrets. His father was an entirely different matter. He'd only seen him once after he had moved to Oregon with his mother and brother when he'd been sixteen. Years later, Jay Wolfe had found Jayson at a hotel following a concert; he'd been drunk and he wanted money. Jayson had given him the opportunity to go to rehab and put his life in order—with Jayson footing the bill. But his father had refused the offer, and he never changed. He'd died a pathetic death after living a pathetic life. Jayson thought of the validation and acceptance Elizabeth had gotten from her mother today, and he wondered how that might feel. How might it have been if he'd been able to see his father one last time, if he'd been able to hear words of love and respect? He couldn't even imagine! Of course, Jayson knew now that his father was progressing on the other side of the veil. The temple work had been done for both of his parents, and Jayson had been blessed with more than one spiritual experience that had let him know they were doing well and moving forward. Such reassurance could not be compared to any amount of earthly interaction. Still, he couldn't help feeling some sorrow over the mortal life his father had lived, fraught with such despicable choices. He turned his mind to the situation with Meredith, finding healing there even for himself. He'd prayerfully endeavored to be free of any ill feelings toward her for many years. But he'd never had a positive encounter with her, either in person or on the phone, and he was glad to see the changes in her. He was glad for his children's sake. And his wife's. It had truly been a good day.

* * * * *

Elizabeth felt significantly better than she had the previous morning while she and Jayson went through the usual morning routine. She felt happy and comforted to think of her mother sleeping in the basement, and looked forward to spending more time with her. She wondered if Meredith might be up to a laid-back trip to the mall, or going out to lunch. She'd often wondered what it would be like to share such a relationship with her mother. She said to Jayson, "I wonder if we could talk her into going to church with us on Sunday."

"I just think that might be possible," he said. "With the way she's been behaving, you could probably have her baptized next week."

Elizabeth chuckled. "We should maybe give her a little more time than that."

After Addie left for school, Trevin having gone earlier, Jayson was about to head to the studio when the phone rang. Elizabeth glanced at the caller ID and said, "It's my mother."

"Good morning," Elizabeth said into the phone, trying not to feel panicked.

"Good morning, dear," Meredith said, sounding weak and frail.

"What can I do for you?"

"I think we need to talk, Elizabeth," she said. "Could you come down here, please?"

"Of course," she said. "I'll be right there."

She hung up the phone, and Jayson asked, "What's wrong?"

Elizabeth repeated the conversation, while panic threatened to overtake her. "Now, calm down," Jayson said gently. "Just . . . go talk to her. I'll watch the kids. Take as long as you need."

"Okay," she said, breathing deeply. "Thank you."

Elizabeth prayed while she descended the stairs, then she knocked lightly at the door to her mother's room before she opened it and peered in. "Come in, Elizabeth," Meredith said, holding out a hand from where she was propped up in the bed with pillows. Elizabeth attempted to take in the difference in her appearance without showing her alarm. In the absence of makeup and her efforts to mask the problem, the problem—whatever it might be—was glaringly evident. "I look horrible, I know," Meredith said, "but I just couldn't get myself up to do anything about it. I'm afraid yesterday took all of the best I have to give."

"What are you saying, Mother?" Elizabeth asked, taking Meredith's hand as she sat on the edge of the bed. In spite of her suspicions, she'd never imagined that the situation could be so severe.

"I hope you'll forgive me," Meredith said, "but I didn't want anyone to know . . . because I didn't want everyone being nice to me just because I was ill. I was determined to see my family and be as normal as I possibly could. And I did." She smiled with great satisfaction. "I think yesterday was probably the best day of my entire life."

Elizabeth took all of this in, grateful at least for having had some inkling that something was wrong. She could see now that it was helping soften her own shock. But the shock was still there, and she could hardly think clearly. She had a dozen questions and at least that many emotions rolling around inside, but she tried to remain steady and focused and simply said, "Tell me what's going on, Mom."

Meredith sighed. "I haven't been feeling well for a long time."

"How long?"

"A year, maybe two. There were different symptoms. I ignored them. I was busy. Then I started losing weight, and began having pain. I went to the doctor about a month ago. They did tests, and I kept telling myself it would be nothing . . . easy to solve. I was told that I was so full of cancer there was no hope of any surgery or treatment that would make any difference."

Elizabeth gasped, then sobbed. "Mom?" she said like a child.

"They told me I had a month, maybe two."

Elizabeth sobbed again, then put her free hand over her mouth.

"I'm sorry to spring it on you this way," she said without visible emotion. "I just . . . wanted to see my family again, and wanted to try to repair some damage." She smiled. "It's evident you've all gotten along marvelously without me, but I do thank you—all of you—for being so kind and gracious. I was hoping for a good day with my family. I didn't expect it to be *that* good."

"And now what?" Elizabeth asked, wondering how bad it really was.

"Now I just need you to take me to a hospital and help me get checked in. Everything else is in order. I'll just leave my luggage here. There are some things in there for you; the rest you can throw away, and—"

"Mom?" Elizabeth said hotly. "How can you be so . . . cold about this?"

"I am not cold about this, Elizabeth. I've just had my time to cry. I've cried and screamed. I broke several things. I was like that for days and days. But I knew I had to get it out of my system, because I couldn't call you up or come here and be blubbering all over the place. Now, I've seen my family, and I've hopefully mended some bridges. And now it's time for me to go."

"Go?"

"I just need you to take me to a hospital and—"

"And what? Just drop you off and leave you there to die so you won't inconvenience me?"

"I guess that's it, yes."

"Mom!" she said again, unable to believe what she was hearing, what she was feeling.

"Elizabeth, listen to me," Meredith said intently. "I don't think motherhood ever suited me very well." She chuckled. "I don't need to tell you that. Now I think I should have tried harder. Just because it wasn't easy or comfortable for me, doesn't mean I shouldn't have made the effort to be a good mother to my children." She sighed deeply. "Now that my life is coming to an end, I hold no delusions about the kind of mother I was. I don't expect anything from you, Elizabeth, because I haven't ever put enough into our relationship to be able to expect anything. I know that. I'm okay with it. You've been more . . ." she finally showed some emotion, ". . . kind and gracious to me than I ever expected or deserved. I was hoping for tolerance enough to be able to see the kids, and to . . . have the chance to . . ." her tears increased, ". . . to tell you how sorry I am . . . that I was so horrible. I'm sorry I wasn't there for you. I should have been here . . . when you had your babies . . . when you . . ." She got so upset that she couldn't speak at all. Elizabeth eased closer and wrapped her arms carefully around her mother, and together they wept for several minutes. Meredith finally said without relinquishing their embrace, "I should have been here when you lost Robert and Bradley. It's my greatest regret." Elizabeth eased back to look at her. "I just couldn't face it. I could only think of losing Derek, and I didn't know how I could be any good to you when I couldn't keep myself together, and I knew I would probably just add to your stress if I showed up. So I didn't. But I should have. And I'm sorry. I would never expect you to forgive me for all the cruelty and neglect, but—"

"Of course I forgive you, Mom. I forgave you a long time ago."

New tears swam in Meredith's eyes, and they hugged again. Elizabeth eased closer and leaned on the same pillows, keeping her arm around her mother. Meredith cried harder, and Elizabeth just held her, crying her own tears more quietly, marveling at the quiet strength she felt filling her from deep within. While a part of her felt tempted to scream and cry and protest, a power beyond her own seemed to whisper that there would be a time to grieve. Now was the time to bask in the newfound bond with her mother, and to heal old wounds.

"It's all right," Elizabeth murmured. "You're here now, and I'm so glad you came. I'm not going to take you to the hospital, Mom. I'm going to take care of you right here."

"No," Meredith protested, looking at her straightly, "I can't let you do it. Everything's arranged. I've already sorted everything I own, and I sold most of it. I sold the condo. I didn't want you to to have to deal with anything. All the legalities have been taken care of. All the paperwork is in my luggage."

Elizabeth glanced at the luggage, then at her mother again. "Are you saying you had no intention to return to Oregon—at all?"

"No need. I knew there wasn't time. Everything I own is now right there in my suitcases, but as I said, it's just—"

"Don't you have any friends there?"

"None that will miss me for long. I've said my good-byes there. I was very lucky that I sold the condo so quickly, and a dear neighbor who has struggled with finances since her husband ran out on her, she . . ." Meredith laughed softly, "well, she and I never had much in common, but she was very kind after I got sick. And she absolutely loves garage sales. I just gave practically everything to her. We got someone to move it all into her garage. I hope it will help her and her children. They're very kind people."

Elizabeth blew out a stilted breath. She could hardly take it all in. She tried to comprehend the enormity of this, and realized that she couldn't. She could only deal with one issue at a time. She prayed, she listened to her thoughts and feelings, then she asked her mother, "Is there some medical reason for you to go to the hospital right now?"

"Nothing beyond the fact that I do not want my grandchildren to see me like this, and I don't want any of you to find me dead. And I won't have you dealing with whatever it will take to get me to the end. Hospitals deal with this kind of stuff all the time. My medical insurance is still in place. It's all taken care of. The papers are in the—"

"Will you stop worrying about the papers?" Elizabeth insisted, sounding mildly sharp. "Stop being an attorney and just be my mother. I don't *want* to take you to a hospital. I want you to be here."

"Be realistic, Elizabeth. If you—"

"Mom," she interrupted gently, "how long do you have?"

Meredith sighed. "The nurse that checked me before I left said it would probably be only a few days."

Elizabeth started to cry again. "A few days?" She shook her head, trying to take it in. "I need some time to think, Mom. We'll talk about the hospital later. Do you need anything right now? Are you hungry? Do you need help getting to the bathroom, or . . . anything?"

"No, thank you, dear. I'm fine. I'm not hungry."

"You . . . rest then," Elizabeth said and pressed a kiss to her mother's forehead before she moved toward the door. "Call me if you need something . . . anything."

"I promise," Meredith said. "Thank you."

CHAPTER 8

Elizabeth hurried up the stairs and straight into Jayson's arms. He closed the fridge and wrapped her in his embrace, well aware that she was very upset.

"What happened?" he asked gently.

"She's dying," Elizabeth muttered. "You were right. She was fighting very hard to appear normal. But it's worse than I ever imagined."

"What?" he demanded, taking her by the shoulders to look at her.

"She's full of cancer; there's nothing they can do. She only has . . ." Elizabeth choked the words out, ". . . a few days at most." Jayson gasped, and Elizabeth sobbed, crumbling in his arms again. He guided her to the couch in the living room where he held her and let her cry until she managed to say, "She wants me to take her to a hospital to let her die. She's sold everything in Oregon. Everything she owns is in her luggage. Everything is in order, she tells me; everything is there."

"Good heavens," Jayson said. "I can't believe it."

"I can't either," she said. "But I'm not going to waste what little time I have with her by blubbering all over the place. I can cry after she's gone. I want to talk to her and be with her and . . ." she sobbed, ". . . I want to go shopping and out to lunch and sightseeing and . . . it's not going to happen."

"I'm so sorry," Jayson said. "I'm so very sorry." He looked at her and wiped her tears. "What do you need me to do? I'll do anything."

"I don't know," she said. "You have work to do, and—"

"Elizabeth, you and I both know that no work I do in the studio is ever as important as the needs of others—especially family. Anything else can wait. I can't very well expect God to inspire me if I'm not willing to serve where I'm needed. What do you need?"

She tried to think. "I just . . . want to spend as much time with her as I can, so—"

"I'll take care of everything else; the house, the kids—everything. You just take care of her and yourself."

"Okay," she sniffled, "thank you. I'm sure Dad will help."

"I'm sure he will. What else?"

She started to cry again. "She wants me to take her to the hospital. I'm sure I could be there with her, but I think about . . . when your mom went." She looked up at Jayson. "I want her to be here, but she's refusing."

"Do you want me to talk to her?"

"If you think it would help, go for it," she said. "I guess I should call Dad."

"I think you'd better," he said. "The rug rats are being reasonably calm at the moment." He kissed her brow. "It's going to be all right, Elizabeth. I know it's hard, but we're going to get through it together." He looked at her firmly. "Consider what a miracle it is that she's here under your roof. Think how hard it would have been to hear about this after the fact when you were contacted for legal purposes."

"Oh," Elizabeth put a hand over her heart, "you're right. That would be horrible. I *am* grateful she's here . . . and she's been so wonderful. If it's her time to go, it couldn't be under better circumstances."

"So, let's keep perspective and get through it."

"Okay," she said, "thank you."

"Hey," he said, "we're family. We always have been. You flew to LA to be with me when my mom died. And we weren't literally family then, but . . . you did it anyway."

Once Jayson had gone downstairs, Elizabeth called her father and repeated the news. He was stunned and got emotional. He said that he and Marilyn would be available to help in any way, and he said they would bring dinner over for everyone that evening. Will asked how she was doing, and Elizabeth started to cry again, but she admitted that she was feeling strengthened and sustained and more grateful than sad. After she got off the phone, she wondered if she should go see how it was coming with Jayson and her mother, but she thought it best to let them talk privately. Instead she plopped onto the couch, near where the babies were playing, and just tried to take it all in.

* * * * *

Jayson knocked lightly on the open door to Meredith's room. She opened her eyes and turned her head toward him. He hated the way her appearance brought back memories of his mother's death, but he pushed that away and stepped into the room. "Your daughter's been tattling on you."

"She told you everything?"

"She did. She always tells me everything." He moved a chair close to the bed and sat on it.

"I don't want to be a bother, Jayson. I was really hoping to hold out a little longer so I could . . ."

"What? Get a cab to the hospital and leave us completely ignorant?"

"Maybe," she said. "It would have been a lot less bother . . . a lot less drama."

"May I tell you something, Meredith?" Jayson asked, taking her hand.

"Of course."

"You know that I lost my mother to cancer," he said, and her eyes softened with interest and compassion. "It was long and slow for her . . . for us. I was pretty much unemployed at the time, but my brother was working with another band. With the help of nurses who came to the house, it was pretty much just me and my mother battling the disease for a long time. When the end was near, I called Will and Elizabeth. She hadn't wanted me to tell them how bad it was, but she knew they needed to see each other again before she left, and I never could have gotten through it alone. They were both on the next flights there. Will and Elizabeth were both there with me during those final days. They held me together. We were all with my mother when she left. They've held me together since. The point I'm trying to make is that . . . death is a part of life, Meredith. Sometimes we don't have the opportunity to be with someone we love when they go—like Derek. We didn't know it was coming. It just happened. It was over. But if there's any positive aspect to being taken by some dreadful disease, it's the opportunity to be prepared, to do the things you want to do, and say the things you want to say. You've done that, and I want you to know that I admire and respect you for it. You've initiated a great deal of healing in the last few days. There are people here who love you, and I'm one of them." He chuckled and shook his head. "I never imagined feeling this way, Meredith, but I do. I've always cared about you, wished the best for you. But you've become very easy to love since you've come back to us."

Meredith started to cry. Jayson handed her a tissue and kept one for himself, knowing he wasn't far behind her. "I'm asking you . . . begging you . . . not to leave our home now. We don't want you to die in a hospital. We want you here. As difficult as death is, it's also very sacred. It's like a new birth for you into the next life where you can learn and progress in entirely new ways. Let us share that with you, Meredith. We've done it before. We can do it again. We wouldn't want it any other way. Elizabeth is your daughter, and that makes me your son. And Will at the very least is a good friend, but he's also the father of your children. He's a good man, and he genuinely cares. And Marilyn really likes you. I think she would do anything to help you get through whatever lies ahead in the time you have left."

She wiped tears and tightened her hold on his hand. "Don't make me take you to a hospital. Instead, let me call and make some arrangements to have a nurse come and be here with you, and we'll do everything we can to keep you comfortable, and we'll spend all the time together that we can,"

Marilyn wiped at a steady stream of tears. "You make a very convincing argument, Jayson. I don't know how I could possibly protest." She sobbed and said, "If I were to be completely honest, I don't want to die alone. I just . . ." she sobbed again, "I don't want to be a burden . . . especially when I've done nothing to ever contribute in a positive way to this family."

"That's not true," he said. "You've made Elizabeth very happy since you showed up yesterday. Your acceptance and validation have meant a great deal to her."

"Even though I was only willing to give those things from my deathbed . . . so to speak?"

"It's never too late for a child to hear such things from a parent. I never got to hear such things from my father. I wish I could have."

"Do you Mormons believe in deathbed repentance?" she asked.

Jayson chuckled. "We Mormons believe that it's never too late to change your heart. We believe that God is loving and merciful and His arms are always open." He leaned a little closer. "We also believe that this life is not the end, and you can keep working toward understanding such things after you pass through the veil."

"The veil?" she asked, and Jayson gently explained the principle of the veil between life and death, between the temporal world and the spirit one.

He finished by saying, "I wouldn't be at all surprised if your son were among those who come to get you when the time arrives."

Meredith smiled through her ongoing tears. "What a lovely thought. You really believe such a thing is possible?"

"I do," he said and shared with her some of his personal experiences that had let him know that his mother—and even his father—was aware of him. And he told her of the times when he'd felt Derek nearby. "You're his mother," Jayson said. "I don't believe it's possible for you to be here among us without his knowing. I think he'll be there."

They talked a while longer, then Jayson left her to rest and hurried up the stairs to find Elizabeth pacing while she waited for him.

"She's staying," Jayson said.

"What did you say to her?"

"I'm not sure I remember," he said, "but it must have been inspired. Why don't you go sit with her? I'll keep an eye on the kids while I make some calls to arrange for some hospice care."

"Oh, thank you!" she said and kissed him. She gathered some crackers and apple juice in case her mother might want just a little something to eat, then headed down the stairs.

Jayson spent a great deal of time on the phone trying to get the appropriate arrangements made. Everyone he spoke to was helpful and friendly, but he spent an inordinate amount of time on hold while the babies became restless and discontent, as if they sensed the stress level in the house. Or perhaps their parents had just been too preoccupied this morning. Jayson nearly melted with relief when Will walked through the front door.

"I'm on hold," Jayson said. "I think your grandchildren are feeling neglected."

"I can help with that," Will said. "What else can I do?"

"For the moment, that's great. If we . . . I'm here," Jayson said into the phone, and Will picked up Derek from where he was trying to climb up Jayson's leg.

Without the distraction of the children, Jayson was able to finish up the arrangements. Then he sat to talk with Will about this turn of events and how it was affecting them, more importantly how it was affecting Elizabeth and what they could do to help her through the ordeal. When lunchtime came they opened some canned soup, and Will helped feed the children. Jayson went downstairs to see if the women were hungry, or if they needed anything. He approached the open doorway quietly, not wanting to disturb a tender moment. What he saw made him freeze as memories fell over him like a bucket of cold water. Elizabeth was curled up on the bed, close to her mother, as if they'd been talking with their heads close together, and they'd both fallen asleep. The moment was tender, and, given their past relationship, miraculous. But Jayson had forgotten that he'd once found Elizabeth exactly the same way with his own mother. It had only been a day or two before Leslie had left this world. Will and Elizabeth had been staying in the house with him and the full-time nurse he'd hired. He never could have survived the ordeal without them.

Jayson had long ago come to terms with his mother's death. He missed her, sometimes very much. He often thought of her and wished that she could be around to be a part of his family. It wasn't unusual for him to think, *Mom would have loved this moment,* or *I wish I could talk to Mom.* But Jayson had found peace with her untimely passing. He now knew it had been her time to go, and he had many blessings in his life to compensate for the absence of his mother. In that moment, however, with the image before him merging into the past, the emotions surrounding her death came back to him. He'd not had the gospel in his life at that time. Elizabeth had been married to another man. He hadn't heard from Macy for so long that he'd feared she was dead. He'd been divorced, and his band had fallen apart. His mother's death had been a very large straw that had led to the eventual breaking of the camel's back.

Jayson had to lean against the wall of the family room, some distance from the door to the apartment, and try to assimilate the emotional intensity of the memories. He had to consciously remind himself of how his life had changed since then. He had a greater understanding of life and death, and he had a beautiful family. How strange that he and Elizabeth and Will would be in the house again, preparing for death and helping Elizabeth get through this. There would be some measure of grief for all of them, but for Elizabeth it was more personal. Before Leslie had died, Elizabeth and Will had both shared individual relationships with her for years, so her passing had affected them deeply. Meredith hadn't shared much of anything with anyone for years, so her departure would not impact their daily lives or tear away any longtime close relationships. But the renewal Elizabeth had found with her mother just yesterday was going to be hard to let go of. He knew it would be hard for her. And Meredith was the mother of Will's children, and the grandmother of Jayson's. He wondered how the children were going to deal with this taking place in their home, but he figured that Trevin and Addie could be close to their grandmother as much or as little as was comfortable for them. He wanted them to understand that death was not something to be afraid of, but that didn't mean they wouldn't have their own level of grieving and adjustment, simply because she *was* their grandmother, and she *was* dying.

He was still standing there trying to get a grip when Elizabeth walked out of the room without seeing him. "Hey, Lady," he said in a loud whisper, and she turned around.

"What are you doing?" she asked.

"I didn't want to disturb you, but . . . when I saw you like that . . . it kind of took me back."

She sighed and touched his face. "Yeah, it's taking me back, too." She hugged him tightly. "How did we get through all of that without knowing what we know now?"

"I have no idea," he said. "I'm just grateful we know what we know now. Are you hungry?"

"I am, actually. Mom's asleep. She hasn't wanted to eat much of anything at all. Is that normal?"

"I think so, but a nurse will be here in about an hour. I've got everything arranged. Let's get something to eat and we'll talk about it. Your dad's here."

By late afternoon, a full-time nurse had moved into a spare bedroom off the family room, some medical equipment had been set up in Meredith's room, and Trevin and Addie had come home from school and been informed of the situation. They both expressed concern and asked questions, and they both wanted to talk to their grandmother. Addie with her maternal instincts wanted to do everything she could to help. They both had a great deal of faith, and while they could somewhat appreciate the impact of what was happening, they'd not had a personal relationship with Meredith. They were both concerned about their mother, however, and their natural compassion was touching.

That evening, Meredith told Jayson and Elizabeth again how grateful she was for their kindness. She kept saying how amazed she was at how gracious everyone had been, even before they had known how sick she was. She asked if she could speak to Will, which was easy since he'd been upstairs with the children. When he came into the room, she asked that Elizabeth stay as well.

Elizabeth sat down, wondering if she really wanted to be included in whatever it was her mother wanted to discuss with her father.

Meredith looked directly at Will and thanked him for being so kind. She commented on what a fine woman Marilyn seemed to be, and that she was happy he'd found someone who could appreciate what a good man he was. Will didn't say much. He just listened.

Meredith then said, "You came here to live after Robert and Bradley drowned."

"That's right," Will said, and Elizabeth wondered where this was headed.

"And you lived here in the home with Elizabeth until you married Marilyn."

"That's right," he said again. "By then Jayson and Elizabeth were married, and they didn't really need me anymore."

"We've never eaten as well since you weren't around to do most of the cooking," Elizabeth said, hoping to keep this light.

Meredith said, "I've just been trying to put events together in my head. So much that's happened during these years feels kind of foggy. I remember when you sold the house and left Oregon, I was wondering what kind of insanity had overtaken you." She shook her head. "I just want you to know now that . . . for that . . . and for a thousand things before that . . . and since that . . . I'm so grateful you were there for her when I wasn't. I just want to thank you for being such a good father to our children."

"They're great kids," he said, as if Derek was still every bit as alive as Elizabeth.

They reminisced a little bit about the times when the children were very young and they'd had some good memories to share. And they both shed some tears. Then Meredith got sleepy and drifted off. Will went back upstairs, and Elizabeth talked with the nurse. She told Elizabeth that she'd seen cancer patients do exactly what her mother had done. They'd been able to hold out through a big family event or until they were able to see a certain loved one, and then they would fall apart quickly. Elizabeth was glad to know that her mother wasn't in much pain. She didn't fully understand the reasons; she was just grateful.

That night, the nurse insisted that the family go to bed as usual. She told them she would rest near the patient, but she would set an alarm to check on her at regular intervals, and if anything changed, she would let them know. Elizabeth slept surprisingly well and left Jayson to handle Saturday with the kids while she stayed near her mother. That afternoon, Meredith was actually feeling quite well, and they all decided that a little drive would be nice. Jayson helped Meredith to the car, but at his suggestion Elizabeth went alone with her mother so that they could have some time together. They drove up the canyon a little ways, then went clear to the other end of the valley to see the lake. Before going home, Elizabeth drove her mother past the temple but said little about its purpose. She was saving that for another time.

During the following week, Meredith had ups and downs that kept getting more down. But she was able to spend time with the children individually, and with the family as a whole more than once. She and Elizabeth shared some long talks. And they went out for one more drive, but it was shorter, and when they returned, Meredith was so weak that Elizabeth knew it would be the last time.

As the week drew to a close, the time Meredith was awake grew less and less, but Elizabeth earnestly talked to her about the things she knew to be true about life and death. She taught her about temples and eternity, and it seemed the most natural thing in the world for Meredith to quietly request that Elizabeth take care of those temple ordinances for her after she was gone. Elizabeth informed her that she would have done it anyway, but she promised to do it at the very first opportunity after the waiting period was over.

While Meredith slept, Elizabeth remained close to her, pondering and praying and allowing her spirit to take in events that were more miraculous and comforting than they were upsetting. She'd grown accustomed to living her life without her mother, so the day-to-day adjustment would not be so difficult. And though she was losing her mother mortally, she'd gotten her back emotionally, and she could treasure forever the healing that had taken place between them.

Meredith passed away early Sunday morning. Elizabeth sat on the bed with her as she left. Jayson and Will were in the room. It was a peaceful event without any drama, and a beautiful spirit was present in the room. After she was gone, they all cried, then they talked for a while about all of the deaths of loved ones they'd survived, and they speculated over who might have come to greet her. Derek would surely have come. Elizabeth wondered if her son Bradley might have been there as well. She'd like to think so.

By early afternoon, a mortuary had come for the body, and all of the medical paraphernalia had been removed. Elizabeth sat in the little apartment alone, trying to get up the nerve to go through her mother's luggage. It was all she had left. Ironic, she thought, for someone who had once been so worldly. She smiled to think of how many pairs of shoes her mother must have gotten rid of. They never would have fit in ten such suitcases. She pondered the enormity of life and death, and how the possessions gathered through a lifetime were mostly meaningless when the end came.

Elizabeth finally got up the nerve to open one suitcase and found it filled with what would be expected for a short trip: a couple of changes of clothes, a makeup bag, an extra pair of shoes, a sweater, a couple of magazines. She then realized that the other one hadn't even been unzipped. Had there been nothing in it that she'd needed since she'd arrived? Elizabeth took a deep breath and opened it, stunned to see a couple of boxes a little larger than an average shoe box. But these were high-quality and expensive, with a Victorian look to them. On top of the boxes was a large manila envelope, and paper-clipped to that was a white, business-sized envelope on which was written simply, *Elizabeth*.

Her fingers were trembling as she opened it, mostly wondering how it might have felt to be doing so if her mother's death had come as unexpected news with no opportunity for healing and closure. Inside was a lengthy handwritten letter, full of many of the sentiments she'd shared verbally during her brief stay. It was as if she wanted to make certain it was said, just in case things hadn't worked out as she'd hoped. At the end of the letter, she clarified that all of her affairs and belongings had been completely taken care of in Oregon, and there was nothing for her to have to deal with. She made reference to the legal documents in the attached envelope, which would make it easy for her to have what Meredith was leaving for her. She apologized that she couldn't have given her more time and love. And that's when Elizabeth cried. She cried for the lost years, and the wasted energy that she had devoted to trying to cope with the results of Meredith's bad behavior. But it was all in the past now, and Elizabeth's tears of sorrow and grief merged into those of peace and gratitude. She finished the letter from her mother, which ended with reference to the two boxes that contained everything she had that was really worth keeping, and since Elizabeth was her only living child, she should have them. Elizabeth set the large manila envelope aside and opened the first box to find it filled with photographs and letters that Elizabeth looked forward to going through more closely another time. The second box had a number of odds and ends, some things that had belonged to Meredith's parents, who were both deceased, and even some baby things that had belonged to her and Derek. Elizabeth finally opened the manila envelope and glanced through the legal papers. Since Meredith had been an attorney, and a fine one, this of all things would be in perfect order. There was a great deal of legal jargon, but the bottom line was evident.

Elizabeth took the letter and the legal papers upstairs and intercepted Jayson on his way to find her, since he'd just put the babies down for naps. They'd missed church today with all that was going on.

"How are you?" he asked.

"I'm doing well," she said, "all things considered."

"I'm glad to hear it. What have you got there?"

"Well, I thought you should be the first to know that I am going to be a rich woman."

She pointed to the figure on the will, and Jayson laughed. "Wow! We can help a lot of humanitarian projects and missionaries with that."

"Yes, we can!" she said.

"I just want you to know, however," Jayson said, "I didn't marry you for your money."

Elizabeth laughed and hugged him tightly. More seriously she said, "Thank you."

"For what?"

"For being here . . . for helping me through this. It's been an eventful couple of weeks, but . . . I've felt very blessed. I'm so grateful she came."

"So am I," he said and hugged her again.

Two days later a graveside service was held for Meredith following a brief family viewing at the mortuary. Will offered a beautiful prayer before the casket was closed, and Jayson dedicated the grave where Elizabeth's mother was laid. The casket and the flowers were beautiful, and Elizabeth's memory of their last few days together had made up for a lifetime of grief between them.

* * * * *

Elizabeth found it almost eerie how quickly life settled back into the usual routine. Her mother had come, instigated miracles, and passed away, all in fewer than two weeks. Elizabeth thought about her mother a great deal while she went about her normal tasks, but most of the thoughts were pleasant. Her moments of grief were insulated with the comfort of the Spirit and the miracles that had taken place preceding her mother's death. Since her mother hadn't been a part of her everyday life, adjusting to her absence in this world was not terribly difficult.

Elizabeth went to visit Layla at every possible opportunity, wanting to give support to both her and Macy. Layla's health problems were still a mystery, but she was in good spirits. Elizabeth suspected that had a great deal to do with Macy's help and support and the special bond the two of them had come to share.

Elizabeth enjoyed being able to do an occasional fireside with Jayson, and each time they did it, her own testimony was strengthened regarding the power of the gospel in their lives, and how abundantly it had blessed their lives. She was actually pleased to see that Jayson had been avoiding any effort to get a haircut. He kept his hair well-groomed, and it looked good on him, although it wasn't nearly long enough to put into a ponytail. More than once following a fireside, she'd noticed a young person with longer-than-normal hair, or someone dressed unconventionally, speaking to Jayson. She knew some people might not agree with her, but in her heart she truly believed that Jayson's uniqueness was reaching out to people who struggled to feel like they were able to fit in. Because Jayson lived the gospel so well, he couldn't help but be a good example.

As autumn settled in, Trevin and Addie were doing well in school, and the babies were growing and changing every day. Jayson continued to work steadily on his album, with some days being more creatively productive than others. Elizabeth continued to teach Sunday School and enjoyed the calling, but her love for it couldn't hold a candle to the pleasure Jayson found serving with the young men.

Jayson quickly started looking forward to Wednesday evenings as one of the highlights of his week. He liked doing activities with the boys, and also being a part of their lessons in priesthood meeting on Sundays. Most of them were great kids, although some were more rowdy, others a little withdrawn. They had a variety of interests and personalities, but Jayson was quickly getting to know them as individuals, and he loved seeing them progress in many respects. They asked a few questions about his career, but Jayson answered them succinctly, then gracefully changed the subject. Not many weeks into the calling, he was pleased to realize that the boys had gotten to know him as just one of the guys, and he became less concerned about their interest in his career, even though it rarely came up.

Jayson and Roger began socializing outside of their Church callings when Roger mentioned that he had started jogging every morning and asked Jayson if he wanted to join him, as long as they could work into it slowly.

"Actually, I'd love to," Jayson said. "I walk the dog every morning, but I think both of us could stand to move a little faster. I need to get in shape for the concert tour."

Roger chuckled. "You have to be in shape for a concert tour?"

"Doing a concert is like playing a game of basketball," Jayson said. "At least it is for me. It takes a lot of energy and stamina."

"Fair enough. We'll get in shape together."

They started running together *and* playing basketball here and there, which they often did with the boys on Wednesday evenings after the activities. The two of them got to know each other quite well, and they went out to dinner a couple of times along with their wives. Jayson liked Roger, and he liked the way that he was so easygoing about Jayson's strange career. Being a lawyer, Roger insisted that his own career was *more* strange.

In the middle of a fairly unproductive day, Jayson was glad to get a call from a sister in the ward, asking for his help. "My daughter is very ill," she said. "I called the bishop's house, and his wife suggested I call you. She said that you're at home during the days most of the time, and I was praying you would be available. Would you very much mind coming over to help my husband give her a blessing?"

"I would be honored," Jayson said and hurried to their home. It was far from the first time he'd been called on for such things because he was one of few men available during the days. But he was glad to be of use in any way he could, and there was nothing more valuable he could share than his privilege of holding the priesthood. There were a few retired men in the neighborhood, but that meant they traveled more, or they worked in the temple on certain days.

A few days later he got a similar call from a sister in the Relief Society presidency, asking if he could help her get an elderly sister into her car for a trip to the hospital. The wounded sister had fallen and injured her ankle. It wasn't an emergency, and once they were at the hospital, they could have help getting her inside, but she needed a strong man to help get her to the car. Again Jayson was more than glad to be able to help, and he felt gratified with what fifteen or twenty minutes of effort could do for his own spirits.

While Jayson only spent a few hours a week with the young men, he worked more than full-time in the studio, applying himself diligently to the new album. Some of the music came quickly and with great force; other pieces were a struggle. But gradually he was getting enough pieces written to make an album. He just didn't feel entirely satisfied about a lot of what he was doing. He'd started laying down tracks to record the music. Because he could do the guitars, pianos, and vocals himself, he could record each piece separately and complete most of the tracks on his own. He could play the drums just enough to give a basic rhythm until the real drums could be recorded. Elizabeth sometimes did backing vocals, or played the violin or flute. Once he reached a certain point, his brother Drew would be coming to record the drums and they would finish up a great deal of the recording. Jayson knew that uncharted territory lay ahead in recording and performing the Mozart piece with so many different instruments. But he wasn't going to worry about that until he got farther along. He just wished he felt more confident about what he had.

At one of the many points when he felt somewhat stuck, he called his brother, if only to complain. Elizabeth had surely heard far too much of his whining. Drew wasn't home, but Jayson left a message, and his brother called back a couple of hours later. But the call came right in the middle of dinner, so Jayson told him he'd call him back. Once the children were down for the night, Jayson finally got ahold of Drew when both of them had the time to talk. After the usual catching up, Jayson readily admitted, "I'm really struggling to put this album together, little brother."

"I thought it was going pretty well. The last time we talked, you were on fire."

"That was then. The title track is good. I've got it under control as much as I can until I pull in other musicians. But the rest is like Swiss cheese. I've got a lot of bits and pieces, but it's just full of holes . . . not linking together. It's starting to make me crazy. The record company is waiting; they want a summer tour. Time is running out. I hate the pressure. I don't want to be making music like this. I shouldn't have to be doing it like this."

"But when you took on this project, you knew you could do it. I know you can do it."

"That's what Elizabeth says."

"Well, she's right. Maybe you're just trying too hard. Would you like me to come out and see if I can nudge you along a little?"

"I would love it!" he said.

"Okay, well . . . we have kind of a busy week, but I could probably come next week. I'll talk to Valerie. In the meantime, relax and don't be so hard on yourself. Stressing about it surely isn't conducive to tapping into your creative juices."

They talked a while longer, and Jayson knew his brother was probably right. He decided to take a few days and focus on other things, knowing that with his brother here they could likely make some progress. He spent some extra time with his family, figuring he was overdue on dates. First off, he insisted on spending a day taking care of the little ones so that Elizabeth could go out with friends for the entire day. He ended up also watching the child of one of those friends in order to make the outing possible, but he was fine with that. The ladies went to the temple, out to lunch, spent some time at the mall, and visited an art gallery. The next day he took Addie bowling after she got home from school, then they went out to eat. And the day after that, he and Trevin got something to eat at Trevin's favorite place before they haunted some music stores, trying different instruments and stocking up on essentials, like strings and guitar picks.

As always, time spent one-on-one with the kids brought him to a greater awareness of his own love for them. And they were such good kids. Addie was doing great in school and got along well with a number of different friends. Her maternal nature was continually a blessing in her helpfulness with the younger children. She was usually on top of her home-work and loved to read, but it took some effort to get her to do her chores and keep her room clean.

Trevin was sharp and smart and responsible. He never had to be nagged to do his homework or chores. He wasn't particularly fond of reading, except for his scriptures, but he was fairly obsessed with playing guitars. Jayson was proud of him for many reasons beyond their growing bond with music. He was so much like his mother, and—Jayson had to admit—like his father. He remembered well the man Elizabeth had once been married to. Robert Aragon had had his challenges, and Jayson had been aware of those. But he had definitely been sharp and smart and responsible. And Robert had been a very good father. Jayson had learned a lot about being a good father by observing Robert with his sons. And Trevin had gotten some of the best of Robert. He always got fairly decent grades in school, and he never gave his parents any grief. Jayson was stunned that a kid could be that good. But then, a number of the young men in the ward were that good. They were just good kids. They'd been raised with love and strong values, and many of them chose to honor those values of their own free will. Trevin was right up there.

Trevin was also helpful with the younger kids, though not as conscientiously as Addie. Still, it had become a natural, almost unconscious thing that had occurred with the children. When Trevin was around, he looked after Derek, and they seemed to have a bond as brothers, even with more than a decade between their ages. Addie helped with both children, but she definitely was more connected to her sister, and she handled Harmony amazingly well for a third-grader. They were all great kids, and being their father was one of Jayson's greatest joys.

Jayson took one of his other greatest joys out on a twenty-four-hour date. Will and Marilyn came to stay with the kids Friday night while Jayson and Elizabeth spent the night at a bed-and-breakfast in Salt Lake City. Their date included a nice dinner out, and the following day an excursion to Temple Square and a matinee movie before they returned home to find everything in such good order that Jayson threatened to leave Will and Marilyn in charge more often. They even stayed through the evening and cooked dinner for the family, which extended Elizabeth's period of relaxation. Macy and Aaron came by, since Will had invited them over to eat his cooking. Trevin was also at home, as opposed to being with friends, as he usually was on a Saturday evening. While they all relaxed throughout the evening, talking and laughing and playing a little music, the world just seemed close to perfect.

CHAPTER 9

On Sunday, the family pitched in to help with making dinner and dessert in double amounts so they could take the extra to Macy's other family. While they were there they had a nice visit. No one had yet figured out what was wrong with Layla, but she had been able to return to work enough to keep the family's income going. Work took everything out of her, however, and her time at home was spent mostly in bed, with Macy keeping everything under control. The Relief Society was helping, the kids were all getting better at doing their chores, and all in all, Macy was handling it rather well. She was frustrated that she hadn't been able to get pregnant, but they all kept praying that it would happen, and she admitted that a part of her was glad she wasn't dealing with pregnancy symptoms while there was so much for her to do.

Everyone was excited when Drew called to announce that he was coming to Utah in a couple of days and bringing his family with him. Jayson and Drew had always been close, and Jayson loved spending time with him, whether in work or leisure. Drew's wife, Valerie, fit comfortably into the family. She and Elizabeth had become quite close. And their daughter, Leslie—named after Jayson and Drew's deceased mother—was near Derek's age. Drew and his family had stayed in spare rooms of the house for many weeks on numerous occasions while the brothers had worked on recording and rehearsals. Now, with the apartment off the family room, it was even more convenient, and the arrangement had become comfortable and familiar. The first twenty-four hours of their visit they just spent time together and caught up on life and playing with each other's kids.

On the afternoon following his arrival, Drew asked, "So, how is the album coming since we talked?"

"I haven't done a blasted thing with it, little brother," Jayson said. He loved to call him that, since Drew was older, but also shorter.

"Okay, let's review."

"I guess it boils down to some fine-tuning on the tracks I've been working on. Of course, with you here, we can get the drums figured out and recorded. And then I need to get some great musicians . . . somehow."

"For the Mozart thing."

"Yeah."

"Got any ideas?"

"Yes, actually. There are orchestras associated with some local colleges, and I've already spoken to the directors. I'm basically asking for people who can do Saturday rehearsals and recordings for several weeks, and then be able to take the summer off and tour with the band. With any luck, we'll get people who can do both. I figure that shouldn't be too hard for some college students."

Drew chuckled. "I bet there's some incentive in recording and touring with Jayson Wolfe."

"I hope so. I want them to be good. I need it to sound the way it does in my head, and I'm not a music teacher."

"So you can do auditions."

"If I get enough people who are interested. Right now I'm just praying for enough people who are willing and talented. The pay isn't bad, either."

"How many songs you got?" Drew asked.

"No enough," he said. "I just feel like I need at least one more really great number. Something strong; dance music. The kind of song that . . ."

"Pumps the crowds and rocks the radio," Drew said.

"You read too many entertainment magazines."

"I don't read them at all. That line is from one of the reviews Gray Wolf got in *Rolling Stone*."

"That was a long time ago. I don't know that Jayson Wolfe solo has that much impact."

"I think you're kidding yourself if you believe that," Drew said and shrugged. "You're my hero, big brother. I know you won't let me down."

"I might if I can't come up with a real power number. This album is great, but I've only got one, maybe two, that will make good radio hits. They're going to want another one, and I'm blank."

"So let's jam," Drew said. "We always came up with great stuff when we just started messing around."

Jayson laughed. "Now, why didn't I think of that?"

"And maybe Mom will help us out."

"Maybe she will," Jayson said as they both stood up and moved to the studio, needing no more encouragement. He slapped his brother on the shoulder. "I thought you weren't into religion."

"Just because I'm not into going to church on Sundays doesn't mean I don't believe my mother lives on. And we both know she's been there for us."

"Yes," Jayson said, "we both know that."

Jayson picked up his favorite electric guitar and turned on the amp while Drew made himself comfortable on the drum stool, making some minor adjustments. There was little he enjoyed more in his career than playing with his brother. They'd grown up together doing this very thing, and they'd rocked stages around the world. It was in their blood. Drew had always been content to be behind the drums and let Jayson be the front man. So their talents complemented each other greatly. And Jayson honestly believed Drew was one of the best drummers in the world. He was humble about it and currently had no desire to pursue any career beyond being Jayson's personal drummer for his solo work. They both had enough money to get by for the rest of their lives; therefore, playing music together came from loving music and loving each other. It was always great!

"Okay," Jayson said, "let's see what happens. If I can come up with the music, the lyrics will come."

"That's the spirit!" Drew said and did a dramatic drumroll.

They started out doing bits and pieces of old stuff that they were comfortable with. Then they started messing around with strange combinations and sequences, mostly laughing like a couple of kids when it all sounded ridiculous. Then Drew said, "Wait a minute. What was that? Do it again."

Jayson tried to remember and picked it out. "Okay," he said, liking it. He did it over and Drew added drums that fit perfectly. After the fifth time through the same few bars, Jayson went on, just letting his fingers work almost on their own. A few minutes later he was so deeply engrossed in an intricate guitar solo that he was stunned—and psyched. It was working! He stopped suddenly and held up his hands.

"What's wrong?" Drew asked. "It's sounding great."

"Yes, yes it is," Jayson said, but it was what he heard in his head that sounded *really* great. "Horns. It needs horns. I can hear them." He played some bars again while he hummed a counter melody that would played by multiple brass instruments.

"That's great," Drew said and added the drums, and they both laughed when it worked.

Jayson was thinking how this album was getting more and more complicated when Drew said, "It all works out very nicely since you'll have some horns in that little orchestra you're going to hire." Jayson felt like he'd been slapped in the face when it was so obvious, yet it hadn't even occurred to him. The very next thought that came to him came out of Drew's mouth before he could voice it. "And since you're going to pay all these musicians to tour with you, you'd better get your money's worth and put some orchestration through the whole album."

"Yes!" Jayson said as if he'd just been awarded a gold medal. "Yes, yes, yes! That's it! That's what's missing." He laughed. "That idea came to me when I first got the Mozart thing, but I'd forgotten." He laughed again. "You're a genius. Boy, have we got our work cut out for us."

"Yes," Drew laughed, "but it's sure going to be fun. Now let's try it again before you lose what you just came up with."

A couple of hours later they had what Jayson would call the rough draft of a decent song laid out. Now that he'd become more comfortable with it, he decided to just let the guitar rip and see what happened. They did it from the top, and Jayson told his brother to just follow him on the bridge. The speed and intricacy that Jayson saw in both of his hands made him laugh out loud while he was playing. It really *was* going to be a great song.

When they finished, Drew laughed and threw his sticks in the air. "Oh, man!" he said. "How long have you been playing that thing?"

Jayson had to think a moment. "More than thirty years, I believe."

Drew laughed again. "That was amazing!"

"You're not so bad yourself, little brother. Those sticks were a blur."

"It must be Mom."

"It must be," Jayson agreed.

After supper, both families gathered in the studio to hear the rough draft. They all whooped and cheered with what had been dubbed "the great brother duet." Then Jayson said with a great deal of aplomb, "Ladies and gentlemen, this is what happens when mamas let their little boys play with drums and guitars."

They all cheered again, and Drew said, "Now watch. He'll say that on stage every time we perform it, until we're all *sick* of him saying that."

"You'd better believe it," Jayson said. "Because our mother will be listening, and it will make her smile."

"You'd better believe it," Drew said.

* * * * *

Jayson came awake in the dark, aware of nothing but his own sharp breathing and pounding heart. Was it a dream or a panic attack? Both, maybe. One a result of the other. The pain in his chest as he struggled to draw breath distracted him from being able to remember the content of his dream. He swung his legs over the edge of the bed and dropped his head between his knees, heaving to draw air.

"Jayson, what's wrong?" Elizabeth asked, and he felt her arms come around him from behind.

"I don't know," he said. "A dream . . . I think."

"What? Tell me."

"I'm trying to remember. I don't know."

She coached him through slowly catching his breath, and he managed to calm down enough to say, "I can't remember . . . images. More . . . a feeling."

"What feeling?" she asked, and his heart quickened again.

As if she sensed his elevating tension she urged, "Just tell me. Breathe slowly and tell me."

"It was like . . . when Derek was killed . . . when Mom died . . . when I found out Debbie was cheating on me . . . when Macy ran away. It was like . . . all those feelings rolled into one. It was like . . . I'd lost everything."

Elizabeth listened and prayed for the right answer to soothe him. To her, it was clear. "You've lost a great deal in your life, Jayson; we both have. But we have the gospel now. The only way we could really lose *everything* would be to turn our backs on the truths and covenants we hold dear. As long as we hold on to that, no matter what else happens, we have eternity, and it's not possible to lose everything."

Jayson felt better from her explanation. It made sense, and it did ease the sensation he'd been left with. He asked her to kneel and pray with him, then they got back into bed, but he had trouble going back to sleep. The next day he still had a mildly uneasy feeling hanging over him. Elizabeth suggested they call her father and ask him to give Jayson a blessing. It wasn't the first time Will had done so, simply in the capacity of being a father figure to Jayson. In the blessing he spoke of the peace and comfort that were available to him through making the right choices and honoring his covenants, which he was doing. Will also commanded any evil presence or influence to leave, and Jayson felt much better afterward. He was determined to just keep doing what he was doing and have faith that all would be well. His life was good, and he didn't take it for granted. Still, he wondered how long it could last. Was it too good to be true?

That very day Jayson received a letter that helped with his perspective. The woman at the record company who handled all of his fan mail had sent it, along with a note. *I thought you should see this one and give a personal response. Looking forward to the new album. Fran.*

Jayson opened the enclosed letter eagerly, knowing that Fran wouldn't forward any hate mail. It was handwritten and somewhat lengthy, from a young woman who wanted him to know about her experience of how his music had impacted her life. She'd loved his music from the very first album when she'd been a young teenager, and she had followed his career. When his solo album had been released, she'd seen him on a talk show and was touched as he'd spoken candidly about his family values and the religion he'd found in his life, even though he hadn't been specific. She'd gone to his website where there had been a link to the Church's website. And that had led her to eventually being baptized. Jayson laughed aloud as he read, and then he cried. Then he went to find Elizabeth and handed it to her. He watched her read the entire thing, not disappointed when her reaction was much the same as his.

"That's what it's all about, isn't it," he said. "That's what makes it all worth it."

"Absolutely," she said and hugged him. Jayson wrote the woman a letter in return, thanking her for taking the time to share her experience, and briefly bearing testimony of his knowledge of the gospel truths she had now embraced.

The next morning he went on the usual every-other-day run with Roger, and Jayson told him about the letter and how it made him feel. Roger had served a mission and had performed baptisms. But Jayson hadn't joined the Church until well into his adulthood. The idea of people actually coming into the Church because of his influence and example was a thrill to Jayson, and something that Roger understood.

When they were done, Roger came over to get some papers that Jayson had for him. Since Roger had the day off, they ended up chatting for a long while, and Jayson truly appreciated his friendship. He stayed for breakfast, and afterward they moved into the living room so Jayson could watch the kids while Elizabeth took care of something. Drew and Valerie had gone on some errands.

Roger became distracted by the career wall, and it became evident that while he'd been to their home many times, he'd never gone past the front room. He asked questions, and Jayson told him a little about how he'd met Elizabeth and her brother Derek, about the accident that had killed Derek, and how he and Elizabeth—and her father—had remained close through the years. When Roger had finished perusing the wall, he turned toward the glass cabinet and said, "Are those Grammys? Seriously?"

"Yes," Jayson drawled. "That came up at our first meeting."

Roger chuckled. "I know. I'm just giving you a bad time. Although, that really is cool. And the hat? There must be a story to that."

Jayson told him how Derek had always worn silly hats, even on stage. And that was Jayson's favorite. He appreciated the way that Roger was more touched by the tender memories of Derek more than he was impressed by the Grammys.

"And the shoes?" Roger asked, pointing to the pair of high-heeled, bright red shoes in the cabinet that Elizabeth had worn to perform when they were in high school. Jayson told him why he'd loved the shoes, and how he'd asked her to send him one when they were both married to other people and he'd been recording his first successful album. They'd used it to design a logo for *Red Shoes Productions*. He'd kept the shoe for years, and now the pair was back together.

"After all of that," Jayson said, "Elizabeth finally told me why she'd worn red shoes. It was something to do with the ruby slippers in *The Wizard of Oz*. The idea being that ruby slippers are like the gifts and talents we have with us. They can be a curse or a blessing—usually both. But they're there whether we want them to be or not. In the movie, the ruby slippers drew a lot of attention from the wicked witch, but they were also what got Dorothy home. That's probably a lot of silly metaphorical babble, but we're eccentric people. That's the reason we keep the red shoes with the Grammys—and the hat."

"That is so cool!" Roger said again. "You're a pretty awesome guy to hang around with, Jayson," he added, "but not because you're famous." He became as serious as he would to discuss important matters about one of the young men in their stewardship. "You're a good friend because you're a good man."

"The feeling is mutual," Jayson said. Roger had to leave a few minutes later, and Jayson took a shower, then went to work as soon as Drew got back.

On Sunday, Drew and his family stayed at home to relax while everyone else went to church. Later in the day, Jayson left again to attend a presidency meeting with the other Young Men leaders. When they were finished, Roger asked Jayson if he would stay a few minutes. When it was just the two of them, Roger said, "I've been pondering something, and I've even made it a matter of prayer, and I want to talk to you about it."

"Okay," Jayson said, feeling only mildly concerned.

"You're being talked about behind your back," Roger said, but he said it with a chuckle. "The boys are starting to ask more questions about you and your job, but they're afraid you might be offended if they ask you. I think it would be a good idea to have an activity where the boys see more of what you do and where they can ask all their questions. What do you think?"

"I . . . don't know," Jayson said.

"Well, let me share some of my thoughts with you. First of all, we have a few boys, as you know, who are learning guitar and piano, and I think this could inspire them. But my biggest motivation here is that . . . well, I want the boys to see that it's not all fame and excitement. I don't think they have a clue how hard you work, or what you've been through to get where you are. You've shared some of your experiences with me, and I know you do firesides. But the boys in *your* ward don't know any of that. If they can see that being a musician is not just about being on stage, it might be good perspective for them. And I'm certain the lessons of tenacity and hard work would apply to anything that any of them might do with their lives. Or you can look at it this way. It wouldn't be the first time that we've had a father of one of the boys show us around where they work. Maybe Trevin would like that. Before you came on board, we'd been to the fire station, the military base, a restaurant, and even the prison."

"And I missed all that?" Jayson said lightly.

"Yeah." Roger chuckled. "So what do you think?"

"It all sounds reasonable," he said. "Let me think about it."

"You do that," Roger said, "and if you're okay with it, we'll put it on the schedule. I know you're in the middle of recording, so you need to decide when it would be convenient."

Jayson *did* think about it, and he talked it over with Elizabeth. They decided that Roger was probably right. It would be better for the boys to see the big picture, as opposed to just seeing selective parts of it. At the next presidency meeting, a date was scheduled for the activity, but Jayson became so caught up in the recording that he didn't give it much thought after that.

The response from college students who could play the instruments Jayson needed was a little overwhelming. Drew and Elizabeth helped Jayson do some interviews and auditions. Between the three of them they had a wide range of musical ability and knowledge, and they all knew what was needed for the project to work. After fourteen musicians had been chosen, they were all given copies of the music Jayson had written, and the date for the first rehearsal was scheduled in a few weeks. In the meantime, Jayson and Drew would keep working on the other tracks, with some help from Elizabeth.

One song in particular kept giving Jayson grief. He just felt like something was missing. In the past, he'd always been able to figure out the missing ingredient eventually, but he'd set this one aside several times and it still hadn't come to him. It was Elizabeth who said over lunch in the kitchen, "It almost has an old-time gospel feel to it . . . sort of. What you need is a choir for backing vocals."

Jayson thought about that a minute, trying to hear what it might sound like in his mind. Then he smiled. "You just might have figured it out. Where are we going to get a choir?"

"Duh!" Elizabeth said. "Are you not the man who played the piano for the ward choir not so many months ago? I have a hunch you could get a bunch of them to come over and record. They'd be thrilled!"

"And for the tour?" Jayson asked.

"I don't know. I guess taking the ward choir for one number isn't very practical."

"We should have had those musicians sing as part of their audition," Drew said. "They'll be there anyway."

"I bet they have voices tolerable enough to make it work," Jayson said. "But we have some really great voices right here in the ward to make it sound exquisite on the album. Let's try it." He leaned toward Elizabeth. "I assume you would love to arrange it."

"I *would* love to arrange it," she said.

Elizabeth made some calls and found nine people who would be thrilled to come over on Saturday morning and have their voices included on Jayson's new album. Jayson and Drew went out to purchase some new equipment. With that many people in the studio, they would need the headphones and microphones to handle it, as well as other equipment that would broaden their recording capabilities. They were also anticipating the forthcoming recordings with fourteen extra musicians.

When the day came, Will and Marilyn arrived early to watch the children while Trevin was gone for the day with friends. Drew's wife, Valerie, was also there to help keep everything under control. The choir members all seemed excited as they arrived, and a lot of questions were asked as they were taken into the studio and given some basic instructions. The headphones and microphones were an entirely new experience for all of them. But each person had enough knowledge of music that they quickly picked up on what Jayson wanted as he taught them the simple lyrics of the chorus that would be repeated over and over, growing through the song into a powerful ending. He let Elizabeth lead them while he worked through the lead vocals, and Drew just watched and handled the recording equipment from inside the sound booth. The drums, piano, and guitars had already been recorded and were being heard in the headphones. The first time they tried it all together, Jayson kept getting goose bumps and had trouble not laughing out loud with pleasure. They practiced throughout the morning, then Will brought pizza in for everybody at Jayson's request. Everyone gathered in the kitchen to eat, and Jayson got more questions about his career during the lunch break than he'd ever gotten in all the time he'd lived in the ward. Elizabeth answered most of them. He mostly joked about how he wasn't smart enough to do anything else.

As they returned to the studio and worked on fine-tuning the song, they ran into a few glitches. But Elizabeth had a way of hearing what the problems were and guiding them through it. They all took a couple of breaks but kept working. They maneuvered in some oohs and aahs that started to sound really great, along with the repeating chorus: *How can we know? How can we know? Is this world the end or just the start? How can we know? Oh, how can we know? Search in your soul, oh, search in your heart. The heavens are open and peace is free. Search your soul and find your heart. Oh, that's how we know. That's how we know.*

It was nearly five o'clock when Drew said over the intercom from the sound booth, "I think we've got it." The entire group sat down to listen. Jayson felt very pleased with what he was hearing, but he was surprised to notice some teary eyes among his backing vocalists. When the song ended, they all applauded and cheered, then they sat and visited for nearly an hour before they started drifting away. Each person hugged both Jayson and Elizabeth as they left, thanking them for a great opportunity and some good memories. Jayson promised them each a copy of the CD, and told them their names would be printed in the credits. They were all thrilled.

"Wow!" Jayson said to his wife once the crowd was gone. "That was certainly a memorable day."

"Yes, it was," she agreed. "You gave some of them an experience of a lifetime."

"I don't know about that, but they did seem to enjoy it."

"You are pleased, aren't you?" Elizabeth asked.

"I am; very much. It's perfect."

"I agree," she said and laughed. "What a great day!"

The following day a new young man came to church, and Jayson met him during priesthood meeting. Clayton was just a little older than Trevin and in the same grade. He and his mother had just moved into a basement apartment in the ward. He seemed like a nice kid, and he also seemed glad to be there. He was a little quiet, but then, he was the new kid. Jayson looked forward to getting to know him.

Two days later, Jayson had just poured himself a glass of ginger ale when the doorbell rang. He carried the glass with him and opened the door to see a woman that he recognized as being new in the ward. Her attire was humble, and her short brown hair was worn in a style that had long ago gone out of style. She held a big purse in front of her, as if it were some kind of shield. He knew this was Clayton's mother, but he couldn't recall the surname.

"Hello," he said brightly. Her lack of response brought his attention to her sour expression, most specifically the sharp eyes and tight lips.

"Brother Wolfe?"

"That's right." He motioned with the hand that held the glass. "Would you like to come in?"

Her lips screwed together more tightly, and she asked, "Is your wife at home?"

"Yes, did you need to speak with her? I'll just—"

"I don't need to speak with *her*," she said, stepping inside. "I just wanted to be sure we were not alone in the house."

"Of course," Jayson said, closing the door. He understood that it was an appropriate policy, and one that should be carefully followed. But her tone and manner implied that were his wife *not* at home, she might be in some kind of mortal danger. Realizing he needed his wife in the room—for more reasons than one—Jayson hurried to add, "Have a seat. I'll just go and get her."

He left the room before she could comment, set his glass on the counter, and hurried to find Elizabeth. "Could you come to the front room, please?"

"Is something wrong?"

"Apparently. The woman who just moved into the ward is here, and she doesn't look very happy. I need you to protect me."

Elizabeth stood. "What makes you think it's about you?"

"She doesn't want to speak to *you*, so it must be *me*."

Elizabeth clearly wanted more of an explanation, but he just hurried her to the front room. Their guest rose as they entered. "I'm Bonnie Freedman," she said.

"Yes, I met you on Sunday," Elizabeth said, holding out a hand. But Sister Freedman just kept a tight grasp on the handles of her purse in refusal of the greeting. Elizabeth shot a quick glance at her husband, then said, "Please, sit down. What can we do for you?"

"I told your husband I didn't need to speak to *you,*" she snapped, sitting on the edge of one of the couches. Jayson and Elizabeth sat on the couch opposite her, and Jayson reached for his wife's hand. Bonnie Freedman was momentarily distracted by the large framed photograph of Jayson and Elizabeth singing together on stage. She scowled, then set her angry eyes pointedly on Jayson. "I understand my son is under your stewardship in the Young Men program."

"That's right," Jayson said. "Clayton seems like a fine young man, although I've barely had the chance to—"

"Clayton is misguided and struggling," the woman insisted. "He has no comprehension of the horrors of the world he's growing up in, and I am trying very hard, as a single mother, to guide him appropriately. His rebelliousness concerns me, and I must be vigilant in taking every possible precaution to protect him."

Jayson couldn't comment. Without actually knowing the boy—or his mother—he had no way of understanding what the actuality of the situation might be, as opposed to her interpretation of it. He just nodded, and she hurried on, her lips pursed so tight it was a wonder she could speak through them. "One of the many evils my son contends with is the music that does not promote the values and standards of our religion." Jayson tightened his hand around Elizabeth's. He suspected where this was headed now, and his stomach constricted. "Clayton has brought it to my attention that one of his youth leaders—specifically *you,* Brother Wolfe—has made a grand contribution to such worldly music."

Jayson had absolutely no idea how to respond. He'd never encountered—nor imagined—such a reaction to his career. He heard Elizabeth gasp, but his own shock made it impossible to turn and look at her. That same shock kept him from speaking, which allowed Sister Freedman to assume that his silence left no doubt that Jayson's work was completely unsuitable for her son—or anyone else, for that matter.

"I have come here, Brother Wolfe, to be assured that the things I've learned about you and your involvement with *rock music,*" the words pressed through her lips as if they were filthy and she'd been forced to lower her standards to even utter them, "are completely in the past and have nothing to do with your life since you've become a member."

A spark of anger urged Jayson past the barrier of shock enough to say, "And what, exactly, Sister Freedman, have you learned about me and my involvement in *rock music?*" He mimicked her tone too subtly for her to know that he was mocking her.

"I know how to use the Internet, Brother Wolfe, and it didn't take much effort to learn everything I needed to know."

"I hope you don't believe everything you see on the Internet," Jayson said, attempting to lighten the mood, certain this had to be some kind of joke.

Sister Freedman said sternly, "Are you saying then that the pictures I saw of you with long hair and an earring were not real?"

Jayson sighed. He couldn't believe this. "Yes, that was certainly me. As you can see, I no longer wear an earring, and I could probably use a haircut—although I don't believe that issue comes up in a temple recommend interview."

The woman made a disgruntled noise, then said, "And is it not true that you spent time in a drug rehabilitation facility?"

Jayson exchanged a glance with Elizabeth, if only to be assured that she was as stunned as he. "Yes, that is true," Jayson said, "but the reasons for that are—"

"Personal and private," Elizabeth interrupted firmly. "No one can fully know the struggles that my husband has had in his life. His past is no one's business but his own. The present is between him and the bishop, and he is worthy to serve in the Young Men organization. As I see it, nothing else is important here."

Sister Freedman seemed to take that in, then she said, "Can you assure me, then, that all of this is in the past? You are no longer involved with this . . . *rock music?*"

"I still have the same job, if that's what you're asking me. I am in the process of doing a new album now, and—"

"If you are going to be in a leadership position, working with my son, I must insist that you abandon this nonsense."

"Nonsense?" Jayson echoed then chuckled without humor. "Excuse me?"

"As a member of the Church, you must see the wisdom in putting such things behind you and—"

"This is my career, Sister Freedman. I am a musician, and I have no intention of abandoning anything."

The woman let out a little gasp, then her lips pursed more tightly. "Are you saying that if your career was selling alcoholic beverages or tobacco that you would not let such work go upon being baptized?"

"I do not sell alcoholic beverages or tobacco," Jayson said. "I make and sell good music to a world that needs it."

"Your attitude is astonishing, Brother Wolfe," she said.

"I was thinking exactly the same thing," Jayson countered. He took a deep breath and added, "Allow me to explain something, Sister Freedman, that might not have occurred to you before. Contemporary music encompasses many varieties with a wide range of values. I am well aware of many musicians who promote a great deal of evil with their music and the way they present it. I can assure you that my music does not fall into that category. I have always endeavored—even before I became a member of the Church—to have clean lyrics, positive messages, and an uplifting sound in my music. I can assure you that since I joined the Church, I am even more careful about such things. I can also assure you that I would never do or say anything in my work with the young men that would be inappropriate, for any reason—no matter what my career might be."

Jayson waited for the silence to be followed up by some apology or comment that she was glad to know where he stood. But her nostrils flared and her eyes blazed as she rose to her feet. "It's evident that you're not willing to listen to reason, Brother Wolfe. But I can assure you that as long as you keep this up, my son will not be participating in any activities where you will be present."

"Excuse me?" Jayson said again, but the woman was moving toward the door.

"You heard me."

"Are you threatening me?" he asked, following her.

"I'm simply making it clear where I stand and how I feel about your lifestyle."

"My *lifestyle?*" Jayson knew he sounded angry—because he *was* angry. He'd never been so astonished in his life. After his years living in LA, submerged in the music industry, he'd been exposed to so many ugly and disgusting *lifestyles* that he had trouble believing *his* lifestyle was being condemned. "My lifestyle is that I have a temple marriage and a beautiful family and I love the gospel. Is that what you mean?"

"You *know* what I mean," she said and opened the door. "Thank you for your time." She closed it again and Jayson stared at it for half a minute before he turned to see Elizabeth with her mouth hanging open—literally.

"That really did just happen, right?" he asked.

"If I hadn't heard it myself, I wouldn't have believed it," she said. "I think you'd better call Roger."

"I think I'd better," he said and went to make the call.

CHAPTER 10

Repeating to Roger everything that had been said, Jayson was freshly struck by the ludicrousness of this woman's attitude. Roger agreed with him completely and validated his feelings. He assured Jayson that he would discuss the matter with the bishop, and they would go on as planned. He felt certain that the whole thing would blow over quickly, and he felt confident that the bishop would talk with Sister Freedman and reassure her of what everyone else knew—that Jayson was worthy to serve in this calling, and his career was not the evil that this woman seemed to think it was.

Jayson felt more calm after he got off the phone, but he had trouble sleeping that night as Bonnie Freedman's words rolled through his mind like the memory of a nightmare. He kept telling himself that one woman's opinion was no reason for him to get up in arms. But he wondered about this woman's son, and how this might affect him if he was being denied the privilege of coming to the youth activities—just because Jayson was there.

At breakfast Jayson told Drew and Valerie what had happened. He waited until Trevin and Addie had gone to school, not wanting to sound gossipy in front of the children. He especially didn't want Trevin having any prejudices toward Clayton or his mother. Drew and Valerie were not members of the Church, but they could certainly appreciate the ridiculousness of Sister Freedman's attitude. Drew echoed what Roger had said, certain the issue would blow over quickly. Jayson wished he could feel the same way. Maybe he was just paranoid. Either way, he'd be glad when it *had* blown over. He wondered what made this woman so narrow-minded and self-righteous. And he worried about her son. He'd seen some minor problems with other young men when their parents were too strict or extreme, and he hoped that Clayton would be able to see life beyond his mother's dysfunction.

On Wednesday evening, Clayton was not in attendance. Jayson wasn't surprised, but Trevin said to him later, "I wonder why he didn't show up. I invited him. He said he really wanted to come."

Jayson only said, "I hope he'll be there next week."

After the kids were in bed, Jayson had to talk it all through with Elizabeth again. She was patient and allowed him a safe place to vent his feelings. She assured him repeatedly that this woman's opinion had no bearing on what Jayson knew in his heart, and they just had to let the bishop and the other leaders deal with the situation with Clayton as best they could. He knew she was right, but that night Jayson couldn't sleep again. Not wanting to disturb Elizabeth, he went to the basement to watch TV.

Elizabeth got up in the night when Harmony woke up wanting her usual drink of water. When she found her husband missing, she went to the family room in the basement and found it dark except for the light from the TV. Jayson was sitting low in the big chair, with the remote in his hand, looking a little dazed. But it was *what* had his attention that caught *her* attention.

"Since when do you watch your own music videos? I thought you couldn't tolerate that stuff."

"I can't," he said, toneless. "Most of them are really very strange."

Elizabeth sat beside him, wondering about the source of his thoughts. "Yes," she said, wanting to urge him on. "That's the nature of music videos, as you have told me more than once. And much of that is out of your control; it's in the hands of the director and the record company. We both know that. At least you insisted on certain boundaries. At least your videos were never disgusting, as many are."

"No, but they're strange." He sighed. "I wonder how they might look to Sister Freedman."

"Oh, for heaven's sake," Elizabeth said and snatched the remote from his hand, turning off the TV. "You think she's sitting in front of the Internet watching this stuff, trying to build a case against you, or something?"

"Yes, I think she is."

"Well, that doesn't make a lot of sense, does it? If she thinks your work is evil, why would she expose herself to it?"

"Since when does the woman make any sense?"

"And since when does the opinion of one dysfunctional person have such bearing on the way you feel about yourself? This is ludicrous, Jayson. You know your heart. You know where you stand with the Lord. How many times do we have to go over this?"

"I don't know," Jayson said and went up to bed at Elizabeth's insistence. He *did* get some sleep, but he had trouble focusing on his work with Drew while his mind kept wandering to things Sister Freedman had said. They kept jumping into his head like poisoned darts. He talked to Drew about it again, and his brother insisted that they needed to work and he needed to get a grip. Jayson did his best to focus on the music and did better throughout the next couple of days. On Saturday they had their first rehearsal with the mini orchestra, and it went fairly well, even though they had a long way to go to make it sound the way Jayson could hear it in his head. They had to actually remove the drums and a few other things to make room for all of the musicians to sit comfortably and play their instruments without colliding. Even then it was a tight fit, but it worked. After they left, the drums were set up again so Jayson and Drew could continue their work on recording drums for the other songs.

On Sunday, Jayson noticed Clayton and his mother in sacrament meeting, but the boy didn't come to priesthood meeting. He knew he was the reason, and it made him sick to his stomach. He was surprised to hear it announced that this Wednesday's activity would be at his home, where the boys would get to see what Jayson did behind the scenes to write and record music. The boys seemed enthused, and a couple of questions came up, but Roger told them to hold their questions until Wednesday. Jayson told them his wife would be making some really great cookies that they could have after the activity if they behaved themselves. He knew from experience that food was always a great motivator. He just wished that Clayton Freedman might be there. But he knew his mother would *never* allow him into the den of iniquity.

When Wednesday evening came, Jayson felt a little nervous, but Valerie and Drew watched the babies so that Elizabeth could be there with him. And of course she assured him that all he had to do was talk about what he knew, and it would be easy. He felt sure she was right. He didn't want to admit to her that it was the haunting thoughts of Bonnie Freedman's accusations that made him feel like having the boys here like this was somehow wrong. He knew it wasn't, and reminded himself that he knew where he stood with the Lord. And that's all that mattered.

The boys were very impressed with the studio. Jayson showed them the sound booth and how the recording equipment worked, then they all sat on the floor of the studio for questions.

"Are you famous?" one boy asked.

"To some people, I am," he said.

"How come we've never heard of you?"

Jayson chuckled. "Well, the technical answer to that would be that the bulk of my audience was established several years ago when I did two CDs with a band called Gray Wolf."

"My brother listens to them!" a boy piped in with enthusiasm. "That's you?"

"That's me," Jayson said. "But I didn't do any music for a while after that, then I did a solo CD, which was a big hit with the people who liked the early music. The fact is that my audience is mostly between the ages of twenty-two and thirty-eight."

"How do you know that?" a boy asked.

"It's called marketing research. There are people at the record company who do that kind of stuff."

"How many different instruments do you play?" one of the leaders asked.

"I play the piano and guitars mostly," he said. "I can pick a beat out on the drums when I'm writing music. I play the mandolin a little."

"Which are you best at?" another asked.

"I think the piano and guitars are pretty equal," Jayson said with a chuckle.

Roger asked, "When you say guitars, you mean more than one? How many exactly, and what are the differences?" Jayson knew Roger already knew the answer to that, but he wanted the boys to hear it. He stood up and pointed the guitars out, since they were all there in the studio—some hanging on the wall, and some leaning in stands. He explained the differences between the acoustic, the electric, and the bass, and why he had more than one of each.

"Which is your favorite?" a boy asked.

Jayson pointed to one and said, "This is my favorite to play." He pointed to another, "And this one is the most special to me, because it was a gift when I graduated from high school."

When it was asked who had given him the gift, he told a brief version of how he and Derek had been friends in high school and had started a band along with Jayson's brother and Derek's sister. Then Derek had been killed in a car accident. Jayson had been angry over the death and had smashed his own guitar. Derek's father had given him the new one, and he'd always cherished it. He then pointed at Elizabeth and said, "My wife is Derek's sister, and we named our little boy after Derek."

The boys thought that was cool, but there were many comments made about how hard it would be to lose a friend that way.

"How many pianos do you have?" a young boy asked, thankfully changing the subject.

"I have three," Jayson said. "I have that one," he pointed, "which is a classic grand, and another one similar to it in the front room. And I have that one," he pointed to the other side of the room, "which is electric, and it makes all kinds of great sounds."

"Is that the piano you take on tour with you?"

"No, this one stays here. When I go on tour, we rent a piano that is used for touring musicians. A company is hired that transports and sets up all of the instruments and lights and other stuff."

Jayson then let the boys each take a turn being silly at the microphone while Elizabeth recorded it and played it back. He let Trevin play some guitar, which impressed his peers, and he asked the others who played instruments to each take a couple of minutes, which also impressed the boys. Then Roger talked Jayson into playing something for them. Even though Roger had warned him that he expected him to do so, he still felt a little awkward. Rather than playing a whole song, he played bits and pieces of a few different ones on both piano and guitar.

Then Roger said, "I think you should play that newest one you were telling me about."

"What was I telling you about?" Jayson asked, honestly not remembering.

"The one you said that you and your brother came up with. He's here, isn't he? I think we should hear it. You told me about the lyrics. I think these boys would appreciate the lyrics. I want to hear you and your brother play. And you should tell the boys how long the two of you have been playing together."

"Okay," Jayson drawled, then he told the boys the two-minute version of how he and Drew had been begging their mother for drums and a guitar when they were still in elementary school, and how she'd made them learn some piano first. Elizabeth went to get Drew while he was telling them, and he was surprised to see his brother enter the room, which meant he wasn't going to get out of this. It wasn't that he minded playing the song. It was just a little weird to be playing in the studio for someone besides family.

"All right," Jayson said as he put the guitar strap over his head and turned on the amps for that and the microphone. "This is just drums and guitar. When the song is done it will have bass guitar, piano, and some brass."

He heard an echo, "Brass?"

"Horns," he clarified. "So, use your imagination."

Drew hit the sticks together for a one-two-three and they were off. A quick glance showed immediate astonishment on nearly every face in the room, then Jayson focused solely on the music, and his audience faded into the background, as it always did—even if his audience consisted of thousands. After playing the intro, he put his mouth to the mike and sang the lyrics he'd written a couple of days after he and Drew had come up with the music.

"The designated driver has had one too many drinks. The hero on TV takes a puff and blows his smoke. The pretty lady drinks a shot to calm her rattled nerves, while boys and girls wonder if this is some kind of joke." And the chorus: *"Whatever happened to good clean fun? The kind that doesn't take a pill or booze to loosen up. Laughter's free and doesn't leave a hangover. Come on, boys and girls, let's get addicted to good clean fun!"*

He heard some applause, which distracted him for a moment, then he went straight into the second verse. *"Are the AA meetings just a hoax for losers who are bored? Is the surgeon general lying when he says this stuff can kill you? Do the rehab centers fill their rooms just for fun and games? Does Big Brother simply push this stuff so he can later bill you?"*

Jayson and Drew then went into the lengthy bridge with the elaborate duet they had constructed in their memorable jamming session. And then the chorus again: *"Whatever happened to good clean fun? The kind that doesn't take a pill or booze to loosen up. Laughter's free and doesn't leave a hangover. Come on, boys and girls, let's get addicted to good clean fun!"* Following a strong finish, there was great cheering and applause.

"And that," Jayson said, taking off the guitar, "is what happens when you practice."

"That was so awesome!" more than one boy said, while most of them looked amazed. Jayson knew they weren't necessarily easy to impress. He just hoped they were impressed for the right reasons.

Elizabeth announced that punch and cookies were in the kitchen, and they all practically ran.

"Okay," Roger said quietly to Jayson on their way out of the studio, "I was convinced that you were good. But I didn't know you were *that* good."

"Don't let it get out. Sister Freedman would be very unhappy to hear it."

While the boys were eating refreshments, Jayson gave each of them a copy of the solo CD he'd made after he'd joined the Church. The decibel level in the house went down significantly after the boys left, but Jayson felt like it had gone well. And Elizabeth agreed. Jayson just wished he could stop thinking about Clayton's absence, and the reasons for it.

* * * * *

In the next few days, all of the recordings were finished up except those that required the orchestra musicians, who would continue rehearsals on Saturdays. Drew and Valerie and their little daughter returned to LA. Drew would be coming back as needed to help finish the recording when they were ready. The same day they left, Macy called to report that Layla was doing poorly again. She wasn't back in the hospital, but she was pretty much down in bed and not able to work.

"What can we do?" Jayson asked her.

"I have an answer to that this time," she said.

"Good," Jayson said, wanting to actually be able to help, as opposed to feeling helpless.

"I think you and Mom should come and visit her, and I think you should play a song for her."

"Really?" he asked, surprised.

"You've probably forgotten that Aaron told you once that his mother took him to a Gray Wolf concert—long before they ever met you. She loves your stuff. It would lift her spirits. And while you're here, you can help Aaron give her a blessing."

"I'd be honored," he said, "on both counts."

They arranged a time when Aaron could be there as well, then Jayson went to tell Elizabeth what was going on. After he'd brought her up to speed, she asked, "What's bugging you?"

"What makes you think something is bugging me?" he countered, sounding far too defensive. She scowled at him, silently calling him a hypocrite. "Is it necessary for you to be so perceptive? Can't a guy keep a secret?"

"No secrets with us, Jayson Wolfe. It's Sister Freedman, isn't it? You're still so bugged over it that you think about it night and day."

Jayson scowled back at her. "How *can* I keep a secret when you read my mind?"

"I don't have to read your mind. You haven't been the same since she came to give you her edict. I don't know how to convince you that it doesn't matter. This is between you and the Lord, and you know where you stand with Him." He sighed, wishing he could explain how he felt, then she said, *"However,* if it's bugging you this much, then maybe you should try to talk to her again. Prayerfully, with caution, and without anger."

"Okay," he drawled, taking that in. "You're coming with me, then?"

She hesitated. "I will if you really want me to, but . . . I don't know if I should. I don't know if it's good for her to feel alienated from me, too. I'm in Relief Society with her, and—"

"You're taking sides?"

"I am *not* taking sides. You know very well where I stand on this, Jayson. But I don't know how all of this is going to play out, and I just don't feel good about going with you."

"Obviously I can't go alone."

"No, of course not."

"And I don't think I should take Roger. We wouldn't want to alienate him too, since he's the Young Men president. If she finds out he's my friend, Clayton won't stand a chance."

"Okay, you can stop with the sarcasm," she said. "Before you take this any further, you'd better get yourself in a more positive frame of mind. You have to remember . . . what would Jesus do?"

"Jesus had much more patience than I do," Jayson said.

"You still have to *try* to have patience like Him, and you have to try to see this woman as He would see her. You don't know what's going on in her heart, or where all of this is coming from. So . . . pray first. Maybe you should take Dad. He's a great diplomat. He'll let you say what you feel like you have to say."

"But he'll keep me from getting out of line."

"Yes, he will."

"Fair enough. You talk him into going with me. I'll pray to be able to do what Jesus would do."

"That's more like it," she said and kissed him. Taking his face into her hands, she added, "It's going to be okay, Jayson. We've been through much worse than this."

"So we have," he said and kissed her again.

That afternoon, Jayson and Elizabeth left the kids with Trevin after he'd gotten home from school so they could visit Layla. Macy met them at the door and took them to the family room in the basement where Layla was lying on the couch, reading a book.

"You have company," Macy said.

Layla looked up and set the book aside. "Oh, hello!" she said when she saw Elizabeth, then Jayson. She looked weary and worn, and even thinner than the last time they'd seen her. But her eyes lit up. "You brought your guitar?"

"I did," he said and bent over to give her a hug after Elizabeth had done the same. "Elizabeth is going to sing for you."

"Not alone, I'm not," Elizabeth said, and Jayson chuckled.

They all sat to visit for a short while, asking Layla about her symptoms and the situation. She cried as she expressed her frustration in not being able to find out what the problem was. She couldn't believe that with all of the medical advancements of the twenty-first century, an answer couldn't be found. Jayson and Elizabeth fervently agreed with her. Aaron got home from work while they were visiting, and they all exchanged hugs in greeting.

"Oh, enough about my health," Layla said. "I'm sick of talking about it. Play a song for me. It will be the highlight of my month."

"What do you want to hear?" Jayson asked.

"Oh, how about a Gray Wolf classic?"

Jayson chuckled. "It's been a long time, but I could probably pull one or two out of my hat. They don't sound like much with just me and the guitar, though."

"That's a matter of opinion," Macy said and nudged her father. "Just do it."

Jayson embarked on a laid-back mini concert, with many mistakes, laughter in between, and a variety of songs. Elizabeth did some vocals with him on a few, and Layla started to cry more than once. He finished with an arrangement he'd come up with of the hymn "Be Still My Soul." Nearly everyone cried.

Jayson finished and looked around at all the tears. He resorted to his typical line to break such awkward silence. "It was that bad, eh?"

"It was wonderful," Layla said. "All of it was wonderful! I love every-thing you do, and you're so sweet to come and do this for me. You truly have a remarkable gift." She sniffled and laughed softly. "I just can't believe how music can bring the Spirit into a room."

"Amen," Elizabeth said and winked at Jayson.

Jayson set the guitar aside and said, "Macy asked if I would help Aaron give you a blessing. Are you okay with that?"

"Oh, of course!" Layla said. "I'd be very grateful."

Jayson stood beside Aaron, who said quietly, "Would you do the blessing part? I think she's sick of hearing me over and over."

"Never," Layla said. "But it's all the same priesthood. Whatever you decide is fine."

"I'd be honored," Jayson said and uttered a silent prayer that he would be guided to say the right things to give Layla comfort and guidance. After

Aaron did the anointing, Jayson put his hands on Layla's head and was amazed at how quickly and clearly thoughts came to his mind and then through his lips. After speaking several points of comfort and spiritual assurance, he heard himself promising her that with time the answers would be found and her body would heal, but she needed to be patient and trust in the Lord.

When the blessing was over they all visited a short while longer. Layla once again thanked Jayson and Elizabeth profusely for coming, for their music, and for the priesthood blessing. When they left, Jayson felt better than he had since Bonnie Freedman had come to visit him. In the car, Elizabeth said, "There's some perspective for you."

"Yeah, I guess I need to keep perspective," he said, but he still felt like he needed to try to talk to Sister Freedman again.

That evening before Jayson left to pick up Will and pay his visit, the executive secretary called to make an appointment for Jayson to see the bishop, and to bring Elizabeth along.

"Do you know what it's about?" Jayson asked.

"I'm sorry," the secretary said, "I just make the appointments."

A time was set, and Jayson hung up the phone, feeling sick with dread. He *knew* this had something to do with Sister Freedman. He just knew it. He told Elizabeth about the appointment and how he was feeling, then she prayed with him before he left, hoping that Sister Freedman would be home so he could get this over with. And maybe what the bishop wanted had nothing to do with her, and this could all be put behind them.

After Jayson picked up Will, they talked over the situation during the very brief drive. When they weren't done talking, Jayson pulled over a few blocks from their destination so he could get himself in the proper frame of mind. Will suggested they pray together, and Jayson was grateful, knowing he needed all the help he could get. As they drove the last few blocks and got out of the car, Jayson felt calm, and he was determined to remain that way. He felt an inner peace that helped him believe the Spirit was with him, and he uttered another silent prayer that it would go well, that he could help this woman understand where he was coming from. Even if they could agree to disagree, perhaps some compromise could be made on Clayton's behalf.

They went up the driveway of the large home to the outside stairs that went down to the basement apartment. Jayson took a deep breath and knocked at the door, praying sister Freedman was home, yet almost hoping she wasn't. The door came open quickly, and Sister Freedman scowled when she saw him.

"Hello," he said. "I'm sorry to drop in on you like this, but I was hoping we could chat for a few minutes. This is my father-in-law, William Greer."

"Hello, Sister Freedman," Will said with his usual natural diplomacy.

"Hello," she said. "Are you a member of the Church?"

"I am," Will said. "Would it be all right if we come in for a few minutes?"

"I suppose so," Sister Freedman said and showed them in. Jayson noticed that the furnishings were old and showing wear, but the room was immaculately tidy. He could smell something cooking. Or perhaps it was the residue of what they'd had for dinner. He wondered if Clayton was here. He hoped not, but didn't want to bring it up.

Sister Freedman motioned them to the couch, but her pinched expression made it clear they wouldn't be staying long. She sat down across from them and remained on the edge of her chair.

"If you've got something to say, Brother Wolfe," she said, "you should say it and go."

"Very well," Jayson said and sought for his kindest, most patient voice. "I just want to know why, Sister Freedman. Why do you hate me so badly?" As soon as he said it he thought that he could have worded the question more maturely than that, but it was already out.

She made a disgruntled noise and looked away. "I don't hate *you*, Brother Wolfe. I hate the music you play and the lifestyle that is naturally attached to it."

"There are a lot of people who hate the music I play; my ex-wife is at the top of the list." He said the last lightly, hoping to ease the tension, but her frown deepened. Perhaps the very fact that he had an ex-wife was a point against him. He hurried on. "But that doesn't automatically make it evil. I can firmly say with a clear conscience that there is nothing about my music that inspires a lifestyle that God would disapprove of."

She looked at him then, her eyes blazing. "How can *you*, who are so caught up in such a lifestyle, possibly *know* such a thing?"

"I know because I strive to live close to the Spirit, and the Lord has let me know that He not only approves of my career, He is the one who gave me this gift."

She gasped as if he'd spoken blasphemy and she might somehow become contaminated by his words. "I hate to be the one to tell you, Brother Wolfe, that you are clearly deluding yourself. I think you should spend a little more time on your knees and find out where you're *really* getting your inspiration."

Jayson was so stunned that it took him a moment to come up with a cohesive thought. He shared a quick glance with Will, noting his astonishment. But apparently he was going to let Jayson do the talking. He didn't know if that was a good thing when he felt his astonishment turn quickly to anger. Still, he kept his voice calm, recalling Elizabeth's repeated admonitions to do so. "Who are you to tell me," he said, "how much time I need to spend on my knees, and where I'm getting my inspiration? You don't know anything about me."

"The fruits of your labors speak for themselves," she said.

"And what do you know about the fruits of my labors?" Still he kept his voice calm, and his questions in the tone of gentle inquiry. "Would you like to read my fan mail? Have you spoken to any of the thousands of people who have let me know that my music has helped them get through tough things, lifted their spirits, even helped them become more spiritual?"

"How people of the world may define such things is of no interest to me."

"But destroying me and *my* spirit is apparently your concern?" He hated the way he had admitted that he felt as if that's what she was doing—destroying his spirit.

"This is between you and God, Brother Wolfe," she said sternly.

"Now you're contradicting yourself. If this were between me and God, you wouldn't be telling me what I should and should not be doing."

The conversation went downhill from there, and Jayson was amazed at how calm he remained, right up to the moment that Will interrupted Sister Freedman by coming to his feet and bringing Jayson with him, holding firmly to his arm.

"Thank you for your time, Sister Freedman," Will said and ushered Jayson out the door before she could say another word.

"That went well," Will said with sarcasm before they were up the stairs to the driveway. Jayson couldn't even speak. Will took the keys from him and told him to get in the car. He drove aimlessly for more than five minutes before either of them made a sound. It was Will who said, "I don't even know what to say." He let out a sardonic chuckle. "I didn't doubt that you were telling me the truth, but that is *unbelievable.* It's like she has no purpose in her life except to persecute *you.*"

"You think?" Jayson said, appreciating the reassurance at least. The fact that this had been bothering him so deeply was perhaps due to how his instincts had sensed that her disdain for him was not nearly so minimal as everyone had been trying to tell him.

Will shook his head and chuckled again. "I can't believe it. I just can't believe it."

He pulled the car into Jayson's driveway, and Jayson said, "I'm supposed to take you home."

"I think we need to talk to your wife first."

"Okay, I can go for that. I think my calm is beginning to wear off."

In the house, Elizabeth asked Jayson, "How did it go? Did you stay calm?" She then noticed that her father was right behind him. "Oh, he remained amazingly calm," Will said. "In fact, I would say his remaining calm falls into the realms of superhuman. I just remained quiet. My tongue is bleeding from biting it, but I did remain quiet."

"What?" Elizabeth demanded.

"It was an absolute disaster," Jayson said, and between himself and Will, they told Elizabeth the gist of the conversation, while her expression became steadily more astonished.

"But that's not the worst part," Will said and motioned toward Jayson to explain.

"What could be worse?" Elizabeth asked.

"She called me a sex symbol, Elizabeth." Her mouth came open, but she didn't speak. "She said I should be ashamed of the way I've paraded myself in front of cameras and audiences, using my good looks to incite women to have obscene thoughts."

"She actually *said* that?" Elizabeth was so astonished she could hardly breathe.

"Do you think I made it up?" Jayson countered, feeling somewhat justified by how upset she was.

Elizabeth glanced at her father. "She really did," Will said. "And your husband actually remained calm when she did. I mentioned that already, didn't I?"

"Well . . . well . . ." Elizabeth stammered. "Maybe I *should* talk to her. I mean . . . what does that imply in regard to our marriage, our family?"

"Good question," Jayson said. "So, why don't you help out the situation by going over there and alienating yourself from her? I think that's pretty well clinched. If you have the nerve to be married to me, you're already going to hell."

"Don't curse!"

"I'm not cursing. It's a place. It's in the Bible. It's where all people who play rock and roll—and anyone who listens to it—are going to end up unless they listen to Bonnie Freedman and change their evil ways." While Elizabeth was stewing, he asked, "Do *you* think I've done that?"

"What?"

"What she said? Do you think I've used my good looks to—"

"You're asking me questions you already know the answers to."

"I know what *I* believe, but maybe I *am* delusional. I want to know what you think. You've had a front-row seat through my entire career. You've seen every television appearance; you've been to the concerts. You've got every magazine picture glued in some scrapbook. I want to know what you think. What you *really* think, Elizabeth. And don't patronize me just because this is tough on me. I have to know the truth. If I'm doing something wrong, I've got to make it right."

As if she were testing him, she said, "Why don't you tell me what *you* think—honestly. And then I'll tell you what *I* think—honestly. I want to know what you really believe, and if I think you're off base, I'll tell you."

Jayson looked at her, then at Will. "Fair enough," he said, then pointed at his father-in-law, "but only if he gets his turn, too."

"Only if I get to be completely honest," Will said, and Jayson wondered what he might have wanted to say all these years, but had been too polite to say it.

"You first," Elizabeth said, motioning toward Jayson.

"I've never *tried* to be a sex symbol. I'm disgusted with the way musicians and actors use themselves to sell their music or films. I've never so much as unfastened an extra button on my shirt, even when the photographers have told me to. I got in an argument with one of them once over it and left the shoot. I understand that my face sells records. That's because I'm the guy who wrote it, who's playing it. I've never really thought much about where I fall on the good-looking-to-ugly scale. I just go to the photo shoots and do my best to promote what I do appropriately. I've never worn anything too tight or inappropriate when I've performed—or *ever*. Whatever the public makes of hanging my posters in their houses or coming to my concerts is not *my* problem."

Jayson was startled to hear Will applauding.

"What's that supposed to mean?" Jayson demanded.

"First of all," Will said, "I'd like to say that your mother was an amazing woman."

"Yes, she was," Jayson said, waiting for the point.

"I wanted to marry her, you know."

"Yes, I know," Jayson said. All of that felt like a dream now. She'd been gone for so long.

"I bring her up because she taught you well. Everything you just said came from her, and I know it did. But you made the choice to do what she taught, and you *should* be applauded for it. You're working in an industry that's gone mad with many different levels of evil. There's some really great stuff out there, but you have to be careful when you go looking for it. Now, for my complete honesty. I have considered you as good as my own son since you were sixteen. I have watched your fame evolve. I've seen you hit the top, drop to the bottom, and claw your way up again. And I have *never* seen you do anything that has made me ashamed or embarrassed to call myself your father. You have always handled yourself as appropriately as it could be possible under the circumstances you've faced. And since you came into the Church, your behavior has been especially exemplary. I'm proud of you, Jayson, in the purest sense of the word. And I will stand by you through this, whatever it takes."

"Amen," Elizabeth said quietly.

"What?" Jayson asked, not because he hadn't heard her, but because he wasn't sure what she meant.

"I said amen, which means I fervently echo every word he said. If you need it clarified, I'll say it. I've loved you for as long as I've known you. I *have* followed your career as closely as any devoted fan. I've never seen any evidence of anything in your speech or behavior, or what you produce, that has ever made me feel even a little bit awkward or uncomfortable." She smiled with a glisten of tears in her eyes. "You're my hero, Jayson Wolfe. You have an amazing gift, and you cannot let one person's opinion hold you back in any way."

Jayson let all that sink in, and tears came to his eyes. He had the love and support of the people who mattered most to him, and he knew where he stood with the Lord. So, why did this woman's words sting him so deeply? For all the good he'd just heard—and believed in his heart—was there still some measure of truth in what Bonnie Freedman had said? Was that why he couldn't let go of it? He finally said, "How do you convince a person like her that it's possible to feel the Spirit when you're playing a loud electric guitar?"

"I don't know if you can," Elizabeth said

"Convince her or feel the Spirit?"

"Convince her. I don't think you could ever convince her, and you should stop trying. What I know is that you feel the Spirit."

"How do you know that?" Jayson asked.

"Because *I* feel the Spirit when you play that loud electric guitar. It's exhilarating. It's fun. A person can't play the way you play without divine intervention, Jayson. We both know that. Every good gift comes from God. Many people choose to use those gifts for evil purposes, but you haven't.

Your ability to play that guitar the way you do has brought you to the attention of a lot of people who have been impressed enough to find out more about you and look into your beliefs. Do I need to remind you that at least one person has come into the Church as a result of your influence? There could be more that you don't know about. You have never done anything related to your career that you should be ashamed of. But even if you *had,* you should have the right to be forgiven and not judged for it. If you had albums and photos out there from before you were baptized that were *disgusting* it shouldn't have any bearing on where you stand now with God—or members of the Church. Are you hearing me?"

Jayson nodded, still feeling emotional. "Yeah, I hear you. Thank you; both of you."

"I can understand why this is upsetting, Jayson," Will said. "It's upsetting to me, so I can only imagine how it must feel for you. But you just need to take your feelings to the Lord; give them to Him, and He will ease your pain and confusion."

Jayson nodded again, knowing he was right.

CHAPTER 11

Jayson felt decidedly nervous as the appointment with the bishop drew nearer. He kept glancing at the clock and consciously telling himself that the reason for this meeting surely had *nothing* to do with Bonnie Freedman's opinions of him. He'd done his best to take the advice of Will and Elizabeth and prayerfully let go of the difficult feelings he'd been dealing with. But so far he hadn't had much success. He didn't know if the problem was him, or if there was something he was supposed to learn from all of this. Likely both.

In the car on the way to the church building, Elizabeth took notice of his wringing hands. "What are you so concerned about?" she asked while she drove and he looked out the window. "It's probably a new calling."

"I haven't had this one all that long."

"Well, sometimes changes occur for all kinds of reasons and with odd timing. Or maybe they'll just add a calling onto the one you have. It happens, you know. They probably need a pianist in one place or another. They *always* need a pianist, and you can do that on top of your other calling without any stress whatsoever."

"I thought we weren't supposed to speculate over Church callings."

"Okay, so I'll stop speculating," she said. "I just don't think you should be nervous."

"I'm happy to do anything the bishop asks me to do; I'll serve in whatever capacity he wants. As long as it's about that, I'll be fine."

Elizabeth looked astonished. "What *else* are you thinking it could be?" She gave a wry chuckle. "Are you in some kind of trouble that I don't know about?"

He looked at her with a complete absence of humor. "Nothing you don't know about," he said far too seriously.

"Then I have no idea what you're talking about."

"I'd bet the royalties from a gold record that this has something to do with Sister Freedman."

Elizabeth actually laughed. "That's ludicrous."

Jayson let out a dubious snort. "Yeah, we'll see. If it isn't, I'll give you my next royalty check."

"You give me all your money, anyway. You hate managing the money, remember?"

"Then if I'm wrong, you have to give it all back to me," he said.

"I'll look forward to that," she said and pulled the car into the church parking lot. As they walked into the building holding hands, she added, "You really *are* nervous."

"I have a sick knot in the pit of my stomach," he admitted.

Elizabeth stopped walking and forced him to face her. "Why, Jayson? Even if this interview *does* have something to do with this woman, why should it matter? You know where you stand with the Lord. You know your intentions, your purpose. One woman's opinion should not have this much weight with you. It shouldn't!"

"Well, for some reason it does."

"Why, Jayson? I don't understand."

"I don't understand, either. I just know that I have a sick knot in my stomach. When I figure out how it got there, I'll let you know. Come on. We don't want to be late."

They arrived at the door to the bishop's office right on time, but the door was closed since he was in there with someone else, and they ended up waiting nearly half an hour. Jayson prayed silently and tried to focus on reading from the scriptures that had been left on the little table in the waiting area, but he just couldn't shake the eery sense of foreboding surrounding him. He couldn't figure if it was some messenger of Satan just trying to discourage and frighten him, or if the Spirit was trying to prepare him for an inevitable trial on the path ahead. Either way, he wanted to have this over with. He didn't begrudge the time the bishop was spending with whoever might be in his office. He just wanted to know why *he* was being called in, and what the outcome was going to be. Maybe Elizabeth was right. Maybe it had *nothing* to do with Sister Freedman, and he would be pleasantly surprised. Then again, maybe *he* was right. Either way, he felt like a kid again, sitting outside the principal's office waiting to be reprimanded for his inadequacy. He'd never gotten into trouble for doing things he shouldn't when he was a kid. He only got into trouble for not doing enough. He'd always been so caught up with the music in his head that he'd often let all of his school work go. And he'd been frequently lectured about it.

"What are you thinking about?" Elizabeth asked.

"The principal's office," he said, and she gave him a puzzled stare. "It's not important," he added.

When the office door came open, a young couple emerged. Jayson knew them only vaguely. They were chatting casually with the bishop as if their visit had been friendly and relaxed. They all exchanged greetings before the couple left, then Bishop Bingham invited Jayson and Elizabeth into his office, closing the door behind him. After they were all seated, the bishop asked some kind questions about how the family was doing. Then he asked, "And how is your work coming along, Jayson?"

"It's getting there," he said. "We should have the recording all done in a few weeks."

"And then it's on to the tour?"

"Not until summer, but there will be promotions and rehearsals in the meantime."

They talked a little about each of the children while Jayson waited for the axe to fall. The bishop finally got to the point and said, "We're making some changes in callings again. Sometimes it takes some shuffling around to get things right. I'm extending the call for you to once again play the piano for the choir. Our pianist was put into Primary after that pianist moved out of the ward."

Jayson swallowed carefully. "I would be happy to do that, Bishop. I'm assuming this would be on top of my calling with the young men."

It only took a split second of seeing the bishop's expression to know what was coming. Jayson wasn't surprised but was still entirely shocked when he said, "Actually . . ." He drew the word out the length of five words. "We're making some changes there as well. Since you will be very busy with the release of the new album, we thought one calling would be enough for now."

"I can handle both, Bishop. Except when I'm actually on tour—which is many months away—I'm more than willing to put in the time."

"And we appreciate your attitude, Jayson. We just feel this is best for now."

"We?" Jayson echoed.

"My counselors . . . and I."

Jayson squeezed Elizabeth's hand and glanced over to see her biting her lip, as if she wanted to keep him from saying what she probably knew he was going to say. Well, he figured it had to be said. He could never live with wondering. "May I ask you something, Bishop?"

"Of course."

"Tell me honestly . . . does this have something to do with Sister Freedman?" The bishop's astonishment was immediately evident, but he said nothing. Jayson added firmly, "You're my bishop; you can't lie to me."

"I would never lie to you, Jayson, or anyone else."

"But you would omit details of the situation in order to spare my feelings?" Jayson suggested. More silence. "I need to know, Bishop, if this has something to do with Sister Freedman."

"For what purpose, Jayson? I don't want there to be any hard feelings or ill will among members of this ward."

Jayson thought about that for a long moment, at the same time counting to ten and reminding himself to remain calm. "Is that why I'm being released? To avoid ill will among members of this ward?"

The bishop's sigh communicated more than anything he'd admitted to so far. Jayson waited—and counted—and silently asked God to help him see and understand whatever might be taking place here in a Christian manner. "Jayson," the bishop finally said, "I really believe that the details of this situation can simply be avoided, and that we can all just live and let live."

Jayson inhaled sharply, and the shock of reality felt like cold water in his face. Still, he managed to keep his voice even. "So, you *are* releasing me because of Sister Freedman." It wasn't a question.

"I'm releasing you because I believe it is the right thing to do under the circumstances."

"Under the circumstances?" Jayson countered, sounding much more calm than he felt. He reminded himself that this man was his bishop. It would not be appropriate to question his decisions, but he did feel the need to clarify, "I think I have a right to understand what's happening here, Bishop. I respect your right to make these decisions. But I *do* need to understand it."

The bishop sighed again, even more loudly. "Truthfully, I'm having trouble understanding it myself. I'm fairly new at this bishop stuff, and I've never dealt with anything like this before. I'm just trying to do the best I can to keep peace and work all of this out."

Jayson swallowed carefully, and again had to consciously will back his emotions to keep them from getting out of control. "So . . ." he began with caution, "help me understand this. Are you saying that in order to keep peace—by peace, I assume you mean with Sister Freedman—you are releasing me from my calling?" The bishop said nothing, and Elizabeth squeezed Jayson's hand with a silent reminder to remember who they were talking to. Jayson made certain there was no lack of respect or hint of anger in his voice when he responded to the silence by asking, "Is that or is that not a true statement?"

Following another sigh, the bishop said, "I prayed very hard about this, Jayson, and while I don't claim to handle every situation exactly as the Lord would have me handle it, I've done my best to—"

"Keep peace?" Jayson interrupted, sounding only slightly upset.

"She's very upset about this, Jayson. She firmly believes that your influence on her son is not a good thing."

Jayson mustered more self-discipline to help him remain calm, although he felt more like crying than shouting. "And what do you think, Bishop? Do you think my influence on her son is not a good thing?"

"I do not question your influence or anything else about you."

"Did you tell *her* that?"

"I did."

"And . . . what? Her bishop's word that I'm worthy to hold my position is not sufficient for her to let go of these ridiculous notions that my music will destroy her only child? It's all right and expected for *me* to have sufficient faith to accept my bishop's word regarding a difficult situation, but not for her?"

"Jayson," Elizabeth scolded gently. "We can't possibly understand the entire scope of the situation from our perspective."

"No, we certainly can't," Jayson said, and the silence became brutal as if no one knew what to say without sounding hurtful or upset. Jayson prayed silently while at the same time feeling wholly unworthy of having his prayers answered when he felt so angry. Feeling his high water table coming dangerously close to the surface, he knew the best option for the moment was to get out of here, give the matter some distance and thought, and deal with it later under more reasonable circumstances. He hurried to get to the one point that mattered at the moment. "I just need to know, Bishop, that this change in callings comes from the Lord, and not from some avoidance of a problem."

The bishop was quiet for a long moment, then said calmly, "That is for you to find out. It's between you and the Lord. Why don't you give the matter some time and prayer, and we'll talk about it more another time."

"My thoughts exactly," Jayson said and came to his feet.

Jayson rushed out of the bishop's office, then moved even faster to get out of the building before he burst into tears and started sobbing like a baby. He made it to the car but couldn't open the door. A quick glance assured him he was the only one in the parking lot, other than Elizabeth, who was close behind him. He put his hands on top of the car and hung his head between his arms, heaving for breath. This was it! This was the sensation he'd had when he'd awakened from that dream. The moments in his life when he'd felt this way paraded before him. Derek's death. Elizabeth telling him she didn't love him and couldn't marry him. Debbie cheating on him. Macy running away. His mother dying. This was the kind of grief that was impossible to reason with when it was in your face. He couldn't breathe. He couldn't think. He only knew that he was in pain, and he couldn't even rationally understand why. He reminded himself that Elizabeth *had* married him—twenty years later—and Macy *had* come home. He'd found peace over the deaths of his loved ones and events that had scarred him. But right now, the path to finding such peace felt impossible to traverse. But why? This wasn't a death or a tragedy. It was a Church calling—and a belligerent woman who just couldn't leave well enough alone. Why was he taking it so hard?

Jayson felt Elizabeth's hands on his back. The sensation was eerily familiar as he considered how many times she had been with him through the tragedies of his life. "Why are you so upset?" she asked.

"I don't know," he muttered. "I was just . . . trying to figure that out."

She put her arms around him from behind. "I owe you a lot of money."

"How's that?"

"You bet me the royalties from a gold album. You were right."

"Oh," he groaned and put a hand over his chest, heaving for breath.

"Jayson," Elizabeth sounded panicked, "what's wrong?"

"What's *wrong?*" he snarled, pressing his anguish into anger. "I've just been . . . cut off at the knees here."

"I really don't think it's as serious as all that. I can understand why this is hard for you, but—"

"Can you?" he demanded.

"I know you're upset, Jayson, but you don't have to take it out on me."

Jayson looked at her hard, feeling for the first time in years that she *didn't* understand. But then, he wasn't sure he understood it himself. "You know what?" he said. "You're right. Let's go home. I'm sure I'll get over it."

In the car Elizabeth broke the silence by saying, "Talk to me."

"There's nothing to say. Apparently I am not worthy to do anything in this church but play the piano, so—"

"That's not true and you know it."

"I know no such thing," he insisted. "How else would you explain it?"

"I don't know. Obviously you need to pray about this in order to find some peace and—"

"Peace?" he snapped.

"Yes, Jayson!" she came back just as strongly. "This has *nothing* to do with whether or not you are worthy. You *are* worthy, because you're a good man, a righteous man, a faithful man. You cannot let this upset you so badly. I think you need to calm down before you jump to conclusions."

"You know what? I don't want to talk about this anymore. Let's just drop it."

"Fine," she said, and there was silence until the car was parked in the garage. Jayson got out and went to the studio. Elizabeth went to check on the children.

Jayson flipped on the light in the small space between the exterior door and the studio door that created a sound barrier. He closed the door and leaned against it, putting a hand to his chest, feeling that tightening again that made it difficult to breathe. Without turning on any other light, he went into the darkened studio, guided by the beam of light behind him to a place on the floor, in the shadows near the piano. He sank to his knees, and hot tears finally came while he wondered what he'd done to bring this on. He wondered why God would punish him this way. He kept thinking of the things that Elizabeth had said. Why couldn't he see it the way she saw it? Why did it feel like somebody had reached down his throat and torn his heart out? He didn't understand why he felt the way he did. He only knew how he felt. And he hated it.

* * * * *

After the children had all gone to bed, Elizabeth really began to worry about her husband. It wasn't like him to not show up for the children's bedtime, no matter what was going on. She figured he needed some space and time, so she'd left him alone and had taken care of the bedtime rituals on her own. But now she was worried. She kept thinking of his reaction to what the bishop had said, and wondered why it was giving him so much grief. For that matter, she'd considered his reaction to all of this business with Bonnie Freedman to be excessive. Before now, she'd just figured he would calm down when he'd had some time to realize that in the grand scheme of things, this woman's opinion wasn't that important. But for some reason it was important to Jayson, and Elizabeth now felt bad that she hadn't given more validation to his feelings.

She went to the studio to find him, perhaps expecting him to be picking out something on the piano or the guitar, which was a typical way for him to think and calm down when he was upset. But there was a light on only near the door, and the light was out in the studio. For a moment she thought he wasn't there. Then she saw a shadow of him, sitting on the floor, leaning against the wall. She stepped quietly closer. It was seeing his hands that made her heart drop and her stomach tighten. He was methodically and unconsciously rubbing his left hand with his right. Instantly she was catapulted back in time. The gesture was something Jayson had once done a great deal, but she'd completely forgotten because she'd not seen him do it for years.

Following a severe injury to his left hand, Jayson had struggled for a very long time to be free of the pain enough to play music again. The accident had been the final straw after many tragedies in his life, and he had become addicted to the painkillers he'd started taking following the surgery. He'd come close to committing suicide before he'd finally come to stay with her and her father, and then he'd gone into drug rehab. The detox and subsequent counseling had been a nightmare for him, and had been difficult for Elizabeth as well. And now she'd been taken back to the moment she'd walked into his room at the facility when he was nearing the end of his detox.

She held her breath as she entered the room and found him sitting on the floor, leaning against the bed, his head down. He wore jeans and a button-up shirt that was only partially buttoned. His feet were bare. He was nervously rubbing his left hand with the fingers of his right, as if to rub out the pain and stiffness that she knew was there.

"You have company," the attendant said, and Jayson's head shot up. Elizabeth couldn't keep from gasping. He looked more ill than her father, who had been vomiting all night. His eyes looked sunken, his skin sallow. He looked thinner, more fragile. He looked broken.

"Thank you," Jayson said, his voice weak. The attendant left the room, leaving the door open.

Elizabeth watched Jayson take hold of the edge of the bed and come unsteadily to his feet. She rushed toward him and took hold of his arm to help him, immediately wrapping him in her arms.

"Oh, Elizabeth," he muttered near her ear, holding to her tightly.

She took his face into her hands and pressed her brow to his, just as she'd done the night before he'd come here. "Are you okay?" she asked.

"*Better now . . . that you're here.*" *He teetered slightly, and she urged him to the edge of the bed, sitting beside him.* "*Sorry,*" *he said,* "*I haven't been able to eat much, but that's getting better.*"

He folded one leg onto the bed and turned to face her fully, taking both her hands into his as she did the same. Elizabeth looked into his strained and weary eyes. She said intently, "*Talk to me. Tell me.*" *She watched huge tears rise into his eyes and then fall before he pressed his face against her shoulder and wept.*

"*I never imagined the human body could endure such horrors and survive. I've never been so sick in my life. The hallucinations alone were horrid. A thousand times I wished I was dead.*"

"*Oh, I'm so sorry,*" *she said, wiping his tears with her fingers.* "*But the worst is over now.*"

"*So they tell me,*" *he said.*

"*But?*" *she asked, looking at him closely.*

He chuckled bitterly and returned to rubbing his left hand. "*Today is my last official day of detox,*" *he said.* "*Tomorrow I start into the program. It smacks of military basic training; they're not going to give me time to feel sorry for myself. Private therapy. Group therapy. Heaven knows what else. Now comes the picking apart of my heart and soul to find whatever it is I was trying to bury under the drugs. Well, I know what I was trying to bury, and I don't want to look at it. That almost scares me more than the detox did.*"

"*But you made it this far; surely you'll make it through whatever you have to in order to be whole again.*"

"*Again? Was I ever whole? I don't remember. It doesn't feel like it.*"

"*Yes, Jayson. You were. And you will be again.*" *She took his face into her hands.* "*You can do this. I know you can.*"

"*I don't know it,*" *he said, sounding angry. Then he wept again.*

That memory merged immediately into another, a few weeks later, when she and her father had been asked to join Jayson for a counseling session . . .

Elizabeth took notice of Jayson as he moved to a chair and sat down. The last time she'd seen him, he'd looked significantly better than he had after coming out of detox. Now he looked worse. The evidence of the trauma he'd been through showed in his face. His eyes had a shocked, bewildered quality that she'd first seen there following Derek's death. His feet were bare, and he wore jeans and a dark button-up shirt. The cuffs weren't buttoned, but the sleeves of his shirt weren't rolled up. The top four buttons of his shirt were left undone, leaving a portion of his chest exposed. His hair was more mussed than usual. His clothes looked like he'd slept in them. His face looked gaunt and weary. He was rubbing his left hand with his right.

Elizabeth brought herself back to the present, deeply unsettled over seeing her husband sitting in the dark, on the floor, rubbing his left hand with his right. By the time he'd come out of rehab, he'd been using the hand a lot more, he was playing music again, and she'd not seen him rub his hand like that since that time. Trying to think of what to say, that unsettled feeling slipped into something closer to terror. Jayson had survived more loss and grief than most people could imagine. His counseling in rehab had opened a Pandora's box inside of him, and facing up to its contents—and its creation—had been torment for both of them. And for Will. Elizabeth had assumed the metaphorical box was gone and forgotten. Life had been good for them since then. They'd continued to work through old issues, and they'd both been happy since their marriage. Happy and well-adjusted—or so she'd believed. But her deepest instincts knew that something deep and painful had been unleashed for Jayson in the last few hours. And she was terrified!

Frozen where she stood, unable to speak, Elizabeth felt more prone to turn and leave the room, hopefully undetected, and call her father. He'd been close to Jayson through all of that. He was the only other person who really knew Jayson's heart, turned inside out.

"I really just want to be alone," he said, startling her. She'd been there for several minutes and had assumed that he wasn't aware of her presence.

"Okay," she said, wishing it hadn't sounded so emotional. "I'll . . . uh . . . you know where to find me . . . if you need to talk."

Elizabeth hurried from the room, closed the door and leaned against it. She put a hand over her mouth to keep her sudden sobbing silent. Then she forced herself to her senses and went to the phone to call her father. A glance at the clock assured her that he would still be up. But she would have called him anyway.

Her stepmother answered the phone. "Can I talk to Dad?" Elizabeth asked.

"I'll get him," Marilyn said. "He's right here." She then heard Marilyn say quietly to Will, "It's Elizabeth. She sounds upset."

"What's wrong?" Will asked into the phone.

"It's Jayson," she said and started to cry again. "Something's wrong with Jayson."

"Is he hurt? Is he—"

"We had an appointment with the bishop. He was released from his calling."

"Why?" Will demanded.

"I think it's more important to consider what Jayson thinks about the reasons." She sobbed. "He was so angry, but now . . . now . . . he's sitting in the studio in the dark . . ." She tried to compose herself enough to be understood. "He's rubbing his hand, Dad. Do you remember how he—"

"Yes!" Will interrupted, his tone exactly mirroring Elizabeth's panic. At least she didn't feel like she was blowing this out of proportion.

"I don't know what to do, Dad. If this is some kind of breakdown, or something . . . what do I do? I don't think I handled it very well. I didn't know he'd get so upset. I brushed it off too easily. I don't think he wants to talk to me because I'm the one he was arguing with."

"I'm on my way. I'll have my cell phone if you need to call me in the next five minutes. I'm coming."

"Okay," she said and hung up. Then she cried again. She started pacing before her father arrived, and she opened the door before he got to it. Once inside, he hugged her tightly, and she cried some more. "I'm so scared, Dad. I haven't been this scared since . . ."

"Since when?" he asked, looking into her eyes. "Are you reverting to old pain as well?"

"Maybe I am," she said.

"Since when?" he repeated.

"Since . . ." she sobbed, "I realized he'd almost taken his own life."

"That's not going to happen," Will said. "He's a *lot* stronger now than he was then. He'll be able to work through this. He has a stronger foundation in his life. He has the gospel. He has you, the children."

"And you."

"And me. I'm going to try to talk to him. He'll be fine. I wouldn't expect you to sleep, but why don't you lie down? I'll come and get you if I need you."

Elizabeth nodded and watched Will walk away, praying that he was right.

* * * * *

Jayson lost all sense of time while his thoughts wandered through a barrage of painful memories that left him reeling. And all of it seemed to interconnect with the one-million-dollar question. What had he done wrong? What had he done to be cut off this way?

He realized he wasn't alone and looked up to see Will standing nearby. "What are *you* doing here?" Jayson demanded, then looked away.

"My daughter called me," he said. "She told me you were upset."

"There's no reason for you to come over here in the middle of the night."

"It's not the middle of the night, but even if it were, I'd be here."

"Why?"

"She's scared," Will said, and Jayson shot him an astonished glare. "Does she have reason to be?"

Jayson said nothing. Maybe she did.

"Does your hand hurt?" Will asked.

"No, why?" Jayson asked.

Will looked down, and Jayson's eyes followed to see that he was methodically rubbing his left hand with his right. And he hadn't even realized it. He felt a little scared himself, as the gesture connected to horrific memories. Then Will just had to say, "The memory of pain, then?"

Jayson forced his hands apart, then pushed them brutally into his hair. "Maybe she does."

"Does what?"

"Have reason to be scared."

"Are *you* scared, Jayson?"

"Are you?"

"A little."

"Yes, I'm scared," Jayson said. "I don't . . . know why I'm so upset. I don't understand it." He shook his head. "I just . . . feel like I've . . . lost everything."

"Do you want me to list everything you *haven't* lost?"

"No, I do not! What I feel may not make any sense, but I still feel it."

"I can respect that," Will said. "So, why don't you tell me how you feel?"

"What are you? My shrink?"

"No, I'm the closest thing you've ever had to a father; the man who went through a fair amount of counseling with you. And I'm not leaving until I feel like you can look at what's going on with some kind of reason."

"And what if I can't?"

"I'm not saying this is going to get resolved tonight. But I would think we could at least get some idea of why you're so upset and figure out how we're going to get through this."

"We?"

"We're family. We always have been . . . since the day you came home with Derek. You know it's true, and arguing that point will only waste time. Even if you had never married Elizabeth, you would still be family to me."

"I know." Jayson sighed. "And I'm grateful. It's just that . . . I've put you through a lot. I don't see why you have to hold my hand through this, too."

"Maybe I'll get even one day," Will said. "Maybe I'll get Alzheimer's before I die and make you all crazy."

"Are you trying to make me feel better?"

"Is it working?"

"No."

"Talk to me, Jayson. However long this takes to work through . . . days, months, years . . . we are not going to pretend that everything is all right. We're going to keep talking about it."

Jayson sighed, then groaned. "I don't know why it's getting to me this way. Maybe a normal person could just let it roll off and not feel so . . ."

"So . . . what?"

"I . . . don't know."

"Just say what you're thinking. I don't care if it sounds reasonable."

"I feel . . . hurt . . . offended . . . betrayed . . ." Emotion broke his voice. "Cut off."

"Okay, and . . . did I hear you say that a *normal* person wouldn't feel this way, so you're calling yourself *abnormal?*"

"Since when have I ever been normal?" Jayson snapped, hearing a snotty teenager in his own voice.

"Oh," Will sounded exaggeratedly enlightened, mildly sarcastic, "you mean . . . extremely gifted, unique, eccentric, unable to fit into any mold because . . ." he drew the word out, "you are extremely gifted? Is that what you mean by not being normal?"

"This is silly," Jayson said and stood up.

"You bet it is," Will said and stood as well. "You're in your forties, Jayson. You have achieved a level of success that millions of other musicians only dream of. And you're sitting on the floor feeling sorry for yourself because you're not *normal?* Whatever is going on—*really* going on—is something we need to talk about. But that's not going to happen until you get past this sudden need to be *normal.* There isn't a person who really knows you who would want you be normal. And I do not include Sister Freedman or anyone else who does not know you well enough to *really* know you. When you have so many extraordinary abilities that have touched so many lives for good, how could you ever expect the experiences of your life to be ordinary? God knows the real you, Jayson. He made you the way you are. You are normal for Jayson Wolfe. Nothing else matters."

Jayson listened and appreciated the theory. He was grateful for Will's love and understanding. But if they were trying to get to the heart of the problem, he could only think of one thing to say. "I'm not so sure that God has as much to do with it as I'd led myself to believe." He sat on the piano bench with his back to the piano. Will took a chair. "Maybe I was deluding myself to think that I had God's approval to do what I do."

Will let out a disbelieving chuckle. "Are you serious?"

Jayson glared at him. "No, Will," he snarled with sarcasm, "I just made it up to shock you. You asked me to be honest with my feelings. If you don't want to hear them, then—"

"No. I'm sorry." He put up a hand. "It's just that . . . I've known you most of your life. I simply don't understand how you can look back over the steps you've taken to get where you are and honestly believe what you just said."

Jayson put his forearms on his thighs and hung his head, sighing from his deepest self. "I don't know what I believe, Will. I haven't felt this . . . unsteady . . . since rehab. I feel lost and confused . . . and I'm not sure why."

"Then maybe you should try to get some sleep, and we can talk some more tomorrow."

"Okay," Jayson said, mostly because he wanted to end this conversation. And he didn't necessarily want to pick it up again tomorrow. He doubted he'd know what to say then any more than he did now. Either way, he doubted he'd be getting much sleep.

"Would it be all right if I gave you a blessing?" Will asked.

Jayson felt mildly bristled by the question but wasn't sure why. How could he explain to Will that he didn't feel worthy to receive a blessing? He just said, "Sure, why not?"

Will stood and held out a hand to help Jayson up. "Let's go in the house. I think your wife is worried about you."

CHAPTER 12

Will and Jayson left the studio together and found Elizabeth pacing the hallway. "Are you all right?" she asked Jayson when she saw him.

"I'm fine," he said, and she hugged him tightly, as if she'd feared she might never see him again. "I'm fine," he said again and chuckled, preferring to keep his feelings to himself. If he'd had any idea how upset everyone would become over his little breakdown, he would have kept it to himself. He took her shoulders and looked at her straight. "I'm fine, really. I'm sorry if I upset you."

"I'm going to give him a blessing," Will said, "and we'll talk about it some more tomorrow."

"You sounded just like a father," Jayson said facetiously, sounding again like that teenager—flippant this time. He felt surprised by his own attitude, but wasn't pleased to note that Elizabeth was surprised too. The concern in her expression was evident, but he didn't comment.

Will gave Jayson a blessing that offered assurance and comfort. He was told directly that his Heavenly Father was pleased with the way he lived his life and used his gifts. But for the first time since Jayson had gone into the waters of baptism, he found himself wondering if that was really the power of the priesthood speaking, or if it was simply Will wanting to help Jayson feel better. He appreciated Will's efforts, and told him so when they hugged after the blessing was done. He let Elizabeth walk her father to the door, sensing that they wanted to talk about him. He was in bed by the time she came into the bedroom. She went into the bathroom for a few minutes, then crawled beneath the covers, and he felt her close beside him.

"Are you okay, really?"

"Yes, I'm fine," he lied.

"I'm sorry if I didn't take what you were saying seriously. I can understand why this would be hard for you. If you need to talk, then—"

"I think we both need some sleep," he said and rolled over. She didn't say anything more, but he knew she was crying—even though she was trying very hard not to let him know. Normally he would have held her close and insisted that they talk it through. But he couldn't. How could he talk about it when it just didn't make any sense?

Jayson did manage to get some sleep, but he woke up feeling heavy with a boatload of emotions that couldn't be voiced. All of the thoughts that had haunted him the previous evening were still there, even louder perhaps. And the subtle sense of drowning in darkness felt eerily familiar, but he didn't care to face or understand the reason. He lay in bed and tried to gear himself up for the work he needed to do today. He tried to pray, but didn't get past simply repeating several times, *Why, God? What have I done wrong?*

Elizabeth eased close to his back and wrapped her arms around him. "How are you this morning?" she asked.

"I'm fine," he said. "How are you?"

"I'm worried about you."

"No need for that," he said and got out of bed. Not wanting Elizabeth or anyone else to believe that anything was out of the ordinary, he forced himself into the proper frame of mind to interact with the children normally while Trevin and Addie were getting ready for school, and while the babies were being dressed and fed. He went about the usual routine, managing to tease the kids, laugh with them, and behave like a normal husband and father. *Normal?* He scoffed at the word as it appeared in his mind, then he recalled what Will had said about his *not* being normal. While some of it made sense and he wanted to cling to it, his brain was too clouded to make sense of anything.

Once everything was settled, Jayson kissed his wife as he always did and went off to work in the studio. He went straight to the piano to practice the Mozart piece. He had to do it over and over until it came through him like breathing. The two-part song was about ten minutes long, and it took stamina and focus—but he had to practice it until it didn't feel like it took stamina and focus. The orchestra would be coming again tomorrow to rehearse, and he had to start really integrating the piano with what they were doing. He liked the way playing the song pushed everything else out of his head. It was easy to let go of anything and everything he didn't like in his life when he could play like this. As the thought catapulted into his mind, he stopped abruptly. In the silence he could hear his own shallow breathing. The memory of a conversation from his rehab counseling sessions rushed into him with emotion equivalent to what he'd felt then. *Pandora's Box.* The metaphoric place where people would lock away the pain related to certain issues in their lives.

"What's in the box, Jayson?" his counselor Maren asked.

He chuckled, but a deep trembling erupted inside of him in response to the question. "I don't know what you're talking about," he said.

"There's a part of your brain that knows very well what I'm talking about. All you have to do is ask yourself the question, and you'll come up with the answer. So, what's in the box?"

The trembling inside of him increased dramatically, even before she said, "Do you know what kept the box closed and latched and content to stay closed?"

"Apparently you do," he said, amazed at the anger he heard in his own voice.

"Music," she said gently, and he started to gasp for breath. "And when you became incapable of playing the music that kept the box closed, do you know what did the trick?"

She leaned back in her chair and made it evident she wasn't going to answer that question for him. She expected him to say it, and she would sit there until he did. He knew the answer, and the answer made him sick. "Drugs," he croaked.

"You're a very wise man, Jayson," she said with gentle compassion. "And when we can talk about what's in the box, you'll be able to empty it out and get rid of it. Then you won't need drugs, and you will be able to play music because you want to, not to medicate yourself."

Jayson put a hand over his chest. Is that what he was doing? Medicating himself with music? He could close his eyes and heard Maren's voice, seeing her size him up as if she could see right through his efforts to remain disconnected.

"So, what's in the box, Jayson?"

What's in the box? he repeated silently, and the answer rushed up from the core of himself like a volcanic eruption. He groaned, he gasped, he slid out of the chair to his knees and doubled over with pain. He spent the next three days trying to cope with the metaphoric evil that had been unleashed inside of him. And then Maren coolly asked him, "Are you ready to talk to your loved ones about this?"

"About what?" he snapped.

"You won't get away with pretending denial, Jayson. You know what I'm talking about. And you know that if your healing is going to be complete, the people who love you have to know what's going on. They need to understand it in order to help you press forward and have a healthy life."

"My brother has little to do with this."

"He has less to do with this than Will and Elizabeth, but he's still your brother."

"Will and Elizabeth are not even family."

"They are more family than most people find in the families they are born into. They love you. They share your grief. They are a part of your grief." She leaned forward as she always did when she needed to make a hard point. *"They shared a near suicide with you, Jayson. They saved your life. You owe them this."*

"What exactly is this that I owe them?"

"You owe them understanding of how it came to that. If you come clean with them, if you let them help you now, there will be nothing to hide, nothing to bury. Are you ready to talk to them? Are you ready to tell them what's in the box?"

Jayson thought about that for a minute while his insides trembled. Then he said, "How about if you tell them what's in the box, and then I'll talk to them?"

"If you want me to do that, I can do that. Do you think that will make it easier?"

"Maybe," he said. But as the hours drew closer for a prearranged counseling session with Will and Elizabeth, Jayson felt himself on the brink of insanity. He felt uncontrollably cold; he couldn't get warm, couldn't stop shaking from an apparent shivering that made no sense. And then when he thought he couldn't bear the cold, he became suddenly hot from the inside out, feeling a desire to run barefoot in the snow. He had marveled over the last several days that emotional trauma could cause such literal, physical pain. And he felt sure that his symptoms now were from the same source. He felt terrified, and he found himself praying constantly that they would love him enough to endure this and not lose all faith in him.

Jayson's memories became so difficult to look at that he forced himself to just play the song. He needed to work. He needed to finish these recordings. If they were going to get the album released before a summer tour, he had to get it done.

Jayson finished the first part of the song and was startled to hear Elizabeth say during the two-second pause in between, "Roger is here." He turned around to see her and Roger standing near the door. "You didn't hear us come in," she added and left the room.

"Wow." Roger sat down and crossed his ankle over his knee. "Let's pretend you're not you so we can talk about you."

"Excuse me?" Jayson said, trying to sound as light as Roger did.

"If you were anyone else, I could say, 'That Jayson Wolfe is amazing. Such talent is a one-in-a-million. It's a privilege to be his friend.' But since you're you, saying things like that is a little awkward."

"You should know me well enough to know that you can say anything you want to me."

"Okay, fine. I think you're amazing. It's a privilege to be your friend—but not just because what I heard you playing a minute ago was giving me hordes of goose bumps. I like you because it think you're a great guy, and I admire you."

Jayson turned his back to Roger and pretended to be absorbed in examining the piano keys. "You're just saying that because you're afraid I'm taking what the bishop did last night too personally and you want to make me feel better."

"I'm saying it because I mean it," Roger said, then paused. "Did you?"

"What?"

"Take it personally?"

"How should I take it?"

"I don't know, Jayson. It's really between you and the Lord. I didn't know he was going to release you until he called me this morning. I want you to know it had nothing to do with me. I also want you to know that bishops aren't perfect, but this one has a good heart, and he's really trying to do what he believes is right. You can't fault him for that."

"No, I can't fault him for that," Jayson said, wishing they could talk about *anything* else.

"I once had a bishop who was offending people right and left. He had some personal issues that were hurtful to some of the members. I had a hard time with him myself. I took it to the Lord and I learned something remarkable."

"What's that?" Jayson asked, turning again toward Roger while he fought to remain cool and nonchalant.

"I learned that bishops are entitled to be human, and when we raise our hand to the square and sustain a bishop—or any other leader—we're making a covenant to support their decisions—whether we agree with them or not. It's about obedience. We don't know what the Lord might be trying to teach the bishop—or us."

"So, do you agree with what he did?"

"Whether I agree doesn't matter."

"It matters to me."

"I wish you were still serving in the presidency with me. I think you have a lot to offer these boys, and the rest of us. I think you could be the best thing that ever happened to Clayton Freedman—if his mother would let him anywhere near you. But if I were in the bishop's shoes, I honestly don't know what I would do. Regardless of whether the bishop made the right decision, we still have to support him. Not doing so will just drive the Spirit out of our lives, and none of us can afford to do that. The important thing is for you to make peace with this between you and the Lord. He'll make up the difference for whatever anyone else has done to hurt you, whether intentionally or not." He sighed. "I didn't come over here to give you a lecture, Jayson. I just want you to know that I'm with you in this. And if you need to talk . . ."

"Thank you," Jayson said. "I appreciate it . . . really. I admit it's got me unsettled. But . . . I'm sure I just need to give it some time."

"Okay." Roger nodded firmly. "Well, if you need to talk about it, I hope you know you can trust me."

"I do," Jayson said. "Thank you."

"Now, since I took the morning off, I think you should play that song for me again. I missed the beginning."

"I'm just practicing."

"I know. And I'll let you practice with an audience. That shouldn't ruffle you too much."

"No, you wouldn't think so," Jayson said with a chuckle that almost sounded normal. "The good thing is that you won't know if I make a mistake."

"How does *anyone* know if you make a mistake?"

"*I* know," Jayson said. "But when I actually have to perform it with other musicians, *they* will know. And I want the stage performances to sound like the recording as much as possible."

"Wow. I never realized music was so complicated. I've learned a lot about music from hanging around with you."

"I haven't learned *anything* about the law by hanging around with you."

"That's because my job is boring. Your job is cool."

"Yeah," Jayson said while a dozen negative inner thoughts responded with sarcasm and self-recrimination. Maybe his job was just a little too cool for a good Mormon boy.

"Elizabeth said there were lyrics to the second part, and she was telling me about the orchestra thing. It sounds like it's going to be great."

"I hope so," Jayson said and decided he'd rather play music than talk. If Roger wasn't leaving, the former felt preferable. He dove right into the song, going through the entire number, including the lyrics. He wondered why they felt almost eery now, under the circumstances.

"But sanity comes at the edge of reason. The muse is a voice without limits or season. From the end of the world, right back to its start. It's been speaking and

singing to the mind and the heart, Of madmen like me with the heart of Mozart. Oh, bring on the madness! And help me to soar! Let the angels in heaven grant me more, more, and more. May the music inside me, let it always abide me. Let the muse ever guide me, the light never hide me. Oh, hear the beat, beat, beat of the heart, heart, heart . . . The heart of Mozart, yeah, the heart of Mozart."

He had honestly forgotten Roger was there until he finished and heard the applause. "That was truly amazing," he said. "Forgive me if it's annoying. You probably get tired of hearing stuff like that, but . . . I just think it should be said."

"No, it's not annoying when it's sincere. Thank you."

"You wrote it?"

"Yeah."

"The lyrics . . . the music . . . all of it?"

"Yeah."

Roger chuckled in disbelief. *"How?* I mean . . . you told me you didn't go to college. You didn't *learn* this."

Jayson felt more relaxed now that they were talking in his comfort zone. "I learned how to play the instruments well enough to play what I could hear in my head. The only way to learn was to keep practicing and pushing myself. As far as what I hear in my head, and my ability to translate it into music, well . . . I guess it's a gift."

"You guess? Dear Brother Wolfe. Your gift is incredible, and most impressive because you've done so much good with it."

Jayson looked down and took in what he'd said. He'd rarely if ever had a friend who wasn't also a musician. He appreciated the way Roger didn't treat him any differently because of his fame; Jayson had learned to see through such things a long time ago. And Jayson had come to see over time that when Roger talked about the fame, he was usually teasing him. But he knew that last comment had been sincere, and Jayson had needed to hear it. He had to admit that Roger's compliments and observations were a blessing. Sometimes he just lost perspective on what he was doing and why, and he was grateful for a friend who was willing to say what he thought and help keep Jayson on track.

"I've tried," he said and stood. "Let's go see if we can dig up a sandwich or something. I'm starving."

Jayson pulled stuff out of the fridge, and the two of them made sandwiches and shared lunch before Roger went to work. After he'd left, Elizabeth found Jayson in the kitchen, wiping off the counter.

"You okay?" she asked.

"I'm fine," he said.

She folded her arms. "I'm amazed at how you've taken up lying to me."

Jayson looked away and tossed the dishcloth into the sink. "I wouldn't lie to you."

"Now you're lying about lying. I've known you since I was sixteen, Jayson. I know 'fine' when I see it. You're not fine! It's eating you alive, and it's worse because you won't admit it."

Jayson said nothing, wouldn't even look at her.

"Listen to me," she said, "if you're struggling with this, fine. Talk, scream, cry if you have to. But don't lie to me. If I was insensitive to the depth of the problem, I deserve to be forgiven. You cannot shut me out and hope to find peace with this. Are you hearing me?"

"I'm hearing you, and I'm fine."

"Stop it!" she screamed, and his eyes widened. He couldn't remember the last time he'd heard her use that tone of voice. "Do you remember the last time you tried to convince me you were fine? *I* remember it! You told me you were fine, over and over. You told my father you were fine, week after week." A sob jumped out of her throat. "Then the Spirit shoved me out of bed in the middle of the night and told me to call you. If I hadn't, you would have been *dead.*" She sobbed again. "Don't stand there and tell me you're fine when you're not, because I won't tolerate it! With what we have been through, you're a fool if you think you can expect me to."

"By what we have been through, you mean drug rehab and a near suicide?" He said it in that snotty teenager voice, and he wondered when he had regressed to such immaturity.

"Yes, that's what I mean. And the counseling that followed. We went through it all together. And I never stopped loving you. I never judged or criticized you. I never did or said *anything* to warrant having you shut me out like this." She visibly tried to compose herself, and wiped tears from her cheeks. In a voice that was more calm, she said, "Now I'm going to ask you a question, and I want an honest answer. How are you, Jayson?"

Jayson moved to a chair, feeling a little weak. Elizabeth sat down across the table from him and waited. He cleared his throat, glanced at her, and glanced away. He knew she was right. He remembered the counseling sessions where they had committed to being completely honest with each other, to not hold feelings inside, to be willing to share their burdens. And that was before they'd exchanged vows. "I'm sorry," he said. "I didn't realize what I was doing. I just . . . don't want to talk about it."

"Fine. You don't have to talk about it. But don't lie to me."

"Okay," he said. "Fair enough." His voice cracked. "I'm not fine, Elizabeth." Tears came, and he shook his head. "I'm not even close to fine. I'm falling apart inside, and I don't know why. I just figured if I . . . gave it some time . . . it would get better. Maybe I'm just . . . blowing it out of proportion, and it's not as big a deal as I'm making of it."

"If it feels like a big deal, Jayson, then it is." She was thoughtful a moment. "Do you think this has tapped into something that was hiding in that Pandora's Box?"

Jayson bristled at the mention of it, even though he'd been thinking the same thing. Or perhaps his own thoughts were the reason he bristled. "I don't know," he had to admit. "Maybe."

"Should we get an appointment with Maren?"

Jayson wanted to scream *no!* But he calmly said, "I really don't think that's necessary."

"Maybe not. But maybe it is. If you're really having trouble coming to terms with this, then you need to do whatever you possibly can to work through it. I repeatedly promised Maren that I would never let you sink into any level of depression without doing everything that *I* could possibly do. Besides that, I'm your wife."

"So what you really mean," he took her hand across the table, "is that you will call Maren and drag me into her office at gunpoint if you have to."

"Whatever it takes," she said, but she smiled.

"I love you, Elizabeth. I'm sorry I've been so . . . ratty."

"I love you too, and I understand. Really I do. At least I understand that this is difficult for you, even if I don't fully understand why. I *want* to understand." She squeezed his hand. "Help me understand, Jayson."

He thought about it for a minute, trying to find a way to summarize what was really bugging him. "I think I just feel . . . disconnected. I really can't help wondering if I did something wrong."

Elizabeth felt surprised. But she didn't want him to stop talking. *"Have* you done something wrong?" she asked.

"I don't know."

"Well, right and wrong are pretty clear, Jayson. Have you committed some sin you haven't told me about?"

"No, of course not."

"Then you haven't done anything wrong. You have the right to be human, but being human doesn't make you unworthy."

Jayson was assaulted by new tears, but when they were still in high school Elizabeth had become familiar with how easily he cried. He'd long ago stopped trying to hide his tears from her. "Then why was I released?" he asked.

Elizabeth sighed and shook her head. "I don't know, Jayson. It doesn't seem fair, but I do agree with the bishop on one point especially. That is for you to find out. It's between you and the Lord. Maybe we should start a fast together . . . and go to the temple."

"I don't know if I should."

"Should what?"

"Go to the temple."

"Jayson! Getting released from a calling has nothing to do with your worthiness to hold a temple recommend. The temple is where you will get the answers." She softened her voice. "Please tell me why you would think you're not worthy to go to the temple. I'm having trouble getting the connection."

Jayson blew out a long, slow breath. "I just can't help wondering if . . . I've somehow been deluding myself. Maybe my work isn't as inspired as I thought it was. Maybe God *doesn't* approve of the kind of music I play."

Elizabeth was so astonished she didn't know *what* to say. Then she realized there was nothing she could say to talk him out of feeling that way. Instead she asked, "Do you really believe that? Seriously, Jayson, do you really believe that God doesn't approve of the kind of music you play?" He hesitated, and she went on. "Because I thought it was pretty clear, and has been for a long time, that you *knew* this was a God-given gift. You've had multiple spiritual experiences that have affirmed that to you."

"I thought I knew. Now I'm not so sure."

"Then you need to fast and pray and go to the temple until you get the answer. If God's changed His mind and wants you to stop doing what you're doing, I'm certain He'll let you know. But when times get tough, we need to do the things that we know will help bring the Spirit closer to us—not the other way around." She stood up. "Change your clothes. We're going to the temple."

"You're taking me at gunpoint?"

"Do I have to?" she asked, sounding only slightly facetious. "If I did, there wouldn't be much point, now would there?"

"Okay. You're right. Do you have someone to watch the kids?"

"Dad and Marilyn are coming over."

"You already know that?"

"I told Dad I was going to talk to you and convince you to go to the temple. He said if I couldn't convince you, maybe he could. Either way, he said they were coming to babysit, because you and I could probably stand to get out of the house together."

"I don't know whether to feel loved or manipulated."

"Both," she said and gave him a quick kiss. "I love you too, Jayson Wolfe. And we're going to get through this."

He smiled and kissed her in return. "Have I ever told you that you remind me of my mother?"

"Many times. It's a great compliment. But why now?"

"She always believed we could get through anything together. And I guess we did."

"Yes, we did. I miss her."

"I miss her too," he said and went to change his clothes.

Jayson did feel better after going to the temple, but it hadn't magically eradicated the problem as he'd hoped. He did tell Elizabeth how grateful he was, however, for calling him on his inappropriate behavior. Now that she'd made it clear that she wouldn't put up with him keeping the problem to himself, he felt better just in knowing that she shared his burden, and that he could talk to her about it if he needed to.

On Saturday the rehearsal went well, and Jayson felt confident that they could record the piece the next Saturday. The thrill he felt to hear it coming together was indescribable. The effect of all those musicians in his studio was exhilarating to the point that it almost made him giddy. It was a great distraction from the other concerns in his life.

Even though he was feeling better than he had a few days ago, Jayson still found it horribly difficult to get to church on Sunday and sit through the meetings without betraying how confused he felt. But Elizabeth was by his side, and he didn't even see Sister Freedman. He got knots in his stomach when his release was announced, but then he was sustained as the choir pianist. He reminded himself that he wouldn't be allowed to serve in *any* calling if the bishop believed he was unworthy to do so.

When sacrament meeting was over, Trevin didn't take off to go to his Sunday School class the way he usually did. Jayson didn't realize his son was hovering close to him as he moved out of the chapel, until he turned to see Trevin standing there, looking concerned. Elizabeth had already gone to take Derek to nursery before she went to teach her Sunday School class. Jayson was holding Harmony, since it was his job to take care of her during this hour.

"Is something wrong?" Jayson asked him.

"You tell me," Trevin said and leaned closer, saying quietly, "Why did they release you?"

The question pricked Jayson deeply, and he fought for a steady expression and an even voice. Still, he knew he sounded mildly defensive when he said, "I haven't done anything wrong, if that's what you're wondering."

"I *wasn't* wondering that," Trevin said. "I *like* having you in Young Men, and I know the other guys do, too. You haven't been in that long."

Jayson sighed and realized he needed to be careful with how he answered. "Let me get Harmony some fresh water in her cup and we can talk." He started down the hall, and Trevin followed, holding the baby while Jayson got the water. In the few minutes it took to get her settled with a drink and some toys on the floor of the foyer, Jayson had a chance to consider what was most important in how he presented this to Trevin. Whatever Jayson's own struggles might be with this situation, he needed his son to know the right attitudes. He felt an increased gratitude for his conversations with Will, Elizabeth, and Roger, as their advice gave him perspective now. He felt sure that his visit to the temple hadn't hurt any. He and Trevin sat on the couch, and he figured this was more important than being on time to their classes.

Jayson and Trevin had shared a straightforward and mature relationship ever since Trevin had been instrumental in helping Jayson become converted to the gospel. They shared many common bonds, including their mutual love for music. When he had married Elizabeth and officially become Trevin's stepfather, those bonds had deepened. Jayson had made it clear from the start of taking on his role as a father figure that if Trevin behaved appropriately and made good choices, Jayson would treat him with every degree of the respect that he earned. Trevin had never let him down, not even a little. The boy had matured a great deal in the last few years, and they were able to communicate on a level that was more adult to adult. Jayson was grateful for the relationship they shared, which made it easy for him to say, "I don't know why I was released, Trev. I'm disappointed too. I just need to have the faith that things will work out as they're meant to, and do what the bishop has asked me to do."

Trevin looked frustrated, and Jayson knew it was taking him some effort to not express his anger. Perhaps having this conversation in the church building was a good thing for both of them. He asked in little more than a whisper, "Does this have something to do with Clayton's mother?"

Jayson looked down abruptly, mostly because he didn't want Trevin to read the truth in his eyes. Still, he had to be honest. Not certain what to say, he countered it with a question. "Why would you think that?"

"Because Clayton told me his mother was being an idiot; that she hated you."

Jayson met his son's eyes. Quickly calculating the most important facet of this for Trevin's sake, he hurried to say, "I don't believe Clayton should speak that way about his mother, no matter how he feels." ·

"That's what I told him," Trevin said so quickly that Jayson felt proud of him. "But I don't understand why she would hate you."

"I don't understand it either, but apparently she does."

"And Clayton said she wouldn't let him come to the meetings if you were there."

"That's what she told me," Jayson said. He'd not wanted to be the one to tell Trevin about such things, but he felt some relief that he knew, even though it wasn't easy to talk about.

"Is that the reason the bishop released you?"

"I don't know, Trevin. The important thing is . . ." he borrowed Roger's words, "bishops are entitled to be human, and when we raise our hand to the square and sustain a bishop—or any other leader—we're making a covenant to support their decisions—whether we agree with them or not. We need to be obedient. We don't know what the Lord might be trying to teach us, or the bishop. So, even though I'm very unhappy about this, I don't know how much it has to do with Sister Freedman. It's tough for me; I'm not going to pretend it's not. But I am doing my best to have faith. I'm going to serve as the choir pianist to the best of my ability, and I am not going to speak ill of Sister Freedman, just because I don't agree with her. You have to do the same thing. I worry about how all of this will affect Clayton, but I don't know him very well. If he's hanging out with you, maybe you can have a good influence on him. Although," he added facetiously, "if his mother finds out, he could be in trouble—since you *are* my son."

"He said she would kill him if she found out he'd even talked to me. Isn't that a little extreme? Not that I think she would *really* kill him. But I mean, seriously."

"I believe it is extreme, yes. But it's not for us to judge where she's coming from. Have the two of you spent much time together?"

"I've mostly talked to him on the school bus; sometimes he's eaten lunch with a bunch of us from the ward. You probably won't be very happy to know that he's been telling everybody how his mother feels about you."

"Everybody?"

"Kids in the ward, at school."

Jayson inhaled slowly and deeply, telling himself not to respond emotionally. "Well," he said, trying to keep it light, "I've survived gossip before. I've even been in the tabloids. I'm sure I can survive this. I'm more worried how it will affect you . . . and the rest of the family."

"But the tabloids weren't like this, right?" Trevin said. "You didn't have to go to church with the people who read them."

"No, that's true," Jayson said, not letting on how much that bothered him. He wondered what the kids in the ward were telling their parents, and if those parents might start seeing him in a new light. Those who had been indifferent could very well start forming more of an opinion—probably a negative one.

They talked for a few more minutes, mutually agreeing that they were going to keep to the adage of trying to do what Jesus would do, and ride out the storm. Jayson was grateful that Trevin was such a great kid who cared about others and had convictions about doing what was right. He told him so, and they shared a hug before they went to their separate classes.

Jayson prayed silently more than he paid attention to the lesson, and he found himself doing the same thing during priesthood meeting. After church, Elizabeth asked him, "Are you okay?"

"No, I am not okay," he said. "But I am being honest. You should be impressed."

"I am. Why are you not okay?"

"Later," he said, and they got the family home.

CHAPTER 13

While Jayson and Elizabeth worked together to prepare dinner, he told her about his conversation with Trevin. She was astonished but proud of Jayson for how he'd handled it. They both knew they had to heed the advice he'd given to Trevin.

That afternoon, Jayson went to choir practice and thoroughly enjoyed it. Since some of the choir members had contributed their talents to his album, he felt a growing bond with the choir as a whole and was glad to be there. That soothed his aching soul somewhat, and he counted that as a blessing. When he realized the Young Men leaders were having a meeting and he wasn't there, he felt something akin to homesickness, but he tried to focus on what he was doing and enjoy it.

Heading into a new week, Jayson kept his focus intently on his work while he prayed and struggled to come to terms with his feelings. He shared his thoughts with Elizabeth enough to keep them from bottling up inside, and Will came by one day to take him to lunch. They had a long talk, and his father-in-law told him he was handling it all very well. Jayson wasn't sure about that, but he was grateful to have Will and Elizabeth in his life. Memories of his lonely downward spiral toward suicide kept him *very* grateful to not be alone, and to have the perspective of the gospel in his life.

Drew was supposed to fly in for the weekend to run the sound booth for the recording session, but he called Jayson on Wednesday to say that he had the flu, and according to his symptoms it wasn't going to let up quickly. Jayson assured him that they'd figure something out, but long after he'd hung up he didn't know what he would do. He presented the problem to Elizabeth, who said, "Why don't you give Roger a quick lesson? I bet he could do it . . . if he's available."

"It can't hurt to ask," Jayson said, certain Roger would enjoy it.

"Even I can do it," she said, "so it can't be too hard. But I have to lead the orchestra."

"Yes, you do," he said and called Roger at work. His assistant said he was on another line, but she'd give him a message. Roger called back less than an hour later, and he was delighted with the prospect. They made an appointment for him to come over the following evening to get a lesson in running the recording equipment. Of course, Jayson would be there to make adjustments and see that everything went well. He just needed to be playing the piano, and had to have someone handle the buttons and switches at the right times.

On Wednesday evening Elizabeth arranged for Will and Marilyn to come and stay with the children. While Trevin was at the youth meeting that Jayson would have gone to if he'd not been released, Elizabeth insisted that he take her out to eat and to a movie. He was more grateful for the distraction than he could ever tell her—but he tried anyway.

On Thursday Jayson worked hard and felt some fulfillment and antici-pation to realize the album was nearly ready to turn over to the record company. That evening, Roger came over for his lesson in the sound booth. After they were done with the lesson, they talked for a long while, and Jayson was able to express a little bit of his feelings about the present situa-tion. Roger was kind and compassionate, and not the least bit judgmental. He said that he could understand why it was hard for Jayson, but offered his assurance that the problem was not his fault. Jayson wanted to believe him; a part of him *did*. But something deeper just felt disconnected and confused.

Friday brought a beautiful snowstorm and the realization that winter was upon them. Jayson hadn't been unaware of the holidays creeping closer, since Elizabeth had been shopping, and the house was beginning to show evidence of Christmas approaching. But it was the snow that suddenly made it feel like Christmastime. Jayson had spent most of his adult life living in places where it *didn't* snow, and he'd gotten used to it. But he loved the changing of the seasons, and for him it was a bonus to living in this area of Utah. The snow took him back to his childhood in Montana. He had some really great memories associated with snow, and he liked the way it altered the atmosphere of the air through which it fell and everything it covered.

With the snow came a great opportunity for Jayson. A couple of years earlier he had purchased an ATV with a snow blade, which made it possible for him to move a lot of snow quickly. It was great for their own large driveway and long sidewalks, but it was also an easy way for him to clear snow for other people as well. There were other men in the neighborhood with similar snow removal equipment, and they also often helped out their neighbors as well. But Jayson usually had more time on his hands than others did, and he liked the opportunity it gave him. Since it didn't start snowing until every other guy in the neighborhood who wasn't retired or ill had gone to work, Jayson spent much of the afternoon clearing walks and driveways. He started with the elderly neighbors and just worked his way around. He was especially mindful of his elderly friends Bert and Ethel, who had been there for him when he'd been investigating the Church. They were both getting more frail and rarely left the house, and he often checked in on them and tried to help in little ways. Making sure their snow got cleared was easy but gratifying.

On Saturday morning he was out early to clear fresh snowfall from his own walks and drive, and even though he didn't have much time, he did it for the neighbors who were truly incapable of doing it on their own. He was done and back at the house in time to have breakfast before his real work began. It was still snowing but not too badly, and everyone arrived safely. Everything went as well as it possibly could with the recording of "The Heart of Mozart." Jayson felt ecstatic to hear it come off exactly as he'd envisioned it. Now that he'd worked with these musicians for a while, he was getting to know them and was looking forward to touring with them. They were fun to be around, for the most part, and they all seemed to enjoy the experience. After they had all gone home, Jayson, Elizabeth, and Roger sat in the sound booth and listened to the song a couple of times. Jayson kept laughing spontaneously.

"You're pleased, I take it," Elizabeth said.

"It's just how I heard it in my head," he said and laughed again.

"That is so cool!" Roger said, and Jayson laughed again. It *was* cool. He felt happy and at peace, and was greatly looking forward to the next stage of the project. At such moments it was impossible for him to believe that his gift wasn't good. He still had to record the brass on the song he and Drew had come up with. Beyond that, the only thing left to do on the album was some simple orchestration to give depth to a few other songs. But that would only take one day of rehearsals and another of recording, then the album would be finished.

The following day was bright and beautiful, making the recent snow glitter in the sun. The choir performed a special musical number in sacrament meeting. It went even better than it had at last week's rehearsal, and Jayson was glad to be a part of it. He received many compliments afterward, and could only feel grateful that God had given him the ability to play the piano well enough to help bring the Spirit into the meeting.

Following Sunday School, a woman that he didn't know very well handed him a hand-written note. She smiled at him as she gave him the paper, saying, "Thank you for sharing your gift with us. You'll never know what it's meant to me." While he was sitting, waiting for priesthood meeting to start, Jayson read the note.

Dear Brother Wolfe, I've always enjoyed hearing you play the piano for the choir and other musical numbers, but I would be remiss if I didn't take the time to express my gratitude for the way you have blessed my life today. I have a son in college who has not been active in the Church for many years. He was home for the weekend and I talked him into coming to sacrament meeting with me, which wasn't easy. He said that he wouldn't fit in. He wears his hair long, and he doesn't own any typical Sunday clothes. But he came, and after the choir's number, he had tears in his eyes. He whispered to me that maybe he might be able to fit in after all, and it was evident he was referring to his impression of you. It might sound like a small thing, but for me it was huge. Thanks for sharing your talents, and for not being afraid to be different. Even though I'm not familiar with your career, I've heard that you've had some fame. Whatever you might do out in the world, you'll always be famous to me.

Jayson fought back tears while he silently thanked God for giving him something tangible to remind him that not everyone thought the way Sister Freedman did. He smiled to think of this young man making some changes in his life, even if they were little. And he appreciated feeling a sense that Heavenly Father may have prompted this woman to share her experience as opposed to keeping it to herself, so that Jayson would find cause for hope and encouragement. During priesthood meeting, he silently recounted the vast evidence he had in his life of the Lord's tender mercies, then he went to the nursery to get Derek, looking forward to a quiet Sunday afternoon with his family.

Once the family was gathered from their different locations in the church building, Jayson was on his way to the door closest to where they'd left the car parked when he distinctly heard Bonnie Freedman's voice saying, none too softly, "I cannot believe that you would allow him to play the piano in such a sacred meeting, and . . ." Her voice trailed off. Jayson froze, along with Elizabeth and Trevin. The other children were oblivious to the problem. But there were a number of people standing within Sister Freedman's earshot who also froze. The bishop's eyes met Jayson's and widened with alarm, then softened into apology. His taking hold of Sister's Freedman's arm had been the reason she'd stopped talking. He now ushered her into the bishop's office and closed the door. A tortured silence remained for several seconds, and Jayson felt discreet glances coming his way. His heart was pounding so hard he was almost afraid he'd pass out. He refused to show any hint of emotion in front of these people, *or* in front of his children. Counting the minutes it would take him to get the family into the car and get home, he hurried them all out the door, wondering what he'd done to deserve this.

"I'll drive," Elizabeth said, taking the keys from him.

"I think that's an excellent idea," he said, almost feeling dizzy.

"You okay?" she asked after they'd each buckled a toddler into a car seat.

"Not even close," he said, and they both got in.

Following minutes of silence while Elizabeth held his hand in hers, Trevin said from the backseat, "She had no right to say that, Dad. It was totally out of line."

Jayson couldn't speak. He was torn between wanting to bawl like a baby or scream like a raving lunatic. Either way, he couldn't imagine ever being able to go to church again. He was relieved when Elizabeth said, "I agree with you, Trevin. I don't know why she is the way she is, but we've got to be careful not to judge her, even if what she did is certainly upsetting."

"Yeah, it certainly is," Trevin said with fierce sarcasm. No one else made a sound the rest of the way home. Not even the babies. Even they seemed to sense that silence was best.

Pulling into the garage, Elizabeth said to her husband, "I'll get the kids. Maybe you should just—"

"Yeah," he said and got out of the car, slamming the door. Before anyone else got into the house, he was in the studio with the door closed. By the time Elizabeth showed up—and he knew she would—he'd vented his most intense emotions and had now settled into some level of shock. She found him sitting on the piano bench, his back to the piano, his forearms on his thighs, his hands clasped.

"I'm not fine," Jayson said as soon as she'd closed the door.

"I'm not fine either," she said.

"You go first."

Elizabeth ambled across the room as she spoke. "The part of me that believes I should do what Jesus would do and have a Christian attitude toward all people is currently being smothered with a pillow by the angry part of me that wants to bodily throttle this woman for . . ." her voice cracked, "for being so cruel to the man I love more than life." She sat in a chair nearby.

Jayson shook his head. "I don't know what I feel, but it isn't anything close to a Christian attitude." He sighed and pushed his hands into his hair. "I don't want to go back, Elizabeth. I don't ever want to set foot in that building again. I don't ever want to face any one of those people who heard what she said, or the rest of them that will hear it eventually." He let out a dry chuckle of disbelief. "I can just imagine *all* of them Googling me on the Internet, wondering what they might not have known about me. The tabloids. The music videos. Alcoholic father. Ex-wife who sleeps with punk rockers. Drug rehab." He looked at Elizabeth. "How did the tabloids find out about the drug rehab, anyway?"

"I have no idea. It doesn't matter. What anyone at church or anywhere else might think or believe doesn't matter. Going to church is not about social acceptance, Jayson; it's about your relationship with the Savior. And you cannot let anything stand in the way of that."

"I *knew* you were going to say that."

"I'm saying it because I love you, and when you love someone you help them remember who they really are when they're having trouble remembering that themselves."

Jayson sighed again and looked at her. Not knowing what else to say, he attempted to lighten the mood, if only to avoid the topic. "And I thought you only loved me because I could play the piano."

She offered a subtle smile. "No, I was *impressed* with you because you could play the piano. That's when I knew you weren't really a rebel or a loser. That's when I knew you were a dove trying to exist in a world of swallows."

"What?" he chuckled. "Where did you come up with that?"

"It came to me the first time I heard you play the piano. Didn't I ever say it?"

"No."

"I've thought it many times; I should have said it. It's true, you know."

"Is it?"

"Oh, yes," she said, and a long pause followed. "It's not easy living in your head, is it?"

"What?" he said again.

"That's another one of those things I've thought many times but never said. Maybe I need to say it. I just think that it can't be easy living in your head. The blessing feels like a curse sometimes, doesn't it." She wasn't asking.

"Yes," he said, "sometimes it feels like a curse. Sometimes I'd just like to be . . . normal."

"Normal as in . . . you could sit behind a desk all day? Or maybe do construction or something like that?"

"Yeah, something like that."

"It wouldn't suit you. The blessing-slash-curse is with you whether you want it to be or not. Like those ruby slippers." She mimicked the good witch from *The Wizard of Oz*. "'There they are, and there they'll stay.' It's your gift. You brought it with you when you came to this world, and you can never be free of it. But you have to remember, Jayson, that the ruby slippers are the very thing that will take you home."

"We had this conversation before."

"When your mother was dying."

"I sure miss her," he said.

"I do too."

He chuckled. "She would have been *really* ticked off at Bonnie Freedman."

"Yes, I dare say she would have. But maybe from your mother's perspective, the Bonnies of the world aren't so serious. Maybe she can see the big picture, and she knows that this is nothing but a little hiccup in your life's path. Maybe she can see what it is you're supposed to learn from this."

"You think I'm supposed to learn something from this?"

"Isn't that what trials are for?"

"I suppose. But I'm too angry to learn anything."

"You don't sound angry."

"You wouldn't put up with that, Mrs. Wolfe."

"I won't put up with your pretending that you're not angry, either."

"I'm not pretending. I told you that I'm angry. I just don't have the strength to express it. And I'm tired of talking about it."

"We've hardly talked about it at all."

"We can talk about it later; maybe later I won't be so angry."

Elizabeth glanced at the clock. "You need to eat so you can get to choir practice."

"I'm not hungry, and I'm not going to choir practice." Now he *did* sound angry.

"Jayson, you can't just—"

"I'm not going," he said.

"Then you'd better call someone and tell them to—"

"You can call someone if you want. If it's okay with you, I'm just going to hang out here for a while. I'll do the dishes later to make it up to you."

Elizabeth left the room quickly, but he didn't know if she was angry with him or whether she was simply emotional. And he didn't have the strength to follow her and make it right. He was too stunned to even have the motivation to stand up. Twenty minutes later he was still sitting there when Elizabeth stuck her head in the door and said, "Choir practice will be held here. They'll all be arriving in the next five to ten minutes, I'd guess."

"I can't believe you did that," he snarled.

"I can't believe you would sit here and feel sorry for yourself and neglect your Church calling. If you don't want them to come, you'd better hurry and start calling them back. If you don't let them in or you throw a tantrum, you'll only give Sister Freedman's gossip credibility."

Jayson resisted the urge to curse at his wife before she left the room. He knew that resorting to such deplorable behavior would never help him cope with this or any other problem. He went to the bathroom and splashed cold water on his face. As he blotted it dry, he felt hard-pressed to keep from crying. He shoved the tears deep down inside him and forced himself not to think of the utter humiliation and degradation he had felt standing in the church foyer with Bonnie Freedman's words echoing through the room. He managed to have a cheerful façade in place when choir members began arriving. But none of them had witnessed the drama. He was glad for that. If a single person commented to him about the incident, whether in his favor or against it, he would have probably melted into tears. Those who had been to the studio before to take part in the recording chatted about how they loved the place and how great it was to be back. Some said they should practice there every week because there was such a great feeling in the room. Jayson couldn't feel it, and figured they were just a little starstruck.

Those who had never been to the studio before were *clearly* a little starstruck. He had to endure some polite questions about his career and the purpose of the studio before the choir director asked someone to give an opening prayer and they began. Before the practice was over, Jayson realized that the bishop had come in while he'd been playing. He was sitting near the door, apparently enjoying the light banter of the choir as they discussed the song they were working on and teasing each other before going through the number one last time. But Jayson knew he hadn't come by to check in on his choir, and once the practice was over, he was inevitably in for a conversation that he didn't want to have.

Jayson remained in the moment and turned back to face the piano. At the director's cue, he started the introduction, working in a gentle embellishment that he'd come up with on his own. He no longer needed the sheet music in front of him for this number. Once he'd played a song through a few times, he could play it better if he memorized it and wasn't distracted by the notes in front of him. He tried to feel the essence of the song and allow it to calm the turmoil inside of him. *Be still, my soul: The Lord is on thy side; With patience bear thy cross of grief or pain. Leave to thy God to order and provide; In ev'ry change he faithful will remain. Be still, my soul: Thy best, thy heav'nly Friend Thru thorny ways leads to a joyful end.* By the time they'd finished, he was pleased to see that he *did* feel more calm. Still deeply troubled, but more calm.

Following a closing prayer, the choir members gradually filtered out, but not as slowly as Jayson would have liked. He preferred having someone besides the bishop remain. A number of people made comments to him like, "You're so amazing on that piano," and "We're blessed to have you in our ward," and one person said, "You sure make us sound good." Jayson responded as he always did, attempting to be gracious and humble. Finally the moment came when there was only him and Bishop Bingham left in the studio.

"I hope I'm not intruding," the bishop said, taking a chair near Jayson, who remained on the piano bench. "It was nice to sit in on the rehearsal. We're blessed with a good choir."

"Yes, we are," Jayson said.

"I hear that some of them did some vocals for your album."

"That's right," Jayson said.

"I'd like to hear that song."

"It could probably be arranged." He wanted to add that he didn't play that kind of music on Sunday, partly because it came too close to his work, and partly because he and Elizabeth had agreed that a different kind of music in the house on Sundays helped make it a special and sacred day. He feared that making such a comment now, however, would make it sound like he was trying to convince the bishop that he was a good person. And he knew that no matter what kind of music he played in his home on Sunday, it was what he held in his heart that truly mattered. He hoped and prayed the bishop could sense that.

"You really do play beautifully," he said, pointing to the piano. "I've heard you play many times, but I was called to be bishop the same time we ended up in the same ward, and I've always been on the stand with the piano behind me. It was nice to actually *see* you play. You don't use any printed music."

"I prefer to memorize a piece before I perform it. I play better when I can feel it."

"You truly have a gift," the bishop said. "I really do enjoy it."

Jayson tried to sound light as he countered, "That's easy for you to say; you've only heard me play Church music. That other stuff might scare you."

The bishop chuckled. "It might not be my personal listening preference, but I don't think it would scare me. And who knows? Maybe I'll really like it. I'd like to hear it."

"Forgive me, Bishop, if I'm being blunt, but you don't have to listen to my music to make me feel better about what's going on."

"I'm sorry if that's the way it appears. The truth is that I've been intrigued with your career since I first met you, and I've often thought that I'd like to know more about what you do, but like many things in my life, it's been put off. I'll admit that recent events have increased my interest, but—"

"Do you think that listening to it will give you evidence that Sister Freedman is right about wanting to keep her son away from my influence?"

The bishop let out a chuckle that expressed some discomfort. "You don't have any trouble being forthright, do you, Jayson?"

"Depends on the situation, I suppose."

"I mean it as a compliment. I'm learning very quickly—especially in my position—a person can't afford to beat around the bush and hope that others will fill in the blanks the way you want them to. I guess I'm learning the value of forthright communication, especially with things that are difficult to talk about."

Jayson felt a little more relaxed at the sincere evidence of the bishop's humility. "It took drug rehab to teach me that. Now Elizabeth won't let me get away with keeping feelings to myself. She's not afraid to remind me that doing so in the past didn't work well."

"She's a good woman."

"Yes, she is. Beyond the gospel, she is the greatest blessing in my life."

"She loves and respects you a great deal; that is readily evident."

Jayson realized he was meaning *that* as a compliment as well. He could only say, "I love and respect her. She's incredible."

There was a long moment of silence before the bishop said, "If we're going to be forthright, I should probably tell you that I didn't know about that . . . the drug rehab . . . until recently."

"Recently when Sister Freedman brought it to your attention, I'm assuming?" He nodded and Jayson said, "So, I'll be forthright and ask if the fact that I've been through drug rehab concerns you."

"As long you're obeying the Word of Wisdom now, it doesn't concern me in the slightest."

"I am . . . but you already knew that. And the rehab isn't a big secret. I talk about it when I do firesides, along with everything that led up to it."

"I didn't know that."

"People have to call you to approve my speaking in other wards and stakes. You didn't know what I talked about?"

"No, but I know what kind of person you are, and I've spoken with the stake president, who *has* heard your presentation. I believe he was the first to ask you to do it."

"That's right."

"Since I haven't attended one of your firesides, I wonder if you would mind telling me a little bit about your experiences."

"I would be happy to share anything with you that you're willing to listen to, Bishop. I would like to understand your motives, however. Since we're being completely forthright with each other, that shouldn't be too hard."

Jayson was surprised to see subtle evidence that the bishop was struggling to remain composed. When he spoke, his voice was only trembling slightly. "I have no problem admitting to you, Jayson, that this issue has tested my abilities as a bishop. I don't know that I've handled it the best possible way, but I believe I've done the best I could with my own capabilities. I guess I'm trying to say that I've realized I need to expand my expertise. The most important aspect of this situation is the people involved and how it's affecting them. I don't know how many bishops have ward members who are famous, but since I do, I think it would be prudent to know exactly what you're famous for. The bottom line is that the most important thing I can know about you is how you answer those temple recommend questions. But I am the father of the ward, and I feel like I can serve this situation best by getting as much information as possible. My motives would be twofold: I'm genuinely interested, and I believe getting to know you better will help me help Sister Freedman. Truthfully, Jayson, I'm not worried about this swaying your testimony. I believe that whatever struggles you may face with this, or any other challenge in life, you will come through with your testimony intact. I'm not so sure about Sister Freedman. Because you are in the center of this, I am going to say this much to you in complete confidence, which means I'm asking you not to share it with anyone but your wife. I've prayed about it and believe you need to know in order to help you, because like it or not, this is about you." He sighed deeply. "I am certain that she is emotionally ill. I don't know why, and I don't know to what extent. I also don't know how to help her. That much said, I wonder if you could tell me a little bit about the things she has gotten so upset about. I would like to hear it from you, not from the gossip on the Internet."

Jayson was surprised at how much better he felt. This man's humility, openness, and willingness to listen left him feeling validated and strengthened. He was wondering where to start and how much detail to give him when the bishop said, "Tell me where you grew up; about your family."

"I lived in Montana until we moved to Oregon when I was sixteen. I have one older brother, and we've always been very close. Our father was a violent drunk; our mother was a waitress who had survived a great deal of abuse. She divorced my father and devoted her life to taking good care of us and teaching us well. She was religious and taught us basic Christian principles. She recognized the musical gifts in us from a very young age and always encouraged them. She believed in us. But she minced no words about the need for us to use our gifts for good. I would have never dared even put a bad word in one of my songs. My mother would have boxed my ears."

The bishop chuckled. "Your brother is in the music business too, then?"

"He is. Every success I've had, he's been there with me. He lives in LA with his wife and daughter."

Jayson told him briefly his history with Elizabeth and her family, his first marriage and divorce, and the struggles Macy had gone through. He told him in two sentences how he'd fought his way to the top in the music industry, and then how everything had fallen apart, that his mother had died of cancer, and then he'd hurt his hand and it had needed surgery. "I felt like I'd lost everything," he said, "and then when I lost my ability to play music, I spiraled out of control. The drugs were prescription; I never touched street drugs or liquor or tobacco. But I came within a minute of committing suicide before I started to work my way out of that mess. I came here to stay with Elizabeth and her father, and they made me face up to my problems. They supported me through the rehab, then Macy came home, and as you can see we've lived happily ever after."

"It was after the rehab that you joined the Church?"

"Yes. It was Trevin who was the missionary," he said, and the bishop smiled. "I was pretty stubborn, but he got to me. However, it was long before that—in rehab, actually—that I gained a testimony of the healing power of the Atonement. I guess you could say that when I felt the Savior take my pain from me, I was able to fully heal. I just had to figure out that this was His true church. You know the rest."

"Actually, I think I'm just getting the tip of iceberg. But I appreciate your willingness to share."

"I appreciate your willingness to listen."

"I'd like to know how you feel about what happened today."

Jayson felt his rising mood take a nosedive. He looked down and cleared his throat loudly. "I . . . well, quite frankly, I'm having a hard time knowing how I will ever be able to walk back into that building again, and especially face those people who overheard what she said. And I'm certain it won't stop there. Trevin tells me that Clayton's been telling many of his peers about the problem. I don't believe most people intend to be gossipy. They simply talk about things that are going on. I'd like to think that these people would consider the source and not judge me too hastily. But I'm still having trouble with it. I *really* don't want to go back."

"But you will," the bishop said. "I know you wouldn't let something like this keep you from worshiping the Savior as He has directed."

Jayson remained silent enough to sort out his honest feelings in a way that he could express them appropriately. "I have no problem with my relationship with the Savior. And I know that what you say is true. I just need a little time."

"How much time?" the bishop asked. When Jayson didn't answer right away, he said, "You're playing for the choir next Sunday, are you not?"

"No, actually . . . that's two weeks from today. So, I guess I have two weeks . . . unless I get a substitute."

"No one can replace you . . . especially at the piano."

"Someone else replaced me just fine while I was serving with the young men."

"And do you think you'll feel differently in two weeks?"

"I don't know; I hope so. I'd like to think so."

"How about one week?"

"I guess we'll see."

"But I need an answer right now," the bishop said. "I don't think you're the kind of man to turn down the bishop, even if you don't agree with him."

"An answer to *what?*" Jayson asked, feeling as nervous as he felt suspicious.

"I would like you and your wife to speak in sacrament meeting a week from today. Trevin will be the youth speaker that day. He's already agreed. The topic for this month, as you would have noticed today, is the healing power of the Atonement. And since the choir isn't doing a number, I would also like you and your wife to do an appropriate musical number between your talks. Something from the hymnbook. If you sincerely don't feel like you can do it, all you have to do is say so, and you can let me know when you *do* feel ready, because I'm going to keep asking until you do it. I can understand why the timing must feel difficult for you, but I truly believe that the timing is good. I don't know whether or not you'll believe me, but it was my intention to ask you before today, and I just hadn't gotten to it."

Jayson swallowed hard and attempted to ignore his pounding heart, because he knew what it meant. He knew from times when he had felt prompted to bear his testimony, or to raise his hand in a class and make a comment, that the pounding of his heart, combined with the warmth of the Spirit, was something he *couldn't* ignore—not with any peace, anyway. He finally forced the words out of his mouth, praying that when the time came the Lord would sustain him. "I will do whatever you ask me to do, Bishop. If that's what you want, I will give it my best. I can't speak for my wife."

"Why don't you ask her, and tell her to call me if there's a problem. Otherwise, I'll just plan on it. And thank you. I'm certain you'll be blessed for your efforts, and I will keep you in my prayers."

"Thank you," Jayson said, already consumed with dread for the next Sunday. "Are you sure?"

"About what?"

"Having me speak in sacrament meeting?"

"I'm sure."

"Would you like me to get a haircut before Sunday?"

The bishop chuckled. "No, Jayson. In fact, I might be disappointed if you *did.* I wouldn't want you getting a haircut just to try to prove something to somebody. There are certain callings that might call for a more conservative haircut. But it's not one of the temple recommend questions."

"Funny, that's what my wife said. You haven't been conspiring with her on that, have you?"

"No," he chuckled. "But she's a very wise woman."

"Amen."

"And perhaps we should consider arranging one of your firesides for the ward. Maybe these people need to see that side of you."

"I'm not sure that's a good idea right now. Maybe next Sunday will be more than any of them want to know."

"Or maybe right now would be the ideal time." Bishop Bingham looked at him straightly. "I believe that most people, given the opportunity to hear your experiences and testimony, could not think ill of you or what you're doing, for any reason."

Jayson wanted to think so, but he couldn't comment.

"Now, is there anything else you'd like to talk about?" the bishop asked.

"Not at the moment."

"Will you call me if you change your mind?"

"About speaking in church, or talking to you?"

"You won't change your mind about speaking in church, now will you."

"I'll be there," he said, wondering how he would do it. Recalling how he'd felt standing in the foyer a few hours ago, he couldn't even imagine how he could pull it off.

"I should let you get to your family," the bishop said, "and I should get home to mine." He stood up, and Jayson did the same. They shared a firm handshake, then the bishop surprised Jayson by giving him a brotherly hug. "You take care now, and keep up the good work."

"You too," Jayson said and walked the bishop to the door.

CHAPTER 14

Jayson found Elizabeth in the kitchen, wiping off the counters. The dishes were all washed. "Hey," he said, "you did my job."

"I thought you could use a day off. Trevin helped me while Addie played with the babies. The little ones are asleep, and the big ones are downstairs playing a game, hence the peace and quiet. We ate without you, but I can heat some up for you when you're ready."

"Thanks, but . . . I think I'll wait."

"Fasting?"

"I think I'd better."

"How did choir practice go?" she asked.

"It was good. This is one of those moments when you want me to thank you for being manipulative and conniving when it's for my own good."

"You don't have to thank me. You just have to admit that you're glad you didn't miss choir practice, because they need you and they're counting on you."

"Okay, I'm glad for that. And thank you. What would I do without you around to save me from myself?"

"You will never need to find out," she said and wrapped her arms around him. She took his hand and urged him to the front room. "The bishop stayed a long time. Did you have a nice chat?"

"Mostly, I suppose."

They sat on the couch, and she kept hold of his hand. "Are you going to share?"

"He wants us to speak in sacrament meeting a week from today." Her eyes widened. "The topic is the healing power of the Atonement, and he wants you and me to do a musical number from the hymnbook."

"What did you tell him?" she asked. "I mean . . . I thought you were never going to church again."

"I said that I didn't ever *want* to go again."

"Then you don't have plans to apostatize?"

"Not today." He scowled, but she smiled.

"What did you tell him?" she repeated.

"I told him I would do whatever he asked of me. I said I couldn't speak for you. I'm supposed to ask you and you're supposed to call him if there's a problem."

"Oh, if you can do it, I can do it."

"Then I guess we're stuck," Jayson said. "I was hoping you could call and tell him there's a problem . . . like, for instance, you didn't want to be seen at church with someone like me."

Elizabeth leaned toward him and put a hand on his face. "I want to be with you forever, Jayson Wolfe. Why wouldn't I want to be with you at church? Now, tell me what else the bishop said."

Jayson recounted the conversation, and Elizabeth got a little teary a couple of times. He stretched out on the couch and put his head in her lap, loving the way she pushed her fingers through his hair over and over while they talked. He was grateful for choir practice, the bishop's visit, and his wife's love and understanding.

Later that evening Jayson pulled himself out of his bad mood long enough to stop by the home of the sister in the ward who had given him the note in church. She smiled when she opened the door to see him. He simply thanked her for the note, telling her that it meant more to him than he could ever tell her, and she had surely been prompted to share her feelings with him. He then gave her a copy of each of his CDs, saying that it might be something that either she, or her son, or both might enjoy. "Maybe he doesn't like this kind of music," Jayson said, "but if he does, maybe it will help."

She thanked him profusely, and Jayson left her home thanking God for the little things that kept him going. But that night when he was having trouble sleeping, mostly due to the memory of today's incident at church—interspersed with his prior conversations with Sister Freedman—it was difficult to keep perspective. The thought of speaking in church on Sunday felt so horrible that he wondered if he should call the bishop back and decline. But making that phone call seemed equally hard, so it came down to two choices that mostly favored following through because it would eliminate the need to talk to the bishop again.

Jayson didn't get to sleep until sometime after three, and he didn't wake up until nearly ten. He'd slept through the usual morning routine but still had trouble wanting to get out of bed. After he'd laid there a long while, he wasn't surprised to have Elizabeth peek in to see how he was doing. He resisted the urge to pretend to be asleep, knowing she wouldn't believe he could sleep all day.

"You okay?" she asked, sitting on the edge of the bed.

"You expect me to answer that honestly, don't you?"

"I do."

"No, I am not okay. And no, I don't want to talk about it."

"How about talking about it just a little?"

"Okay . . . I feel utterly un-Christian and selfish. I feel like stomping my foot and declaring that I will never go back to church if I can't be there and be who I am. I want to call Sister Freedman up and tell her exactly what I think of the way she's treating me, and I want to call the bishop and tell him to get somebody else to speak in church *and* to play the piano for the choir. I'm considering a change in profession. Maybe I should quit music and go to law school or something so that I can do something meaningful with my life. I know that all of what I just said sounds ludicrous, but it's how I feel, and you asked for honest."

"Yes, I did. And I think it's good for you to admit how you really feel, even if I know when it comes right down to it, you *will* behave like a Christian. I don't think it's in you to be any other way."

"Oh, I have my moments."

"As any human being does."

"You know one thing I just don't get?" he said.

"Tell me."

"Sister Freedman didn't want me influencing her son, so that problem got remedied, then she throws a fit over my playing the piano. Apparently that's *not* going to get remedied. But it's like . . . she sees me as if I were excommunicated, or something—as if I'm not worthy to participate in any way. Does she really believe that my profession makes me unworthy to be a member of this church?"

"Apparently she does. But your speaking in sacrament meeting is certainly going to put that to rest."

"Is it?"

"Either that, or Sister Freedman will become inactive."

"I think the bishop's afraid of that."

"But he asked you to do it anyway."

"None of us want her to be inactive, or to be so unhappy. But what can anybody do?"

"That sounded suspiciously close to a Christian attitude," Elizabeth said.

"Well, don't expect it to last," he said with a chuckle and pulled her into his arms, kissing her the way he figured a man should kiss his wife at least once a day. She laughed softly and kissed him again, with even more passion.

"Have I ever told you," she said, pressing a hand over the side of his face, "how blessed I am?"

"You mention it occasionally. Is there something in particular you're referring to?"

"Oh, yes!" she said and kissed him. "There are a lot of people out there who would die just to meet you and have your autograph. There are thousands who will be going gaga over the new album and the concerts. But I'm the woman privileged enough to know you better than anyone else. I'm the one who gets to sleep in the same bed with you, and live in the same house, and clean up after the same children. I'm the one who gets to be with you forever."

"It is I who am blessed," he said. "I would be nothing without you; we're nothing apart."

"You're talking like a songwriter again, Jayse. It just spews out of your mouth without even trying."

"Sorry, I can't help it."

"I know. That's what I love about it." She kissed him again. "I love you, Jayson Wolfe."

"I love you too," he said and kissed her, easing her fully into his arms. He was really beginning to enjoy it when he heard Derek and Harmony both start crying from across the hall—which meant they were fighting. He and Elizabeth both chuckled, and she dragged herself away from him to break up the fight.

Jayson took a shower and made the bed, since the deal was that the last one out of the bed had to make it. While he was fixing himself a sandwich—since it was closer to lunchtime than breakfast—Elizabeth found him there in the kitchen. She was holding Harmony on her hip. "I forgot to tell you something. Actually, I keep forgetting to tell you. When I think about it, Trevin's around."

"What about Trevin?" he asked, feeling a little panicked. He knew

Trevin was having a hard time with the present issues as well, and they probably hadn't talked about it nearly enough.

"It's a good thing," she said. "You know he's been pretty focused on the electric guitar."

"Yes, and doing very well."

"Last week he borrowed your bass guitar. He asked me if it was all right, because you were gone. I told him it was fine, and you probably wouldn't miss it, because you only use it when you're writing or recording bass. You didn't miss it, did you?"

"No, I didn't even notice it was gone."

"That's good, because I think he actually wants to surprise you. He's been working on it in his spare time—a lot. And I think it's really clicking."

"Really?" Jayson chuckled. "A little of his uncle in him?"

"More than a little, I think. Anyway, I didn't want you to notice it gone and wonder. But you can pretend you don't know."

"Okay, I'll pretend," he said.

"There's something else I need to say, Jayson," she said with a seriousness that really piqued his attention. "I owe you an apology."

He chuckled. "I cannot even begin to imagine what for."

"When you got released . . . and you were so upset . . . I didn't take your feelings seriously enough." He looked at her sideways and opened his mouth to protest, but she stopped him. "Hear me out. I should know you better than anyone. I should be more sensitive to such things than anyone. And I wasn't. I want you to know that I'm sorry. I'm sorry I didn't understand, or at least *try* to understand."

"It's okay, Elizabeth. You have nothing to apologize for. You *do* know me better than anyone, and you've been there for me every step of the way."

"Okay, but . . . I've been praying about this and . . ." Harmony got wiggly in Elizabeth's arms. "Just a minute," she said and took the baby to the living room where the toys were. She came back to find Jayson sitting at the table, his sandwich ready to eat, but he was ignoring it. She sat down across from him and began again. "I've been praying about this, wanting to understand what it was that I missed, and I think I got the answer, Jayson. And the wonderful thing about the answer, in my opinion, is the evidence that God knows you so perfectly. You see, it occurred to me that the way you respond to emotional things is different than the way I do. That sounds like a no-brainer, but . . . for you and me . . . it's different than it is for most couples. I've known right from the start, from the first time I saw you play, that your intensity with your music is an integral part of you. Because writing and performing music is an emotional process, it would be ridiculous for you to expect that you could separate that emotional intensity from other areas in your life. Is this making any sense?"

"I think so, but . . . it's falling into the category of I'm weirder than everybody else."

"It's a good thing, Jayson. It's just that . . . I don't know if I ever fully understood the connection before. We *both* need to understand it, because it's just the way you are. It's okay for you to react more emotionally to the events in your life, because it's part of your gift, and you can't separate your gift from who you are. Considering how your excessive sensitivity has played into your ability to write such powerful lyrics and music, no one—not me, not your fans, especially not those who have been touched by your work—would want you to be any other way. I think some things are just more difficult for you, and they don't roll off the way they might for someone else. But that's a good thing." She sighed. "The idea came to me so clearly, but I don't feel like I'm expressing it very well. Am I making any sense?"

Jayson nodded. "Yeah, and I think you're right. I guess I need to let that settle in."

"Okay," she said and kissed him.

While he ate, he pondered what she'd said, but it was difficult to think very clearly about anything when his brain felt so foggy. After eating, Jayson got to work, hating the way dark clouds settled over him when he was alone with his thoughts. During the next couple of days he struggled more than he wanted to admit—even to Elizabeth. But he knew she was aware, even if neither of them knew what to say. He finished a fast and started another one the next day. He prayed. He studied. He tried to prepare for his talk, but couldn't get anywhere with it. Piercing words and skeptical glances kept haunting him every waking minute. He felt sure that he was blowing a great deal of it out of proportion in his head, but there were some things he couldn't dispute, and some things he just couldn't make peace with. At moments he wondered if he ever would.

On Tuesday and Wednesday evenings, the brass players were coming to the studio to rehearse the song they would be playing. Jayson had all of the other tracks for the song laid down, so they just had to listen in the headphones and play their parts. He still needed Roger to come over on

Thursday evening to help record it, so that Jayson could be more focused on making sure it was perfect.

On Tuesday morning Macy called to report that Layla was continuing to struggle, and they were all just doing their best to move forward with faith. Then Macy's voice changed tone as she said, "I'm worried about Debbie."

"Biological mother Debbie?" he asked.

"The only Debbie I know," she said, not sounding amused.

"Sorry. Why are you worried?"

"I think she's drinking, Dad."

"She's been drinking for years."

"I mean drinking too much. The last few times I've talked to her, she sounded drunk."

Jayson felt sick at the thought. His father had rarely if ever been sober, and just hearing such a description brought back horrible memories. He was grateful that Macy wasn't living under the same roof with such behavior. In spite of the challenges she'd had in living with her husband's family, they were good people who lived the gospel. "Do you know why?" Jayson asked. "Is there some reason for this change of behavior?"

"She doesn't say much, but I can't help wondering if her choices are starting to crash down around her, and she can't handle it. I know you gave her a huge settlement with the divorce, but I suspect it's running out. And I don't think she's got the connections with the famous crowd she once had. I'm really worried about her, Dad. I don't know what to do."

"I don't know that there's anything you *can* do," he said. "Do you think she's going to listen to you if you ask her not to drink, or to find better friends? Do you think you could convince her that she can still be happy even if she's wasted all her money on a ridiculous lifestyle? You can pray for her, and you can pray to know if there's anything you can do to help her. If you get a prompting, act on it, but do it wisely. That's all you can do."

"You sound like you know what you're talking about."

"I've been through these feelings with your mother, baby. Even though I had some tough feelings toward her after the divorce, I worried about her. I wanted to shake some sense into her. And I went through these feelings with my dad. You can worry yourself sick, but you can't take away someone else's free agency. Do you think her family knows what's going on? Do you still talk to your grandma and grandpa?"

"I do occasionally. But Debbie thinks they're lame and doesn't have much to do with them."

"If she runs out of money, she might be on their doorstep. Do you think they'll take her in?"

"Yes, but it could be ugly."

"Just pray for her, baby. I will too. I always do, actually."

"You do?"

"I do. She's changed a great deal, as you know. But there was a time when she was the most important person in the world to me. I'll always care about her, Macy. She gave me a beautiful daughter, and she stood by me through some tough years. I can't say I'm not glad things turned out this way, because I love the life I have here, and I wouldn't want to still be living in LA with that old lifestyle. But I worry about her too. We'll just keep praying."

"Okay, Dad. And how are you?"

"I'm fine," he lied. But unlike Elizabeth, she believed him.

* * * * *

Elizabeth was glad that the babies were down for naps and Jayson was in his studio when she opened the front door to see Sister Freedman, holding her purse in one hand and a small stack of papers in the other. She silently asked herself, *What would Jesus do?* before she said in a kind voice, "Sister Freedman. What can I do for you?" Wanting to protect Jayson from any further heartache, she added, "My husband is working right now and can't be disturbed, but if you—"

"It's you I've come to speak to," she said.

"Very well," Elizabeth said, motioning her inside. "Come in, then."

Elizabeth closed the door and sat down, expecting Sister Freedman to sit across from her, as she'd done on the previous visit to their home. But she sat down *next* to Elizabeth on the same couch. Without any preamble or explanation, she started shuffling through the papers she held, saying, "I've been on the Internet looking at the lyrics your husband has put in his music, and I have some questions."

Elizabeth resisted the urge to look heavenward and shout, *I can't believe this!* She swallowed hard and said nothing, exercising extreme self-discipline and praying that she would not do or say something to make the problem worse. Now that she could see the printed pages, certain phrases had been highlighted. She wondered how much time this woman had spent searching through music lyric sites and studying them.

"Apparently," Sister Freedman said, "he has written all of these words himself."

"That's right," Elizabeth said.

"So, I was wondering . . ." She pointed to a highlighted section. "What does he mean here, exactly, by 'saving it for marriage?' What *does* he mean by *it?*"

Elizabeth smothered her own astonished disbelief that was wanting to scream, and instead she focused on the question. She knew the song well and pointed out the lyrics above the specified line. "See here where it says, *'The love I feel for you is too much to feel. I want to hold you so badly that it's too much to hold. But I'm saving it for marriage so you'll know that it's real.'*"

As if Elizabeth had only strengthened Sister Freedman's case, she said, "There is clearly an underlying message in this song."

"Yes, there clearly is," Elizabeth said. "And the message is that it's better to save intimacy until after marriage. We have received letters from parents and teenagers alike, thanking Jayson for this song. This song made a difference to at least a few people. This song made it *popular* for some people to be moral, as opposed to the contrary."

Sister Freedman made a disgusted noise, as if Elizabeth were a child that required great patience. Elizabeth knew exactly how she felt. The prosecutor shuffled through her papers and said, pointing to another section. "And what about this? Here it says, 'I've done it all and I've done it wrong.'" She looked at Elizabeth. "Is he admitting to as unseemly a past as it states here?"

"Sister Freedman," Elizabeth said, feeling like she was speaking to a four-year-old and she needed to be expressly clear and patient. "Just because Jayson wrote the song—and sings it—does not mean that the lyrics all apply to him personally. Most of his songs are not directly personal. In this song he's speaking *as if* he were someone who had lived a life full of mistakes, and was now ready to change. That's why the next part says, 'I'm ready for the higher road. I'm ready to make it right. My soul is not the devil's to own. I'm ready to fight the good fight.'"

Sister Freedman repeated the issue three more times with other songs, always seeming frustrated and dissatisfied with Elizabeth's answers. Elizabeth tried very hard to kindly answer the questions and point out the good, but it became increasingly evident that Sister Freedman had not come to be convinced, but rather to convince Elizabeth that her husband was doing something wrong. She wanted to ask this woman exactly what she'd expected. Did she think that Elizabeth had been unaware of her husband's scandalous lyrics and a practical stranger could come and point out something that would make Elizabeth see the error of her ways in being committed to such a man?

Elizabeth finally came to her feet, saying firmly, "I think we've established that we strongly disagree over the issue, Sister Freedman. I'm sorry that my husband's work is so upsetting to you, but it's obvious there's nothing I can say to change your mind."

Sister Freedman stood as well, saying huffily, "I really don't think you have any idea what kind of man you're married to."

The statement affirmed Elizabeth's suspicions, and made it easy for her to walk to the door and open it. "I'm going to have to ask you to leave, Sister Freedman. I think our conversation is finished. I wish you well in trying to come to terms with whatever it is you're trying to come to terms with."

Sister Freedman's anger was evident as she rushed out the door, but it couldn't have been any more intense than what Elizabeth felt as she closed the door and leaned her head against it. She didn't want to tell Jayson, but she knew she had to, and she knew it would be better to get it over with.

"Something wrong?" Jayson asked, startling her.

"Oh!" She turned around and leaned her back to the door. "You scared me." She was glad he hadn't shown up a few minutes sooner.

He chuckled. "Were you expecting company? Or are you just . . . hanging out by the front door with the hope that you'll get some?"

Elizabeth knew she'd do well to just get to the point. "Sister Freedman just left."

Jayson made a disgusted noise. "I'm not sure I even want to know."

"Yes, you do. The wondering would kill you."

"Okay, tell me. Did she just give you some disparaging message for me? Or were you protecting me from her?"

"I told her you were working and couldn't be disturbed, but she wanted to talk to *me.*"

Elizabeth moved back to the couch, needing to sit down. Jayson sat next to her, his expression hovering between anger and fear. "Let me have it," he said, and she repeated every grueling detail of the memorable conversation.

Jayson remained surprisingly calm. He wondered if seeing how upset Sister Freedman had made Elizabeth was somewhat reassuring. Or perhaps he just felt too weary or in shock to be anything but calm. When she'd finished her report, including her own appalled reaction, Jayson asked, "Does she think she'll convince you to leave me, or something?"

"Or she thinks I can convince *you* of the error of your ways." She took his hand. "It doesn't matter, Jayson."

He resisted the urge to call her a hypocrite. Instead he said, "Look at yourself; look how upset you are, and tell me it doesn't matter."

She let out a long sigh. "Okay, well . . . it doesn't matter enough for us to go on letting it upset our lives. We are *both* going to remain calm, pray for strength and comfort, and press forward. There. I'm calm. If we—" The timer on the stove rang, and Elizabeth stood up. "I'll be right back."

Jayson forced himself to breathe deeply while he prayed for strength and comfort. He stood at the big window and looked out on the dreariness of the day. The snow on the ground had turned dirty and ugly. The sky was gray and dismal. The rain presently falling seemed completely out of place; it was all wrong. In a place where it was supposed to snow in the winter, rain just felt wrong. Perhaps he wouldn't have taken such careful notice of the weather if it didn't so perfectly express the way he was feeling. He was living a life that had so much good in it, and so the things that had gone awry were difficult to understand. It was all wrong. He knew that life was expected to present challenges, and it was naive to think that it wouldn't. But never had he imagined something like this. It was like rain on a day when it should have been snowing. Any other season of the year, rain would have been lovely and welcome. But today it was all wrong.

Elizabeth appeared beside him and said, "What's on your mind?"

He thought of a hundred things he could say, most of them having to do with Sister Freedman, and all of them things she had heard before. Tired of laboring the point, he said, "Winter rain." He explained his theory to her, ending with the firm declaration, "It's just all wrong." He went on to say the lyrical words that had just appeared in his mind, *"I gaze through dirty windows, watching winter rain. It's falling on a world of gray, while I'm drowning in my pain."*

"That's pretty good," she said, "but I resent dirty windows."

He scowled. "I'm speaking metaphorically. Obviously the window I'm looking through is perfectly clean. But the weather is deplorable."

"Okay, it is kind of a gray, yucky day. But if you're looking for metaphors, the rain has cleared the smog out of the air. The air has been stagnant and dirty for several days. If God wants us to find life lessons in the weather, there's one for you. Maybe what seems all wrong now is just a step toward something greater that God has in mind for you."

Jayson inhaled her wisdom and perspective and turned to face her. She smiled at him, and he found the ability to smile back. "There's my sunshine," he said and kissed her. He hugged her tightly. "As long as I have you and God in my life, there will always be sunshine."

"Is that another line for the song?" she asked. "You're talking like a songwriter again."

"No, that's just for you and me," he said and held her while his eye was drawn to the picture of the Savior on the wall. Maybe there *was* meaning in this trial that he couldn't possibly see from his narrow, mortal perspective. Either way, he could only keep pressing forward, putting one foot in front of the other, and waiting for the clouds to clear.

* * * * *

During the rehearsal that evening, Trevin hardly left the studio. He kept saying that he really loved this song, and Jayson was only too happy to have him around. He'd come a long way from the withdrawn child who'd been struggling to come to terms with the deaths of his father and older brother. And Jayson loved him. He noticed Trevin hadn't had a haircut for a while and teased him about being too much like his old man, although Trevin normally wore his hair so short that it would take more than missing a couple of haircuts to make it look out of place at church or anywhere else.

While Trevin sat in the studio with the brass players, wearing head-phones to be able to hear the existing tracks, Jayson noticed that the boy was getting a sinewy look to his arms, and his shoulders were broadening. He'd been near Jayson's height for a while now, but he was starting to look more like a man than a boy, and he was only a sophomore in high school. Jayson also noticed, not for the first time, his striking resemblance to his mother. But looking closer, while Trevin had his eyes squeezed closed and was silently syncing the lyrics, Jayson was caught off guard to see a strong resemblance to Derek—Elizabeth's brother and Jayson's best friend in high school. He'd been an amazing bass player and a remarkable young man. Jayson still missed him, even though he'd been gone nearly twenty-five years. For a long moment, Jayson was taken back to the basement of the Greer home in Oregon where he and Drew and Derek had whiled away endless hours coming up with great music. Elizabeth had joined their little band eventually, and they'd had no idea what magical moments they'd be in the center of, and how abruptly it would all end. Derek had only been a couple of years older than Trevin was now when a car accident had ended his life. Seeing Trevin this way now made Jayson want to cry. The temptation lured his mind to other events—past and present—that made the urge even stronger. Knowing he had work to do and a life to live, he forced back his emotions and focused on the moment.

CHAPTER 15

Jayson was forced back to work when they ran into a couple of glitches with some stanzas that just didn't sound right. The following evening, Trevin went to the usual youth meeting, so he wasn't at practice. Jayson wished he could have gone with him. But the rehearsal went well, and he was pleased. They were moving toward the homestretch of the recording, and he was longing to have it done and move on.

On Thursday morning, Jayson woke up with the dark cloud a lot darker than it had been. The fact that it was still gray and raining outside didn't help. He admitted to Elizabeth that he didn't know what was wrong and why he couldn't shake it. He went to the studio to try to drown it out with music, fearing even as he did that he was engaging in some deep dysfunctional behavior. He took a break to look over some of his original handwritten music for the Mozart song, wondering how it had translated into actuality.

Jayson heard a knock at the studio door and hollered, "Come in."

He didn't know who he was expecting, but he looked up from the sheet music in his hands to see Maren walk into the room. She was the counselor who had guided him through the nightmares and triumphs of his rehab experience, and she had also given Macy some counseling following her own ordeals. He hadn't seen her at all since he'd married Elizabeth. She looked the same, but seeing her brought up mixed memories. She'd helped him more than he could possibly comprehend. But it had been ugly most of the time. He didn't have to guess why she was here now, although he would have expected Elizabeth to drag him to her office, not coerce her into coming here.

"This is a surprise," he said, removing his glasses.

"Is it?" she asked.

"Seeing you walk into my studio, yes. Seeing your face, no. Apparently my wife has been conspiring with you."

He stood up, and she gave him a hug. "It's good to see you," she said with a smile.

"And you," he said, "I think."

"Honesty right off the bat," she said. "I like that."

He sat back down, and she did the same. "So, what did she bribe you with? I dare say house calls aren't cheap."

"And you can afford it. Although I'm not charging extra for the house call. I came because I believe in you and your work, and I was hoping I might be able to help it go a little more smoothly. The concert tickets were a little extra incentive," she added with a soft laugh. "And Elizabeth also told me that you'd play one of your new songs for me. I assume she wasn't lying to me."

"I guess that depends on what kind of mood I'm in after we chat."

"So, play before we chat."

"You have that much faith in me?"

"I'm giving you a choice," she said.

"Either that, or you're trying to get me to prove that I'm using music to medicate myself."

"Are you?" she asked.

"Yes," he said, and she made a noise to indicate that she was impressed.

"You haven't forgotten what I taught you. And you're not only being honest with me, you're being honest with yourself."

"Well, I am since Elizabeth slapped me in the face—not literally. She remembers what you taught her, too."

"I'm glad to hear it. You've had some really good years since we opened Pandora's Box together. You have a beautiful family. Your career has been good. I've kept track of that. I confess that I take pride in having a little contribution in helping you get back to a place where you do all the great things you've done."

"I won't dispute that," Jayson said. There was a long moment of silence. "So, did you have some agenda planned here, or what?"

"I just thought you might like to talk."

"Obviously I didn't have any warning that you were coming, so I'm not very prepared."

"Maybe that's an advantage. You haven't had time to think about what you're going to talk about. So, why don't you just tell me what's going on?" He said nothing and she added, "Something *is* going on, right? I don't think your wife would have called me and offered bribery if there wasn't a justified cause for concern."

"Okay," Jayson said, pondering where to begin, knowing he wasn't going to get out of it, and actually relieved for the opportunity to talk to her now that she was in front of him. "I guess you could say it's a religious problem. And we don't share the same religion."

"I'm not LDS," she said. "But I've lived and worked in Salt Lake City for many years. And I'm a counselor. You think I don't have any understanding of the LDS culture and theology? I can assure you it's come up more times than I can count. So, why don't you try me?"

Jayson was grateful for the comfortable relationship he'd once shared with Maren as she'd helped purge him of a lifetime of pain. In spite of the years since he'd seen and talked with her, their comfort level settled quickly into place. It only took him a few minutes to work up the momentum to tell Maren everything that had happened and how it had made him feel. He quickly realized that she *did* understand the LDS culture and theology enough to get an idea of the dynamics of the situation without undue explanations.

When Jayson felt like he'd said all there was to say, he asked, "So, is my old Pandora's Box back now, or what? If I'm medicating myself with music, am I doomed to have another landslide in my life?"

"No, and no," she said. "First of all, the pleasure and serenity that you get from your music is not a bad thing. Everybody needs something in their life for that purpose. If something occurred that prevented you from being able to play, I think you'd need to be very conscious of finding a healthy way to replace it. I'm not worried about you going over the edge of some metaphorical cliff, or getting into drugs again. You're actually very centered and emotionally healthy, in my opinion. You've done well at maintaining what you've learned. Your religion is good for you. It's given you a strong foundation and more focus. Your relationships with the people you love—and who love you—are also good." She shrugged. "I think you're doing great."

"Well, I don't *feel* great," he said, almost angry.

"This issue is understandably difficult, but I don't think that solving it is nearly as complicated as you might think."

"Okay. I'm listening."

"As I see it, you have two very strong aspects to your identity as a human being. Outside of your relationships, you have your religion, and you have your music. They're both very important to you, and of high value. They are both an integral part of your perception of yourself. If religion or morals were not important to a person, then they could—and would—use their talents in any way that was easy or convenient and have no guilt. But that's not the kind of person you are. For you, being creative must be honored by holding to your moral values, which have become strong religious beliefs. In essence, it's difficult for you to separate the two. If you believe your gift came from God, how can you possibly separate your spirituality from your creativity? The answer is that you can't. And yet, they've been severed. As I see it, you simply have to figure out *why* they've been severed, and then you can put them back together. Am I making sense?"

"Yes," Jayson said. "So far." He thought of what Elizabeth had said about his tendency to be more intense with his emotions because his creativity was so intense. That was making more sense to him now as well.

"Let me ask you a question. Well . . . first let me propose a theory. Let's say that the beliefs we have about ourselves are like plants. Weeds are the negative or false ones; flowers are the positive ones, the ones that help us become our best selves."

"Sometimes your metaphors are really annoying," he said lightly.

"Yes," she smiled, "but they work. Pay attention. You can chop off the weeds over and over, but unless you pull out the root, it will keep coming back. If you have a false belief deeply rooted in there somewhere, then when something goes wrong, it can make that weed grow out of control and smother the flowers."

"I'm with you . . . I think."

"So, what's the weed, Jayson? Where was it planted? And what is it you believe about yourself that's made this issue sever your spirituality from your creativity? In other words, what has made you think that you can't be acceptable in God's eyes and still use your creative gifts, *especially* when, by all logic, you know that you are using your gifts in a way that you believe *is* acceptable to God? The answer is that a subconscious belief is strangling the logic *and* the feelings associated with the issue. So, what's the weed?"

Jayson thought about it and had to say, "It makes sense. It really does. But I honestly don't know."

"Okay, let's talk about it. Is there something from your formative years that might have been difficult, that's possibly been triggered by these events? I'm going to bring up some of the typical things that frequently come up and you see if anything creates any uncomfortable emotions. Your father."

Jayson thought about it. "No. You know as much as anyone that there was a lot of baggage there, but I've dealt with it. I don't think that's it."

"Your mother."

"No." That was easy.

"School."

"What about school?"

"Anything about school. Teachers. Peers. Studies or—"

"I hated school," he said when the thought penetrated his mind and he felt mildly agitated.

"Why?"

"I was a complete misfit, right from day one. I couldn't concentrate because there was music in my head. I rarely got assignments done. I was labeled inadequate and lazy by most of my teachers. I was always in trouble—not because I did anything wrong, but because I didn't do what everyone else thought was right. I was never good enough."

Jayson expected Maren to comment, but she just looked at him for a full minute. "What?" he finally asked.

"Do you hear what you just said?" Jayson repeated it in his mind, and his breathing quickened. "You're not a typical Mormon, are you, Jayson?"

"No," he said.

"Do you think that God is like your school teachers? Do you think He's labeled you inadequate because you're different? If you do, that's a false belief and you need to uproot it. Your theology teaches that God is loving, benevolent, and merciful. I may not share your religion, but I believe that to be true. He is *not* like your teachers or peers from school, and you can't project those traits onto Him. The same applies to the people you go to church with. While some may be criticize you openly, and others may do so silently, you are who you are, and it just doesn't matter what they think. But I suspect that the majority of them are more in awe of you than they are disgusted."

Maren leaned forward and became more intense. "You have a remarkable gift, Jayson, and you're a good man. Both are rare qualities in this world. You should celebrate your uniqueness. Not being a conformist doesn't make you wrong. Your physical appearance and your profession are not some indication of rebellion or disobedience. They are just part of your uniqueness. I don't think I can give you any advice beyond that. I think you need to measure the idea with *your* value system and decide where you can comfortably stand with your religion and still honor your gifts. Frankly, I think that's already in place, and it was fine until somebody pricked a sensitive nerve by telling you, in essence, that you didn't fit in, and were therefore not acceptable."

Jayson let that settle fully into his spirit, and Maren allowed him the silence to do so. "Wow," he finally said. Then again. "Wow." He chuckled. "You're a genius, Maren."

"I didn't tell you anything you didn't already know."

"But you have a way of putting things that just . . . makes them come together and make sense."

"It's a gift," she said with a little smile. "I believe everyone has something they're good at. I know mine, and you know yours."

"Yes, I do," he said and laughed softly, amazed at how much lighter he felt.

"I'm glad you've figured it out. But just because you have it figured out doesn't mean that other people aren't going to continue to see you as different—because you *are* different. There will always be self-righteous and dysfunctional people—in any religious or social circle. That's the nature of the human race. But when you know where you stand with yourself and your own values, such things will be easier to face and deal with appropriately."

Their deep discussion continued a while longer, then merged into lighter small talk until Maren said, "I think you owe me a song."

"I suppose I do. I can only give you the piano, though. If you want to hear the way it sounds in my head, you're going to have to come to the concert."

"Oh, I'll be there," she said. "Elizabeth promised me tickets."

Jayson played "The Heart of Mozart" for Maren, and Elizabeth came into the room before he was done. She noticed the change in Jayson right away, and told Maren she was a genius. After Maren left, Elizabeth wrapped her arms tightly around Jayson and asked, "You're really feeling better?"

"I really am," he said. They sat together in the front room while he repeated Maren's theory, which helped it settle in a little deeper for him.

Elizabeth got tears in her eyes and said more than once, "You seem more like yourself than you have since . . ."

"Since Sister Freedman came to the door; I know. I have a feeling the war isn't over yet. But maybe I can handle the battles a little better from now on."

* * * * *

That afternoon, Jayson actually had fun by himself in the studio for the first time in many days. He went through each of the numbers that he would need to know like breathing, while his mind wandered to the fact that he had to speak in church on Sunday. He was still blank on that, but he figured it would come. Now that he'd talked to Maren, he actually felt grateful for the opportunity to share his testimony of the Atonement and how it had healed him over and over in his life.

Jayson looked up from the piano to see Trevin coming into the studio, as he often did when he got home from school. But his expression made it clear he wanted to talk to Jayson about something. Jayson pretended not to notice and simply said, "Hey there, buddy. How was your day?"

"Good. How about you?"

"Same old stuff," he said. "Just me and the piano."

"You got that song down to breathing yet?"

"I'm getting closer." Jayson turned on the bench as Trevin sat in a nearby chair. "So, what's up?"

"This might sound silly . . . and if you don't like the idea . . . I understand, and I know that these things aren't all up to you, but . . ."

"Just spit it out, son," Jayson chuckled.

"Well . . . today at lunch I was sitting in the bleachers . . . out by the football field . . . eating lunch with some friends, and it was just weird. I couldn't get that song out of my head, and it's like I could see the music video for it . . . there in the field . . . with lots of kids in the stands."

Jayson felt intrigued, mostly with the intensity of Trevin's feelings. He wanted to teach him to listen to and respect such feelings. "Which song?" he asked.

"'Good, Clean Fun,' of course. I love that song! We're recording the last track tonight, aren't we?"

"We are," Jayson said.

"The music's great, but the lyrics are great, too. And . . . I love it. And it just seems to me like . . . having a crowd of teenagers who look more clean-cut and together than a lot of the kids in the world, cheering and singing along with that song would make such a great video. You know," he sang a bar with enough fluency that Jayson knew he'd heard it many times, *"Laughter's free and doesn't leave a hangover. Come on, boys and girls, let's get addicted to good clean fun!"*

Jayson chuckled. He genuinely liked the idea. It didn't take any effort to say, "I like it. You might be on to something. First we have to be sure the record company is going to use that song for a single. I'm pretty sure they will, but they haven't actually heard it yet. If they choose it for a single, I'm sure we could arrange the video. I doubt there would be a problem using the stadium for a Saturday, and I bet we could round up a fair amount of kids."

"Oh, that won't be a problem," Trevin said. "But I don't want to have anything to do with that."

"Okay," Jayson drawled with caution, more from the way he'd said it. "You don't want anything to do with the video, or the—"

"With arranging it," Trevin said. "You see . . ." He hesitated and seemed nervous.

"Just say it."

"The thing is, Dad . . . I don't want you to be offended, or . . ."

"What? I'm not going to be offended. Just say it."

"I really don't want people to know you're my dad." Jayson held his breath, reminding himself that he wasn't going to be offended. But he felt hurt, even if he didn't understand Trevin's reasons. He wanted to ask what part of his career was embarrassing for Trevin. "The thing is," Trevin went on, mostly looking at the floor, "some people around here know who you are, some don't. Like you've said, your biggest audience isn't with high school kids. Of course, kids in the ward know you're my dad. But most of the kids at school don't, and I've heard kids talk about you at school; kids that don't know we're related." Jayson leaned back in his chair, biting his tongue, taking this in cautiously. He felt sick to think of Trevin dealing with any kind of garbage at school because of Jayson's career. "They think it's cool that a rock star lives around here, even if they don't know anything about you and probably wouldn't know you if they saw you. The thing is," he looked up, "I'm proud to be your son, but not because you're famous, and not because people think your music is cool. I love the music, and I love the way you're teaching me. But that's not why I love you. And I don't want people to think that I'm cool just because you're my dad. I want people to like me for me."

Jayson's emotions went from negative to positive in a heartbeat as he understood Trevin's meaning. He silently scolded himself for jumping to conclusions, and thought how wonderful good communication was. He smiled at Trevin and said, "The feeling is mutual, kid. I'm proud to be your dad, but not because people think I'm cool because of it." Trevin chuckled. "I couldn't ask for a finer son. The fact that we both love music is a bonus. I would love you even if you hated my music and you played the . . . tuba or something." Trevin chuckled again. "It's totally fine. I completely under-stand how you feel. I just can't promise that people won't ever find out. I learned a long time ago that fame just comes with the business, whether you like it or not. No secret can be kept forever. And if I film a music video at the school, we don't know what will happen. I *can* promise that whatever happens, we're in it together. Being the child of a rock star isn't easy; ask Macy. But if kids at school find out, you'll be able to discern who your real friends are, and who the shallow ones are. You think about it, and if you still want to do it, we'll see what we can do."

"Okay," Trevin said, seeming completely relaxed. "I figured I could just blend in with the crowd and still be there."

"Yeah, you could."

"Sometimes I've wished we had the same last name, and I've thought about using yours, even though my legal name is Aragon. But maybe it's better this way."

"I'm sure it is," Jayson said. He didn't remark that Addie had been going by the last name Wolfe ever since the marriage. She'd barely started in school at the time, and her last name hadn't been so well-known among her friends. Having the same last name as her parents was less complicated, so Elizabeth had put it that way on the school records, even though her name was officially Aragon. For Trevin, it was different. And that was fine, perhaps better.

"Hey," Trevin added, as if he'd just remembered something important, "are you busy right now? Do you have a few minutes?"

"I'm good until supper, and then we're recording this evening."

"Great," Trevin said. "I'll be right back."

Jayson wasn't surprised when Trevin returned a few minutes later with Jayson's bass guitar. But he pretended to be. He glanced at the empty space on the wall where it had hung, then back to Trevin, smiling.

"Mom said I could use it; I hope it's okay."

"Of course it's okay," Jayson said. "I know you'll take good care of it. But if you really like it, maybe we should get you one of your own."

"Maybe we should see if I'm any good before we do that," Trevin said. "I've saved some money from the work I've done helping Mom, and from the mowing job I had last summer. I'll go in half on it with you."

"Deal," Jayson said, and Trevin put the guitar strap over his head. "I assume you've been practicing something."

"I have," Trevin said and hooked everything up to play it, "but you know the deal . . . bass by itself doesn't sound like much."

"I know the deal," Jayson said. "Just play it."

Jayson recognized the song within a couple of bars, and he was stunned at how smoothly Trevin was pulling it off. By the time he was finished, Jayson couldn't even hope to hide the fact that he was crying.

"What?" Trevin asked, panicked. "Did I do something wrong? Did I—"

"No, of course not," Jayson said and chuckled, wiping his cheeks. "You know me. I cry easier than the average five women."

"Okay," Trevin said, removing the guitar and setting it in an empty stand, "but why?"

"Where did you learn that?"

"It's 'Predator.' One of your first hits . . . off the Gray Wolf CD."

"I know what it is, Trev. I want to know how you learned it."

"I've been listening to the CD. How else would I learn it?"

"I just . . . well . . . I'm amazed at how perfect it is. Do you know the origin of the song?"

"I assumed you wrote it. You write everything you perform."

"I didn't write that one alone. Your Uncle Derek helped me come up with the music. He came up with that bass-line. When we played together, it was magic."

"Is that why you're crying? You miss him?"

"That's part of it," Jayson said.

"What's the other part?"

Jayson shook his head and chuckled. "You look so much like him, especially with your hair not so short. And . . . well . . . you play like him, too. I was wondering if . . . he might actually be helping you. He was a great bass player."

Trevin's eyes widened, then they narrowed. "Is that . . . possible?"

"Oh, yes . . . it's possible," Jayson said. "I've felt Derek with me many times. I can't say for sure how I know; I just know. I believe he's helped me all along. It's not something I talk about very often, and very few people know how I feel, but I think he's remained my partner in music all these years. I didn't really figure it out until . . . well . . . not too long ago. After Harmony was born, I think. I had an experience when I knew, and then I realized that the feeling was familiar, and that it had happened over and over, and I just hadn't recognized it for what it was."

Jayson got the set of scriptures out of the sound booth that he always kept there. He was often wanting to look things up in the midst of his work, or sometimes he would just take a break to read. Together they read chapter seven of Moroni, and discussed the role of the ministering of angels. After a lengthy conversation and Trevin asking many questions, Jayson said firmly, "I believe that, somehow, in ways that I cannot begin to comprehend with my mortal mind, angels from the other side of the veil have something to do with the great musical and artistic gifts that take place here. I can't explain it. I just know it's true."

"That is glorious!"

"Yes." Jayson laughed softly. "Yes, it is."

They talked about more trivial things until Jayson said, "Hey, why don't we do that song together?"

"Could we?"

"I dare say I can remember it. I can't possibly do a show without playing it. My die-hard fans expect it. I have to throw in the old favorites. Let's run through it. Then when Drew comes again, we'll be ready for him."

Trevin put the bass guitar back over his shoulder, and Jayson took up his favorite and flipped all the right switches to begin. The first time they went through it together, they both had trouble remaining synchronized with each other, which was made more difficult without drums. After three tries, they were making it work. Jayson turned on two microphones and started to sing it, coaching Trevin through the backing vocals. Two more times through and they were both laughing and having a great time. Jayson felt himself slipping into performance mode on the sixth round, and he was jumping and moving like a rock star. Trevin got into it with little effort, and they started playing together so well that the memories washed over Jayson, leaving him somewhere between ecstatic and grieving as those days with Derek felt close enough to touch. He finally said, "Okay, I think we're ready to give it to your mother. I'll bet you two nights of dishes that it'll make her cry."

"Is it a bet if I think it'll make her cry too?"

"No, I suppose not. And if we could get your grandfather over here, I bet it would make him cry, too."

"We'll try it on Mom first," Trevin said and went to get her.

Elizabeth came into the studio and said, "Trevin tells me the two of you have a surprise for me."

"We certainly do," Jayson said as Trevin put the guitar strap over his head and settled it into place. Just before the song started, Jayson added, "Watch your son; watch him real close. You've seen *me* do the song before."

"Okay," Elizabeth said, sounding a little nervous. They barely made it to the first chorus before she was crying. By the time it was finished, she was a mess.

Jayson flipped his guitar to his back and went to his knees beside her, wrapping her in his arms. "Hey," he said, "I told Trevin it would make you cry. I didn't think you were going to cry like this. I'm the crier in this family."

"That was so incredible!" she said, wiping her face. She looked up at Trevin, who was looking a little stunned. She reached out a hand for him, and he stepped forward to take it. "You look so much like him; you sound like him, move like him." She looked at Jayson. "It's incredible."

"Yes, it is," Jayson said.

"Tell me more about him," Trevin said and sat on the floor. Jayson did the same, and the three of them talked for nearly an hour about Elizabeth's brother, Jayson's best friend, Trevin's uncle that he never knew. They talked about what a clown he was, and the silly hats he'd wear when they performed every Saturday night in Portland. They talked about his vibrancy and his passion for music. And they talked about the night he was killed. They talked about the devastation, the grieving that had hovered with them for years, and how the gospel had come into their lives and helped heal those wounds as they never had been healed before. Then they talked of how they believed that Derek was still a part of the family, and helping with the music from the other side of the veil. They talked about the day they had done Derek's temple work, and how Jayson had been the proxy for all of his ordinances. While they talked, Addie miraculously kept the children occupied in the house. And they were still talking when Will stepped into the studio.

"What are you doing here?" Jayson asked.

"I was just . . . out and . . . felt like stopping by," Will said. "What are you guys doing?"

"That is so weird," Elizabeth said and laughed softly.

"What?" her father asked, bending to kiss her cheek in greeting.

"We've been talking about Derek—your son, not mine."

"Then that explains why I felt like stopping by. No need to end the conversation on my account."

"I think we'll just play a song for you instead," Jayson said, and they stood up to do a repeat performance. Will's response was so much like Elizabeth's that Jayson also started to cry before they were finished.

"Was it really so many years ago?" Will asked, wiping his tears. He chuckled. "I'll never forget the first time he brought you home with him." He nodded at Jayson.

"Like a stray dog," Jayson said.

"Like a missing puzzle piece that had finally been found," Will corrected. "You changed his life—and mine."

"And mine," Jayson said.

"And mine," Elizabeth added, taking Jayson's hand.

"And now," Will said, looking at his grandson, "it would seem a part of Derek lives on through this amazing young man. I'm proud of you, Trevin . . . for so many reasons. You keep up the good work, and keep being a good boy, and the Lord will bless you."

"I will," Trevin promised, and they started to reminisce all over again until Addie needed help and they had to get supper on in order to be finished before the recording session started. Jayson ordered pizza instead, and they kept talking while they waited for it and ate. Jayson found it difficult to believe how depressed he'd been at the start of the day. Perhaps the sun was coming out a little, even if it was still raining outside. Looking around at his life, he couldn't deny it. He *did* believe in angels, and he believed in miracles. And if God was a God of miracles, then surely he would make it through whatever might lie ahead.

About the Author

Anita Stansfield began writing at the age of sixteen, and her first novel was published sixteen years later. Her novels range from historical to contemporary and cover a wide gamut of social and emotional issues that explore the human experience through memorable characters and unpredictable plots. She has received many awards, including a special award for pioneering new ground in LDS fiction, and the Lifetime Achievement Award from the Whitney Academy for LDS Literature. Anita is the mother of five, and has one adorable grandson. Her husband, Vince, is her greatest hero.

To receive regular updates from Anita, go to anitastansfield.com and subscribe.